The First Love Story of
Vasillor Vasu

VIVEK GANJOO

notionpress.com

INDIA · SINGAPORE · MALAYSIA

ISBN 979-8-89277-928-9

For Avyana

My Love for you
My dear W
If you ever truly want to find-
Is in the twinkle in your eyes,
When you dance in front of a mirror.

Acknowledgements

I would like to thank all the amazing people in my life:

My parents, for everything that I am today.

Vishal, my dearest brother, and his wife, Pratibha, for always believing in me.

Aadhya, for patiently waiting for *Popsi* to play with her.

Sunil, my poet friend, for keeping me motivated.

The entire team at Notion Press who helped me bring this book into the world.

And finally, my wife Neha, for bearing with me and all my idiosyncrasies while I slogged to complete this book.

Chapter 1

Okay! Before I start, let me give you a brief intro about myself. My name is Vasillor...

Sorry, let me start again.

Hi! My name is Vishesh. Yes, That's the name my parents gave me. If you know, Vishesh means "Special". There is nothing *Vishesh* about me, though. The world, by the way, knows me as Vasillor- Vasillor Vasu.

Vasillor? Hmm, you may think as you cross your fingers across your chin (I have seen so many people do that!). To that, let me say: good question. And answer it right away! It was my mother's doing. Back in Dehradun, when I was a kid, she would put so much of that shiny, glittery thing on my lips that the folks over there started calling me "Vaseline Vala ladka". Thankfully, one day "Vaseline Vala" morphed into Vasillor. The name sounded cool (Remember 'The Terminator'?) and I kept it. It made me famous and legendary in a way. There were times when random guys during the interschool competitions would ask me, 'Who is that Vasillor guy in your school?' I can't forget the look on their faces when I proudly proclaimed the ownership of that name.

Oh! Before I move on, let me make a confession- that small white and blue Vaseline bottle has stayed as my lifelong companion. My lips often crack up and crave for it. Talking of The Terminator, let me put on record this as well- I am quite a movie buff! A lot of things that happen in my life run as movie scenes in my mind. And now that we are talking about the mind, let me also tell you this – I call it my Nemesis No.1. My mind likes to confuse me and tell me the things I don't want to hear. Most of the days, we two have our arguments and disagreements.

Now, to the story. My story begins- as most of the stories like these do- from college.

Ah! The excitement of the first day of college. I was all dressed up and ready for the show. I knew the eyes would be on me and I would be noticed far and wide (Absolutely false notion, btw, projected by my Nemesis No.1). I had worn my favorite white half sleeves shirt (half sleeves again folded twice), complemented by the flogged dark-navy denims and pearl-white sneakers. Of course, the top two buttons of the shirt were kept open. I know what you are assuming. And you are wrong. It was not to show off my man-hair. Absolutely not! It was to show something much more macho than that - my encased bullet pendant! It was a farewell gift from a retired Army Major, my neighbor in Dehradun. 'Your college girls will dig it,' he had said. A digital Casio sat on my right hand while the left was decked up with a bunch of bracelets and a *Kadda* I had brought from a Gurdwara.

While on the outside, I looked absolutely macho, on the inside, there was a bit of trepidation. It was the first day of my college in Mumbai, and I didn't know the "rules" yet. Plus, there was an apprehension of a confrontation with the *Seniors*. You know, ragging and all. And I am not a pushover. However, thankfully, the *Seniors* kept their distance; there had been a couple of high-profile complaints and some expulsions last year.

I entered the campus as if I owned it. It was a huge campus, and I didn't know where to go. And I did something that I hate the most: I asked for directions.

I reached Level 3, where I was directed to and looked around for room no. 303. I took a right turn and walked some distance before I realized that help would be needed again, as I couldn't find the room. Grudgingly, I asked for directions from a staff member and was told to turn back. The room was on the left wing. With great self-pity, I walked back to the ground floor, went towards the left wing, and climbed the stairs again. I could hear my Nemesis No1, my Mind -

taunt me: *Macho Man! And you think you will win the world! Fool. You can't even find a classroom on your own.*

While walking through the corridor, I saw two guys standing outside the entrance of a room. I swear, they looked like Laurel and Hardy from afar. Those affable, comic guys! So, I went ahead to seek their help. To my amazement, I found them_in the company of at least half a dozen girls. The girls were standing just inside the door, gossiping and cackling.

I wasn't sure whether the guys were *Seniors* or *Freshers.* So, obviously, I didn't know how to address them. Ragging or no ragging, if they were *Seniors,* they had to be addressed as Sirs. Giving myself the benefit of doubt, I thought it apt to address them as such.

'Excuse me, sirs,' I said. 'Could you, please, guide me to room number 303?'

The thinner shorter one- Laurel for you- turned his head leftwards towards me, looked me up from my sneakers to my gelled-up hair, and said, 'Are you an Idiot or what? You are standing right in front of it!'

I was taken aback by his haughty response. I had expected a response as jovial and breezy as good old comic Laurel's, but this guy's response was so surly. It left me at a loss for the right words and I ended up replying with a fumble, 'Sorry, I… I didn't know.'

Yes, this is one of those moments I want to Shift + Del from my memory!

The heftier, taller one, emboldened by my pathetic response, looked at me, opened his big stupid mouth, and said scornfully, 'you don't only sound like an idiot, you even look like one!'

Now, this was just too much! My blood started to boil, and even my otherwise cowardly Mind started to yell *Fight! Fight!* and started to pump additional adrenaline into my body. *Seniors* or *Freshers,* it hardly mattered to me now. They were going to get bloody noses! But then, suddenly, I remembered my father's advice- the one he had given before seeing me off at the railway station: "Count to fifty before you strike. And drink a glass of cold water."

I was as surprised as you are! Normally, I don't remember a thing my dad tells me. But this! This just came out of the blue. And for the first time, I paid heed to it. I counted to fifty in my head and turned back towards the water cooler, I had passed by earlier. Honestly, it was too difficult for me to do this. But I controlled myself. By the time I had gulped down a glass of water, I had tempered down a bit. *It's my first day. Let me be calm today.* I said to myself.

I reorganized myself, went back towards the class, and said to those guys, 'Will you mind stepping aside, please? You are blocking the entrance.'

'What? What did you say?' They both blurted in unison.

Just then, I heard a girl on the other side of the door say, 'He is right. Right to the T. We are blocking the entrance.'

'Well. Yeah. May be.' The other girls added.

'No, he is right…,' the girl said again. Her voice was firm and assertive. 'Guys. Come on. Let's move from here.'

Our Laurel and Hardy stepped aside with hesitation and made way for me. While I entered the class, I could hear them say behind my back, 'Come on. He asked for it. Only a stupid person would ask something like that?'

Okay! I haven't told you this yet. I wasn't counting just for my dad; I was counting for myself as well. For dad, I counted till fifty. For myself, I counted till three! Three strikes, that's all I give people. And it was strike three. Now, they were on my radar and would be dealt with. Not today. Not on the first day of college. I could wait. I would strike them on the day and time of my choosing.

I left my thoughts at that and moved inside.

The classroom smelled of dampness and sweat, and the slowly whirling fans made very irritating noises. There was nothing to like in the room, expect maybe one thing. The room boasted of individual chairs - the ones with adjustable writing pads and all. This was something new, different from the old benches of the school! Most of the chairs seemed taken, though. People had already put their notebooks on the Pads. It was funny in a way, reminded me of how people put kerchiefs on bus seats back in the day.

I looked around for an unclaimed seat. There seemed to be one to my right in the fourth row. I walked towards it. Just to be sure, I thought I should check with the girl who was sitting in the adjacent seat.

'Excuse me, is this seat taken?' I asked the girl.

'No.' She replied without raising her head. I noticed her dark curls, her high nose, and her long face. She was busy doodling in her book.

'May I sit here?' I asked. (A stupid question in hindsight. She had already said it wasn't taken! I did a lot of stupid things that day.)

'By all means,' she replied, still engrossed in her doodling and without raising her head. 'College property. Who am I to stop?'

Amazing! I thought. Where has all the decency of the world gone? No civility. Just guns blazing. Thud. Thud. Thud. My interactions so far convinced me that everybody in here was snobby and bumptious. I took my seat and turned around to have a good look at the class and its strange inhabitants.

I looked at the two guys who had spoken rudely with me. From their body language, I could see that they were sweet-talking the girls. I looked at the girls they were talking to. How would I rate them, you ask? Well, four of them I rated five. Two looked like a solid six. There were two more, but I couldn't rate them as they had their backs towards me.

I turned my eyes to find a group of guys – the Envy Guys - who I presumed (and rightly so, as I found later) were planning to beat the shit out of the two Romeo Boys. Btw, they named these two guys Romeo Boys because they would always be found hanging around the girls. And why wouldn't they beat them? The Romeo Boys had stolen a march over them. They had befriended most of the girls.

Then, there was another group standing in a corner. They were hotly debating the results of some cricket match and throwing stats at each other- strike rate, net run rate, averages – they had all the numbers on the tip of their tongue. It was uninteresting to me, so I turned back towards the girl sitting beside me. She was still absorbed in her own world, doodling away in her book. I watched her as she moved her pen deftly on the paper - a stroke here, a touch there. It was soothing in a way. I relaxed in my seat and observed her work.

'Here, what do you think?' The girl asked abruptly, looking straight into my eyes.

'About what?' I replied. I could instantaneously tell that she knew I had been watching her work and I felt embarrassed.

'About this drawing.' She replied, pushing her notebook towards me.

All this while, I hadn't even noticed what she was drawing. I had just been fascinated with the way she was drawing. But now she was asking for my comments, and I had nothing on my mind. I took the notebook in my right hand and looked at the drawing intently. I gazed at it for some time, trying to make head and tail of it. It was quite baffling. All I could see was something fluffy like a cloud with the wings of a peacock and the head and neck of a swan. There were trees coming out of the swan's head, and the trees had elephants as leaves!

'Ah… Well…It's …. It's great,' I replied, not sure what else to say, 'What exactly is it?'

'You don't have an eye for the art,' She said, 'Do you?'

'Oh! I do. It is just that I am not wise enough to fully understand your art,' I replied tactfully.

The girl looked at me for a while, making me a little awkward. I could sense that she was measuring me up. Finally, she held out her hand and said, 'Hi. I am Vani.'

'Vasillor,' I said as I shook her hand.

'Vasillor?' She raised her brows. 'A name as silly as my drawing,' She quipped.

I felt somewhat slighted by her comment. My name was surely not silly.

'Vishesh,' I said roughly.

'What?'

'You can call me Vishesh. That's my real name.'

'Hmmm. I am fine with Vasillor,' she said and went back to her doodling.

'Okay.'

She didn't reply. And thus, ended our small talk. As abruptly as it had started. Awkward, wasn't it? *Shit!* I thought. *Where have I landed?*

A couple of minutes later, our professor entered the class. Honestly, for the first time in my life, I felt so happy seeing a teacher! He was my savior, who had come to end the awkwardness I was stuck in.

Our professor, Mr. Kasbekar, didn't take much time to get rolling. He started right away by telling us how lucky we were to be part of this great institution. It wasn't just a college; It was a legacy. He had been a student himself of this very grand college and had decided to stay back after graduation and teach. That's how much he loved this college. 'You don't know how lucky you are!' He repeated himself again and again.

After this emotive introduction, it was all about the usual rules and regulations of the college. 'They must be adhered to. Come what may!' He said, banging his fist on the table. He was turning out to be an emotional guy. 'And one more thing,' he added, 'Minimum 75% attendance. 1% below, and you will be suspended. Understand?'

'Yes, sir!' the class replied.

'Louder.' He yelled.

'Yes, sir!' we all shouted at the top of our voices.

'Good then.' He nodded in approval.

By the time he was done terrifying us with his antics, his time was already up. He hardly taught us anything that day. He finished his session with roll calls and left immediately after. His threats had dampened the mood of the entire class.

It took us two more professors (who were, thankfully, quite jovial) to get out of Mr. Kasbekar's torture-induced zone. And by the time the first session ended, we had recovered some of the earlier enthusiasm about college life.

'I am going to the canteen. Care to join?' I asked Vani during the first break.

'No, thanks,' she replied bluntly.

'Come on! I don't know anyone else here,' I insisted.

'Okay, then,' she said. 'Only because you don't have friends.'

'Okay. Sure,' I replied awkwardly.

We walked towards the canteen in complete silence. I wanted to initiate a conversation, but I couldn't find a common thread between us. I tried to figure her out by reading her body language (I had read somewhere that non-verbal cues were stronger than the verbal ones). She had a confident walk and held her neck upright, hardly acknowledging anyone. She seemed so full of herself, and I doubted she would be interested in any talk I had to offer. Nevertheless, I decided to take a punt and humor her.

'Do you always frighten people with your art?' I asked.

'No. Not always,' She replied, 'Only when I see they can be'.

'Oh, so you mark your targets, then,' I persisted.

'Of course,' She replied with a smile.

'Thank God! You smiled,' I said, 'I thought you were serious types.'

'I am not! I just frighten people,' She replied.

'Hey, give me a sec,' I said as we turned around a corner, 'You carry on. I will meet you in the canteen.'

'Where are you going?' she asked.

I pointed towards the boy's restroom. My bladder was bursting, and I wanted to take a leak. I also wanted to check my look and set my hair.

Inside the restroom, it was crowded. Three guys were at the urinals, and three more guys were standing behind them, waiting for their turn. Two guys were near the washbasin, checking themselves in the large mirrors and tucking in their shirts at the same time. I took my place in front of one of the mirrors.

'Would you please move away?' A tall, slender puppy-faced guy standing at the urinal yelled at the guy behind him, 'I can't go with you eyeing me like a hawk.'

The entire washroom erupted into a volcano of laughter, and I couldn't hide a laugh myself.

'No. I won't budge from here, dude.' replied the guy-in-the-queue, still laughing.

'Shit man!' The puppy-faced guy said as he pulled up his zip. 'You go first.'

'You are such a wuss, Aheesh!' the other guy said, as Aheesh moved away from the urinal and started walking towards me.

I quickly looked away from him and started fiddling with my hair. Aheesh, standing beside me now, turned on the tap, wetted his hands, and ran his fingers through his hair. For a few minutes, he kept playing with the water and his hair. Then he washed his face and splashed some water into his eyes. After that, he started playing with his hair again. I could sense that he was just idling his time, waiting for the washroom to get empty. And as soon as the other guys left, he quickly went back to the urinal without even wiping himself dry. The drops of water dripped down from his hair and his face while he relieved himself.

After he was done, he came back up to me and said, 'You are in our class.'

'I don't know,' I replied.

'No, I saw you', He said, 'You were talking with that girl- Vani.'

'Yes. You know her?'

'No, I don't,' He replied casually, 'Aheesh, btw. Nice to meet you.' He said and held up his hand.

'Vasillor,' I said, 'And I am not going to high-five it.' The guy still had not washed his hands!

'Come on, bro,' he said, pointing at his up-in-the-air hand with his eyes and beaming a high wattage smile.

'No, Thanks,' I said.

'OK. I will wash them first,' he said hesitantly.

The guy was persistent. Left with no choice (and after ensuring that he had washed his hands twice with the soap!), I high- fived his wet hand. Fun fact for you guys- as told by Aheesh himself later – he never wiped his hands after washing them. Ever.

'Are you into gaming?' He asked me.

'No. Not that much,' I replied, puzzled by his question.

'Then, what's up with this Vasillor?'

'Long Story. My friends call me Vasillor. You can call me Vishesh Vasu.'

'Cool,' he said. 'And is that a bullet?'

'Yes.' I replied.

'Super cool!' He said and nodded his head.

'What took you so long?' Vani asked quizzically as soon as we stepped out of the restroom.

Oh boy! It was embarrassing. I wasn't expecting her to be around, and I wasn't expecting a question like this either. A girl standing outside a boys' restroom and asking you what took you so long? How the heck would you answer that? I was flabbergasted, to say the least. I think I blushed and fumbled with the words- 'I… I… met … some guys there and got talking.' I looked at Aheesh. He was in complete shock!

'Have you guys met?' I asked her, attempting to change the flow of the topic.

'No.' She replied curtly.

Not interested in getting to know this crazy girl, thank you! I could read Aheesh's body language, but I was too inclined to move myself away from the awkward situation and paid no heed, whatsoever, to his non-verbal cues.

'Then, let me introduce you guys.' I said and conducted the introductions.

'Lucky bastard, you already got a girl!' Aheesh whispered into my ear as three of us walked towards the canteen, 'You scored on the first day!'

'What? She is not my girl. Are you crazy?' I replied, befuddled at his remarks.

'Oh yeah, that's right. Waiting outside the boys' toilet for you makes me crazy! I am telling you,' Aheesh said, 'She has got a thing for you.'

Chapter 2

Before you guys start assuming things, as Aheesh did, let me tell you what happened a few days later.

'That was really mean. But they deserved it,' I heard a silky whisper from behind me.

Now, this unexpected wisp of words tingled my ears and stirred my body. I had surely heard this voice before; and I tried hard to recall- *Where had I heard it? Whose voice it was? Whose? Whose? Whose?* It was like one of those times when you hear a song, and you know the tune, the lyrics, the tempo; but then suddenly you wonder- Hey, who is the singer? And you forget everything good about the song and wrestle helplessly with your pig-headed memory to remember the name of the freaking singer!

Well, this was the best thing anybody had ever told me, and it made me feel so right. I had my doubts earlier, but her words put me at ease. I took them as a compliment - a compliment she had given me for the retribution (fair retribution, I should say) I had taken on the two *Romeo* boys. You remember them, right? – Laurel and Hardy? The guys who had said I was stupid.

It was the presentation day. We had to present case studies of Business Communication on Fortune 500 companies. Now, when it was the turn of our Romeo Boys, they started the presentation by boasting about the type of research they had done and the hard work they had put in to prepare the presentation. They spoke of the hours and hours they had spent in the library, the multitude of different books and management magazines they had read, and what not. 'It is going to blow your minds,' they declared enthusiastically. They held the entire class in awe and attention! 'Guaranteed A+ in all semesters.' Aheesh said, 'Look at the professor's face. She is so lit.'

Their presentation was turning into more of a stage show, and their fake exuberance was getting on my nerves. So, after a while, I stopped paying any heed to them and started nagging Vani. By the way, Vani had become a good friend now. While she was busy doodling in her notebook, I poked my nose into her work and remarked, 'Now that would put Da Vinci to shame, whatever it is: Rhino-Eagle-man? (Fun fact for you guys: Most of her objects used to have wings and legs. Once she had drawn a train, even the train had wings and legs!) She looked at me, rolled her eyes, and went back to her work.

'Hey! You Red Shirt,' the Romeo boy Laurel yelled at me. 'We are giving a presentation here. Stop horsing around and pay attention.'

The entire class pricked up their ears, upon hearing this. All the eyes turned towards me, and do you know how I felt? Yes. You are right. I felt exactly like Frodo, my friend from The Lord of the Rings, felt under the gaze of the All- Seeing Eye. I had to come up with something quickly to save myself. I had no Sam Gamgee.

I looked straight into the eyes of the Romeo boy Laurel and said haughtily, 'Do I need to pay any attention?'

'What? Yes.' Romeo boy Hardy replied, his tone loud, and anger visible in his eyes. He hadn't expected a counter question.

'I don't think I need to,' I replied defiantly, 'There is nothing new in it.'

'How dare you?' they both yelled in unison.

'I dare because I know this presentation of yours is stale and stolen.'

As soon as I said this, the entire class gasped, and a collective "Boo" emerged. Even Vani looked up from her doodle-book to check on the crisis that had just erupted.

'How dare you?' They repeated themselves. This time, however, their voices were shaky. 'We have prepared it ourselves. Do you know how much time…'

'Five minutes!' I cut them short.

Booooooo… The entire class erupted again.

'It took me five minutes to google and download this presentation. I already have this presentation on my pen-drive. The color, the font, everything is the same.'

To further enhance the impact, I stood up and handed over the pen-drive to the professor.

'He is lying, Miss,' they said, turning to the teacher.

It was of no help now. Their game was over. The shakiness in their voices and their just-turned-red faces had already given them away.

The professor really seemed to be lit now! She sat back in her chair, quietly watching the fracas as it was unfolding. I could tell what she was thinking from the look on her face. *Wow! Finally, something interesting in my class. A conflict, a clash. Wonderful! Wonderful! Who is the Adjudicator? Oh Yes. Oh Yes. I am. Let me enjoy it a little more. How satisfying?* Finally, after a good enough time, she rose as the woman of the moment and with a wave of her hand, quieted the entire class.

'But madam...' One of the Romeo boys tried to speak. She didn't look at him. She just showed him her palm, and he fell quiet. They knew they had lost it. You could tell it from the color of their faces. After a while, they stopped putting up the defense. They just stood there, transfixed to the ground, waiting for the teacher to say something.

Boo. Boo. Cheater-cocks! Cheater-Cocks! The shrill of the class rose again, mainly enacted by the Envy Guys, who were jealous of the Romeo Boys. It was their moment of retribution too, but for different reasons. I looked at them, and they nodded their heads. It was a nod of acknowledgment and appreciation. I had become their hero! As for our Romeo Boys, they looked like lambs in the midst of wolves. They were so cornered. Frankly, a part of me felt sorry for them, but overall, I was exuberant! Revenge is dreadfully sweet.

By the time the teacher intervened and pacified the class again, it was done and dusted for them. And I had a self-congratulatory smirk on my face. I had killed their pride- their *mojo*. And for your information, this act of mine became a precursor to the spiraling downfall of their popularity amongst the girls and opened avenues for other boys! Till the end of the college, they couldn't recover from this. From all of this, though, I learned one big lesson: girls can't stand a cheat! You may be chivalrous, garrulous, handsome, or a humorous hunk, but if you are a cheat, you should just forget it. They will be repelled by you. And they will run away from you. As fast as they can!

It was exactly after this scene that I heard that whisper!

I turned around to take a quick look at the speaker. But all I could catch in that instant was a glimpse of her eyes: dark-chocolate brown eyes. It was as if she was anticipating my move; she was ready with her response. She looked back into my eyes with such intensity that I couldn't stand it and immediately turned back. Momentarily, I felt dizzy from that stark stare, and an awkward, thunderous drumbeat rose in my chest.

How unbelievable, you would say when I tell you that in a fraction of second, three consecutive things happened:

1. My lit professor- with her omniscient eyes- had caught me in the act.

2. A thick white chalk had already flown in my direction like a missile and hit me in the eye.

3. The All-Seeing-Eye of the class was back on me, and I was Frodo all over again.

And though I was looking at the board in front of me - taking notes, feigning ignorance- my adjudicator with all the power vested in her made a redundant statement, 'Over here, my lad,' she said, 'eyes on the board'. For the after-effects, she added, 'And for you, Miss, you can chat him up later when the class is over.'

Ohhhh! A collective gasp went up in the class. The guys looked at me in awe and nodded again, marking appreciation number 2 of the day. I was rising in their ranks fast.

'Silence!' The teacher roared, despite knowing very well that this was her instigation. It was her day to show who the boss was!

As soon as the normalcy restored and she went back to her boring best, I became helplessly restless. I just wanted to turn around one more time to see that face. I just couldn't concentrate on anything else, and I was getting miserable. It was during these tumultuous moments that my gaze fell on her feet, which she had coolly perched on the spindle of my chair. *Ahh!* The most beautiful feet I have ever seen. I would have kissed them right there had I gotten a chance!

Oh! how can I not tell you about her nail polish? The color, which still sends me back to tizzies- Pistachio Green, glistening right under my peeping eyes. I don't know for how long I kept watching and admiring them.

Eleven out of Ten! I rated them.

Now, if you guys are into jigsaw puzzles, then this one is for you-

1.   Silky voice

2.   Dark-Chocolate brown eyes

3.   Pistachio Green polished toes.

Start constructing her, as I did! My mind started giving features to her face- the shape to her nose, the color to her hair, the smile to her lips and all that. It was like one of those software programmes where you play around with different looks, face cuts, hair styling, etc. However, as hard as I tried, something always remained missing. And I couldn't take it. *Just one look!* My mind beseeched me, *and my job would be done*! But I knew I was being monitored by my teacher. I had just become a Hero; I could not be a fallen man now.

'You shouldn't have done that,' Vani admonished me as soon as the class was over.

'Done what?' I asked, embarrassed that Vani had caught me gazing at Ada's feet.

'You shouldn't have put them down.' She spoke.

Oh, that! I immediately felt relieved.

'They deserved it.' I said to her.

'Deserved it?' Vani asked, 'What for?'

'You don't know what for...' I replied.

'Still, you shouldn't have done it.'

This pissed me off a little. She didn't know anything, and still, she was taking their side.

'You don't lecture me on that,' I said sternly.

Yes, I might have been rude. But she wasn't helping the cause either. Soon, an argument broke out between us. She was still admonishing me, and I was in no mood to listen to her lecture on morality. Plus, I had another important thing to do. I had to see that face! But Vani just kept going on and on. And this argument took its toll. By the time we were done, and I turned back to check that face- it was gone. The empty chair stared back at me and mocked me!

'Stop this bickering. Let's go to the canteen.' Aheesh finally interrupted.

I shoved my notebook into my bag, stood up, and started walking towards the door. Vani also joined, but we didn't talk.

Please don't laugh when I tell you what I did as we walked towards the canteen. In my defense, let me say I was possessed. All the way up to the canteen, every girl I passed - I looked at their eyes and their feet. Eyes, Feet. Eyes, Feet. The scanner in my mind just wanted a match. I was so consumed in this process that I didn't realize I was being lecherous and making the girls uncomfortable.

'What are you doing?' Aheesh whispered in my ear. 'You cannot stare like that. Too Obvious. Too Obvious. You will get us beaten.'

'What?' I replied, composing myself, 'I… I am not checking out anybody.'

'Really?' Aheesh said flabbergasted, 'Do you take me for a dumbbell? And what the hell are you looking at their feet for? Checking if they are bent backwards? Look man, I don't know what your deal is. But they are no hags. They are all genuine, hot straight-footed chicks here.'

'Shut up. And keep that chick *gyaan* to yourself.' I replied, taken aback by Aheesh's tongue-in-cheek response.

The food didn't interest me that day. The hunger inside me was for something else, not for food. I quickly took a few morsels and excused myself.

'What is the rush?' Aheesh asked. 'Where are you going?'

'I….' I replied, trying to come up with some excuse, 'I have an urgent call to make.'

'Wait for Vani.' Aheesh said, 'She will ask about you.'

She was still waiting in the queue with her stupid coupons, and I was still mad at her.

'No. She won't.' I replied and went away.

'Will see you in the class then.' I heard Aheesh say.

After leaving the canteen, I headed straight to the classroom. There was a reason why I did that. You see, your idiotic mind makes you believe in all kinds of stuff. Stuff like she would be sitting in her seat waiting for you. Stuff like she would also be dying to meet you. But that stuff is all fake. There is nobody waiting there for you. And when you are ready to browbeat your mind, it hatches up a new idea to console you.

You idiot. My Nemesis No1, my Mind said to me. *Look at your watch. In your eagerness, you came in too early. There is still half an hour to go. She will be here anytime. Just be patient and wait.* Be patient and wait! That wasn't possible. I paced in and out of the class, anxiously waiting for her. After a while, I realized that my lips were parched.

I needed some Vaseline. I searched for it in my right pant pocket where I usually keep it. It wasn't there. I searched in my left pant pocket. Not there either. I searched my bag, throwing out the books and pens onto the floor. Not there! I was getting restless and uneasy. My lips, like my mind, started playing with me. They started drying up more. I could feel the cracks. This was turning into a bad day. How could I have forgotten my Vaseline bottle? Left with no choice, I rolled my tongue all over my lips. It left a sour taste in my mouth.

Tuck! Tack! Tuck! Tack! I heard the approaching footsteps. I quickly picked up my stationery from the floor and rushed towards my seat. Of course, I had to act as if I was busy. I couldn't let her think that I was just idling and waiting for her. So, I opened my notebook and started writing. Writing what? You ask. The cow. The easiest of the essays I remembered. I waited for her to enter. My heart was pounding and pounding!

It wasn't her. Some inconsequential guy entered. Followed by another; and then another. I kept my eyes fixed at the entrance. The Envy Guys came in. The Cricket Guys came in. The Romeo Boys came in. I waited. I waited. Finally, the Girl gang came in. As soon as they entered, I started checking them out- No, not those eyes, not those, not those... Maybe I missed her out. Maybe she would just come and sit behind me. I tried to keep my cool.

'You shouldn't have left like that,' Vani said to me, 'Look, I am sorry.'

I hadn't noticed that Vani had come in and taken her seat beside me.

'I had some work.' I replied, without looking at her. My eyes were still wandering all over the place.

'What work?' she asked me.

'I had forgotten my Vaseline,' I replied.

'Vaseline?' Vani asked, surprised.

'My lips become parched.' I replied, turning towards her.

She looked at the condition of my lips, and said, 'Yes, they are so dry. You okay?'

'Yes. Happens sometimes,' I said.

'Here, use this.' She said, handing over her lip balm.

I took it. It stung as I applied it on my lips.

'Aheesh told me you had a phone call to make.'

'Oh Yeah…. That too,' I replied sheepishly.

'Everything fine at home?' she asked.

'Yes', I said curtly and went back to looking around the room.

Suddenly, there was a pat on my back! *It's Her!* My Mind said to me. My heart raced so fast; I thought it would explode. I could feel the blood rushing inside my arteries and veins. *Finally! Finally!* I turned around to see who my admirer - and my tormentor - was.

'Whoa!' Aheesh said, startled by my quick turn. 'You OK.'

'Fuck! It is you.' My mouth blurted out without consulting my brain.

'Who else were you expecting?' Aheesh replied. 'Why have you turned into a tomato?'

'What?' I fumbled.

'Is something wrong with you? Your face is all red.' Aheesh said.

'Yeah. Look at you.' Vani also chipped in.

'Is everything alright?' Vani asked, 'There is something you aren't telling us.'

'What's it?' Aheesh asked.

'It is nothing, really.' I replied.

They kept asking me whether I was fine or not. No, I wasn't fine. I was dejected. My search for her had failed. But I couldn't tell them that. And their continuous probing was getting on my nerves. At one point, I got so frustrated that I just wanted to walk out of the class. They shut their mouths only after the economics professor walked in.

Well, the rest of the day had no meaning for me. I wanted it to end, but it smirked at me and stretched itself to get excruciatingly long. I couldn't concentrate on any of the lectures. I couldn't understand what Vani and Aheesh were telling me in low whispers. All I wanted was to hear that Voice again and to see those heavenly feet. But the seat behind me was empty.

Sometimes, I thought maybe she was teasing and testing me. She was just checking my patience and would reveal herself to me soon. She must have taken a different seat purposely. And she must still be watching me from her seat. So, I kept styling my hair every now and then and ensured that I don't yawn or pick my nose. My impression shouldn't falter. I kept checking the girls discreetly from the corner of my eyes, hoping to catch someone looking back at me in the same way.

My search continued for the entire day, and for the next day, and for many more days after that. I couldn't find her. I came to the point where I almost convinced myself that she was just a hallucination, a dirty trick played by my Nemesis No.1, my Mind on me. *Well played!* I said to it. *Well Played!*

A week later, I heard her Voice again.

Chapter 3

'Dudeeee!' Aheesh came running and screaming towards me, one morning, in the canteen. 'That girl of yours is a freaking genius!'

'Which girl of mine!' I asked, surprised at his excitement.

'That girl… Vani. Do you know who she is?' he said hysterically.

'I am not sure I follow you, Aheesh,' I replied.

'Google her.' He said as he picked up my phone from the table and handed it over to me.

'What is this all about?' I asked, befuddled.

'Let me do it.' He said and snatched the phone from me. 'What is the password? Forget it, I will use my phone.'

He took out his phone from his pant pocket and sat in a chair beside me. I watched it as he typed Vani's name in google search.

'Here. See.'

My jaw dropped as I looked at the results- her thumbnail photos plastered across the screen of Aheesh's phone and multiple page links with her name. I couldn't believe it.

'Is this for real?' I exclaimed.

'Oh, yes.' Aheesh said.

Who was she?

Well, honestly, she had always seemed atypical. She had a very different, very confident aura about her. Anybody could see that. But in the past few weeks that I had known her, she had never spoken much about herself. She didn't have any airs at all. In fact, to me, it seemed that she didn't want people to know much about her, and that's why she kept to herself.

The Google results were beyond my imagination. Let me tell you what Google said:

'Pure genius!'

'Her Painting- The Butterfly on the Glass … simply outstanding. Breaks the ceiling…!'

'Next Anjolie Ela Menon…'

She even had her own Wikipedia Page! Wikipedia Page! Could you believe that?

I had never ever met anyone famous before. And here was one in my class; one who sat beside me and (mostly) spoke to me only. But why was she living as Clark Kent when she could be out there and live like Superman? That was the real question - what was she doing here, after all? Commerce college was no place for her. What was she here for? What to learn? What degree to get? Hell, why did she even need a degree? It was simply baffling!

I really felt sorry for myself. I couldn't help but remember how I had made fun of her doodles. How stupid I had been! I wasn't even qualified to comment. I was petrified to face her now.

'Wake up, dude! Wake up.' Aheesh snapped his fingers in front of my eyes.

'Don't do that,' I said, embarrassed at being brought back to reality like that.

'Do you know how many awards she has won?'

'No.' I said, and before Aheesh could say anything I added, 'By the way, how did you find all this?'

'Don't know. May be some guy, who had hots for her, did a random Google search and all the info came out. It's all over the campus now. Everyone is talking about her. She has become quite famous!'

I looked at Aheesh with raised eyebrows. *Really?*

'What am I saying? Aheesh said getting the hint, 'She was famous already.'

'Yeah.'

'Hey, Let's put your name in search and see what shows up.'

'No.' I said, 'don't do it.'

But he had already taken his phone away from me and typed my name in.

I don't have to tell you what showed up - hundreds and hundreds of *Vishesh Vasus*. I wasn't there on the first page, not even on the second page. I lay buried somewhere at the bottom of the 30th page. I didn't need to be shown this. I will never forgive Aheesh for making me realize how worthless I was.

'So, what do we do now?' Aheesh asked, after trashing me.

'What do you mean?'

'Do we even continue talking to her?'

'Why would you stop doing that?' I asked.

'Oh! I mean, I would really feel intimidated in her presence now. And what would I even talk about? Besides, I don't want to get snapped by paparazzi.'

'Ha ha. Relax. She is famous but she isn't from Bollywood. Besides, wouldn't it be good for you if you get clicked with her? Maybe when you are ninety, you can show the picture to your little children and talk about her.'

'What do you mean by that?' Aheesh asked, angrily, 'Am I not going to get married till I am ninety.'

'No, you took it the wrong way. I meant you would be married by the time you are ninety. Anyway, have you seen Vani on the campus?'

'No,' he said.

'Why don't you call her and check up on her?'

'Why should I?' Aheesh replied, 'You are the one interested in her.'

'No, I am not.' I said. 'Let's get back to the class.'

On our way up towards the class, I saw Vani coming out of the HOD's Office. I looked at Aheesh; he was in his own world and seemed not to have noticed her. I deliberately paced down and took a left turn towards the water cooler. I wanted to be alone for a moment so that I could organize my thoughts- *Should I just continue to talk to her the way I used to, or should I apologize to her for making fun of her doodles? Or maybe, I could ignore her completely. I could start sitting in the back, as far away from her as possible. Wouldn't that be awkward? Yes. But what else could be done? I was petrified to be around her.*

'You are wasting too much water, Vasillor!' Aheesh yelled from behind, startling me, 'Why don't you carry a bottle?'

Creep! How long had he been standing there?

I had kept the tap on, and the water was just running through my fingers. I had been so occupied with my thoughts that I had failed to notice it. I realized I hadn't even drunk a drop.

'Oh! Yes, I will.' I said sheepishly.

'If you are done, shall we move?' He said.

'Yes, of course!' I replied.

Right then, we saw our Economics professor climbing up the stairs. He was the pedantic types who wouldn't tolerate even a minor deviance. A minute late and he wouldn't allow you into his class. On days when we felt that we wouldn't make it on time, we wouldn't even bother to come to his lecture. Why waste our energy climbing up the stairs, only to be refused entry? Instead, we would walk straight to the canteen and do whatever we wanted to with our spare time. We had started missing his classes too often, and one day, he realized what we were up to. In the previous lecture, he had given us all a strict warning: Miss his class three times in a row, and he would ensure that we wouldn't be allowed to sit in the exams. He was already not a loveable chap, and this move made him the most disliked teacher (The vote was held, and he won unanimously!)

So, as soon as we saw him, we rushed towards our class. It was only after I had settled down in my seat that I realized the plan was something else. I had to go and sit in the back! But it was too late for that now. I had already become a casualty. All I could do now was wait, and hope something good pops up in my head once Vani comes in.

I wasn't expecting Vani to just walk in. No. I was sure she would be ushered in with all the pomp and show. The entire team- the HOD and the faculty- would accompany her, and one by one, they would recite her achievements and read eulogies in her name. She would be presented and showcased to us as a role model, a successful peer we had so much to learn from! I waited and waited, but no such thing happened. Vani didn't show up and neither did the HOD or anyone else. Our economics lecture continued and ended as usual.

'Where is Vani?' Aheesh asked me.

'I don't know,' I replied, 'Call her.'

He hesitated for a while but then finally gave her a call.

'She isn't picking up,' he said.

'Try again.'

I was getting worried for her now. I had seen her in college earlier. *Where could she go and why?* Aheesh tried a couple of times more but there was no response.

'Why don't you try from your number?' Aheesh asked me.

'How is that going to help. She didn't pick up your call; she won't pick up mine.' I replied.

'Why don't you give it a try?' He said.

I took out my phone and dialed her number. To my surprise, she picked up the call.

'Hello, Vani. Where are you?' I asked.

'In the hostel,' She replied.

'What are you doing there? All well?'

'Yes. Nothing to worry about,' she replied.

'Okay, then. You take care…'

'Vasillor, Would you…' She said hesitantly and, after a pause, added, 'Never mind.'

'Yes, Vani? Do you want me to do anything for you?' I asked.

'No,' she replied firmly this time, 'I will see you tomorrow.'

'Okay. Tomorrow then.'

'What did she say?' Aheesh asked me as soon as the call was over. 'Is she Okay?

'Seems so,' I said, 'She didn't tell me clearly what she wanted from me.'

'Maybe she wanted you by her side.' Aheesh said slyly.

'Stop talking nonsense.' I said, irritated with his comment.

'What's your problem? You got a hidden GF somewhere?'

'No.' I replied instantly, 'Not at all. Where did it come from? Why are you asking?'

'Then what's making you so cocky. You know how difficult it is to score.'

'I am not being cocky!' I replied, 'I… I just don't think this is that situation.'

'You are a complete moron then!' He continued with his diatribe, 'She is dropping you hints here and there. And seriously man, guys would kill to have a famous girl like her by their side.'

'Forget it.' I said, 'Clearly you don't know what you are talking about.'

'You, my friend', Aheesh said, 'need to clear the things with her.'

'I have nothing to clear.' I told him, angrily.

'Tread cautiously.' Aheesh said, as he picked up his bag and walked away.

'You shut your pie hole' I yelled at him as he left.

What did she want from me? I wondered.

Chapter 4

'Do you mind?' I heard her ask.

I looked up from the book I was reading. Yes, it was her! Right in front of me. *But was she really?* I knew my mind very well. It could be another of its dirty tricks. Or I might have dozed off in that hot library and was dreaming her up. There was only one way to know. I bit my lower lip hard. The gushing pain assured me that it was all real and happening. She was standing in front of me, looking at me, and talking to me. I was awe-struck and frozen like a statue.

Let me, once and for this moment only, try to be as literal and as poetic as I can be: I was absolutely, completely blown away by the symmetry of her face and the glowing contours of her cheeks; by the fullness of her lips and the shape of her mouth; by the wavy flow of her black and bronze hair and the perfect arches of her eye-brows; and those eyes! There was no way I could help myself and not look at those mesmerizing eyes. The eyes that had left me insane.

It felt like déjà vu. Me looking into her eyes, and her giving me back the same heart- piercing look! But this time I didn't chicken out. This was my moment. The moment I had waited for so long. I kept looking. My gaze was so intense that I could see myself there in those eyes, staring at her resolutely and unabashedly!

'Do you mind?' She asked again. This time she pointed towards the empty chair beside me.

Now, this is the point where all heroes fail. And as you guessed, I failed too. Miserably. Pathetically. My tongue - my wretched good-for-nothing tongue - failed me big time. Imagine the scene: She is standing there, expecting a reply from me. And my mouth opens confidently to address the lady, but my tongue makes absolutely no effort to move, not even for the sake of courtesy. The result: I blurt out some dry air and incoherent babble! And I knew I had crowned myself as the King of Fools in front of her.

Her reaction was bemusing. She gave me a benevolent smile, acknowledging her empathy towards my condition.

'Yea.. Yeah!' was all I could utter in a stuttering voice after a few moments.

'Oh!' She replied, 'I will take another one then.'

'I… I am sorry.' I said, 'I mean, you can take it. There is no one sitting there.'

She pulled out the chair, making a screeching noise in the otherwise dead-silent library. Everybody in the room looked at her, but she hardly cared. She sat in the chair and said to me, 'By the way, I like your guts.'

This statement was in the hearing range of everybody still looking at her.

'Excuse me?' I said, completely baffled.

'That presentation day,' she replied cheekily.

Oh, that! She remembers! I blushed.

How did it feel? What do you think? How would you have felt? Well, until recently, I had dismissed her as a mere hallucination, but now, here she was sitting next to me. My chest was puffed with joy and pride. I mean, it would have been more than enough if she just acknowledged my existence. But here she was, talking about my bravery. Her first impression of me was that of a chivalrous knight. What more could I have asked for?

'I didn't know we would meet in the library,' I said to her.

Of course, I pitied myself. I had looked for her all over the college, except for the library. And that's where we finally met. Lesson for you: If you are searching for someone, please start with the library.

'Neither did I,' she replied. 'I am not a library person, you know. I am here for Shukla Madam's assignment.'

'Oh!' I said, 'But, aren't you a little late? The submission is in an hour.'

'I came to know about it today,' She replied.

'Today?' I asked, surprised.

'Yes. Came back today. I was away. Didn't you notice?' She said.

That explains it. I said to myself. *And... Wait! What did she mean by "didn't you notice?" She expected me to notice! That means something.*

Now, what does a guy do in such a situation? There is a damsel in distress, and it is my chance to prove to her that I am that Hero.

So, I said, 'Here- take my assignment.'

She was extremely surprised by my gesture.

'Are you sure?' She said, 'What are you going to show then?'

I smiled at her innocent reply. 'I can show yours, after you make a copy from mine.'

'Oh!' She said, and blushed. 'Sorry. I thought...'

I smiled.

'Change some words to make it look a little different,' I said.

'Thanks,' She replied, still red in face.

'My pleasure.' I said, 'You now have fifty-five minutes to finish.'

While I was conversing with her, I saw Aheesh looking at me from a distance. I ignored him, but he started waving both his hands in the air, too vehemently for anyone in the library to ignore. I held to my ground and ignored him as royally as I could.

'I think your friend is waving at you,' she said to me.

'Sorry, what?' I replied, feigning ignorance.

She pointed towards Aheesh.

'Oh!' I sighed. 'That's Aheesh. Let me catch up with him.'

I stood up from my chair and walked towards him. I could see everyone smirking at me for knowing a jerk like Aheesh. Who waves arms like that in a library?

'What? You Circus Monkey?' I snarled at him.

'Who is she?' he asked me in hushed voice, 'She is quite a looker.'

The latter part of his sentence calmed me down a little, as if it was somehow my own accomplishment.

'She is in our class,' I replied.

'What's her name?' He asked.

'I don't know.'

I really didn't. How stupid! I hadn't even asked her name yet.

'Haven't seen her in the class,' he remarked.

'Yeah. She was away. Joined back today.' I replied.

'Really?' Aheesh said, 'And what's she doing in the library?'

'Working on Shukla Madam's assignment.'

'You seem to know quite a lot about her, huh?' Aheesh said, raising his eyebrows. 'Wait. Wait. She is coming over here, bro. Why is she coming over here?' He added before hiding behind a book.

'Hey, listen,' She said to me, 'Is it ok if I take your assignment with me? I will finish it in the class. The silence here is killing me.'

'Sure. No issues,' I replied.

'Thanks,' she said and left.

'Douchebag,' Aheesh blurted as soon as she had left. 'You handed over your assignment to her. The assignment that you copied from mine! I worked my ass off for it and you get to be the hero.'

'Yes,' I replied calmly, patting him on the shoulder. 'That's what friends are for. Someday, when it is your turn, I will come to your rescue too.'

'Atleast, you could have introduced me,' Aheesh said.

'Of course, I could have. But you chose to hide behind the book like a cockroach!' I replied.

Aheesh closed his book and said, 'The truth, my friend, is that you are into her. I can read it in your eyes.'

I smiled at his statement and said, 'What is your game? First, you said Vani is into me. Now you are saying I am into that girl.'

Aheesh picked up a pen and started drawing something on the paper.

'Let me teach you some elementary geometry. Do you know what this is? This is an equilateral triangle,' he said, as he showed me the paper. He had written names on the vertices: on the top, he had written Vasillor, on the right Vani, and on the left vertex, Miss X.

Honestly, I couldn't help but appreciate his superb take on my situation. But I couldn't tell him that. So, I said, 'Stop this nonsense and let's get back to class.' I took the paper from him and put it in my shirt pocket. *It was going to be a part of my memorabilia.*

I was dying to reach the class immediately. She had told me that she would be there. I looked at my watch; half an hour was still left, which meant nobody else would be in the class except her. This was a prospect I couldn't afford to lose. I would just sit around somewhere and watch her as she worked on her assignment. And if luck favored, perhaps have a couple of words with her as well. I wanted to shrug off Aheesh, somehow. But he was stuck to me like a magnet. He was in no mood to give me a chance to be alone with her. *Aheesh was starting to get on my nerves!*

On our way up, Aheesh tried many times to engage me in the "triangle" conversation, but I was in no mood to get into a banter with him. To my surprise, the class was empty when we reached there. She had told me that she would be in class, and I had expected her to be there!

'We are early. There is no one here.' Aheesh said, 'Let's go on a round.'

'No,' I replied with a sullen face. 'I will take a seat. You carry on.'

I was disheartened. She hadn't kept her word.

'Okay.' He said and left without any protestations. It was very unusual of him. Maybe he understood.

I took my seat, pulled out my phone, connected my earphones to it, put on some music, and started playing a game. The mix of the music in one's ears and the play on one's fingers is a deadly combination. It gets you so self-absorbed, that everything else means shit to you. And I had gotten so engrossed that I didn't notice when she came in and sat beside me, in Vani's chair.

She placed her hand over mine and patted it. I took out my earphones and looked at her. 'Thank you,' she whispered softly in my ear. That whisper! That silky whisper again! That way of bringing her lips near to my ear and saying things. It was killing me! And wait…… She touched my hand! I could have died an exuberant person that day.

Soon the class started to fill in, and I saw Vani enter. I gave her a completely unnecessary but a friendly wave. She raised her hand to wave back but then stopped mid-way. I guess she wasn't happy to see me with *her* and I could sense the displeasure on her face. I kept waving at her and pointed towards the vacant seat to my right. She walked towards it and sat in it, without saying a word. Not even a Hi. I tried to talk to her, but she ignored me. In the meantime, Aheesh also entered the class. He quickly scanned the three of us, and with a look of utter disbelief on his face, kept moving and sat in the chair behind mine.

I turned towards Aheesh and said to him in hushed voice, 'Come to the front, and sit beside Vani.'

'No. Thank you.' He replied, 'I am perfectly fine. I have got the best seat in the world to watch the drama unfold.'

After some time, when the class was filled and there was din in the air, Vani said to me, 'You could have saved *MY* seat for me.'

'I didn't realize she had taken your seat,' I gave her an honest reply.

'You could have told her to vacate it,' Vani said.

'Really? How could I tell her that? It's college property. Remember?'

'Fine. I don't want to argue with you,' Vani said angrily and took out her notebook and started doodling.

I was still trying to comprehend the situation when Aheesh whispered in my ear, 'What would happen to an equilateral triangle if the vertex named Vasillor is hammered?'

I turned and gave him a dreadful look. It didn't seem to have any impact on him, and he continued, 'It becomes a dead-beaten straight line.'

The sudden fall of the cacophony in the class announced the entry of Shukla Madam. And I was happy. At least now, I won't be bothered by Aheesh, and I won't have to listen to his stupid deductions. Shukla madam started by asking for the assignments, and after collecting them, she double- checked the count with the attendance. The counts matched, everything seemed to be in order. With that done, she started with her lecture for the day. Fifteen minutes later, I heard *Her* say, 'What's your number?'

Now guys, take a moment here!

The girl whom I had been chasing at my wits' end for so many days just asked for my number. Asked my number! The state of my mind? – Implosion, exhilaration. Feelings? - Surreal, strange. Sense of Pride? - Yes, of course. A research question for you: How many guys do get asked out? Yes, find out. I was among those lucky bastards! Crème de la Crème!

I quickly tore a piece of paper from my notebook, wrote down the number on it, and passed it over to her. She took out her phone and punched the numbers in it.

Seconds later, my phone buzzed. I took out my phone and saw that she had sent me a *Smiley*. I smiled and sent one back to her.

Five minutes later, she forwarded me a joke. It was a nice one, and surprisingly new. I chuckled after reading it. Vani heard me, looked up from her notebook, and said, 'What?'

'Nothing,' I replied, 'You carry on.'

My phone beeped again. I immediately put it on silent mode and opened the message.

Wht is ur FRND syng?

Whch FRND? I texted back.

The 1 to ur rt.

Nthng. & Wt does dis FRND mean?

U knw. U & Her… It's the word in the class.

I gave her an astonished look and texted back a confused emoji.

Dn't be Nuts.. Nthng Btwn Us. U can ask my FRND?

K. Nwys.. Hope U saved my No.

Yup… As Miss X.

Thts nt my name !!!!

Thn wht is?????

ADA…

Whts dat??

Thts my name… Ada Khanna.

I smiled and replied: *Bful name. Suits U.*

She sent a *Wink* and a *Thnk U.*

Chapter 5

Ada Khanna.

Ada Khanna.

Ada Khanna.

I couldn't stop myself from repeating her name in my head for many days to come. And she didn't help the cause either. She would send me the lamest of the jokes and forwards. Whenever her message popped up on my phone, a smile spread across my lips. Hmm! How fast time flies when you are chatting and texting. Classes started and ended, days started and ended, and I wouldn't care less.

One of those days, during the lunch break, Vani asked me in the canteen, 'Who are you texting all the time?'

I looked at her sheepishly and said, 'What? Nobody.'

'Really?' Vani asked vigorously.

I snapped and replied curtly, 'Vani, are you keeping an eye on me? Am I supposed to tell you everything?'

She was taken aback by my response and apologized immediately. But I was furious and in no mood to accept her apology. I felt I was right, and she was just being nosy. My mind justified my behavior-*She shouldn't be so intrusive. You never ask her what she does or doesn't? Why should she ask you?*

We ate our lunch in silence. Aheesh, who had joined us back, tried to converse but getting no response from us eventually shut up. We were still in the middle of our meals when Vani stood up and left without saying a word. I watched her as she paced away from us. I realized I had spoken rudely to her and began to feel sorry. I just waited and hoped that she would turn back and ask me to apologize. I was ready for it. But she didn't. She kept moving towards the exit and was soon out of my sight.

'Mind if I join you?' Ada asked.

I was pleased to see her. She was holding a plate in her hand. I felt elated that she preferred to have lunch with me rather than with her friends.

'By all means,' I said to her with a smile.

'Where is your friend?' she asked.

Ha! She is teasing me.

'Well, Aheesh is here!' I said, and turning towards Aheesh said, 'Say hello to Ada.'

'Hi.' Aheesh said.

'Hi' She replied and then added, 'I was talking about the other one.'

'Oh! Vani,' Aheesh replied naively, 'She just left.'

'Left? What was her rush?'

'She had to go to the library,' I replied.

'During Lunch time?'Ada asked.

'Did she tell you that?' Aheesh looked at me accusingly.

'No. I presumed,' I replied.

'Hmm. Anyway, don't you guys think we should complain about the quality of food here.'

'Why?' I asked.

'No'. Aheesh said.

'The other day, one of my girls found a cockroach in her food.'

'Really,' I said. 'I am ok with that. I can handle some additional proteins in my food.'

'Yeah. Me too,' Aheesh chipped in. 'I have heard it's a delicacy in some countries.'

'Yuck. How disgusting?' Ada replied, making a face, 'Perhaps you should be deported to one of those countries then. You can enjoy your Cockroach Curry there.'

Cockroach Curry! Aheesh shuddered on hearing this and threw the spoon he was holding, back into his plate.

'We have to do something about it,' Ada continued. 'Here, we need your signatures on this.'

She took out a paper from her back pocket and handed it over to me.

'What is this?' I asked.

'We are complaining to the college management.'

'Are you serious?' Aheesh said, laughing.

'Yes. What's funny about it?' She retorted.

She unfolded the paper on the table and pushed a pen into my hand. 'You sign here.'

I signed as she asked me to. How could I not?

'Your turn,' she said and passed the pen and paper over to Aheesh. He signed too.

'Now, where's your friend?' she asked, looking around the canteen.

'She is referring to Vani,' Aheesh said.

'Really?' I said. I wasn't sure whether Aheesh was also teasing me or just being stupid.

'Is she coming back?' she asked.

'I don't know.' I replied.

'Well. You should have asked her.' Aheesh said.

'Why don't you go and ask her?' I replied irately.

'Okay! Guys.' Ada interjected, 'Let me go first. After that you can fight each other till death if you wish.'

As she rose to leave, I asked her, 'Is that all? You came here for the signatures?'

My question was so sudden and so direct that she stood there stunned. I could see her color change as she struggled with an answer.

You know, it still baffles me. I had never been so straightforward before. Where did I get the courage from?

She didn't answer and instead sat back in her chair, facing Aheesh.

'Tell me Aheesh.' She said immediately, 'Do you find any of the girls in our class interesting?'

'Well… Ah… I find a lot many, frankly,' Aheesh replied shyly. 'Nita….'

'Too bad. She already has a boyfriend.'

'Preeti?'

'Taken.'

'Ruchi?'

'Seeing someone.'

'God! Is no one available?' Aheesh said in desperation.

'Divya is.' Ada replied casually.

'Really?'

'Yes.'

'Thanks for the tip,' Aheesh said.

'No sir, a cold drink for the tip,' She replied.

'You are cunning!' Aheesh said.

'I need that cold drink now. Thums up.' She said like a boss.

'Yes, madam,' Aheesh said and got up to get her the drink.

'Who are you interested in?' She asked me after Aheesh had left.

Oh! She is turning the tables now.

'Why do you ask?' I said.

'Just curious. Have nothing better to do till Aheesh gets me my Thums up.'

'None from the class.' I replied, dryly.

'What about you?' I asked, 'Any catch?'

'No one good enough here.'

'Huh' I said, raising my brows. *How pretentious!*

'Yup!' She said, making a *pap* sound with her lips.

We didn't talk after that, and I waited anxiously for Aheesh to return. No sooner had he put the bottle on the table than she grabbed it and got up from her chair.

'Thanks.' She said to Aheesh, 'Gotta go now.'

She must have taken only a step forward when she turned back and said, 'So… you two aren't a couple then?'

'No. I told you earlier.' I replied.

'Wait a minute! Is she referring to us?' Aheesh asked, bedazzled. 'Why are you marring my reputation?'

She laughed at his statement. 'No, I am not talking about you. I was talking about him and Vani.'

'Ohhhh! Now, are they? That's news for me too.' Aheesh said, cunningly.

'Bro, I told you we aren't,' I said to Aheesh. 'Have you gone crazy too?'

'Don't worry,' She said, 'I was just pulling your leg. Why are you so touchy on the subject? Raises suspicion. Anyway, see you around then. And thanks for the signatures.'

'She knows too!' Aheesh said animatedly, after she had left.

'It's because of people like you! You are all mistaken.' I replied furiously.

'Whatever!' Aheesh said. 'She is gutsy though. I like her. Hope to see her around more often.'

'Sure do.' I replied, as I watched her high- fiving her girls.

Sure do.

Chapter 6

There was a bit of a cold war between me and Vani for some days. She gave me a royal snub every time I tried to talk to her. She started conversing more with Aheesh, which completely zapped him. And one day he told me starkly that if I didn't mend his current situation with Vani and rescue him from this *thing* that was happening to him, he would be left with no choice but to change his seat and his friends too! I said I felt sorry for him, but there wasn't much I could do.

'Don't feel sorry for me,' he said, 'Just say sorry to her.'

'For what?' I replied.

'I don't know. For the weather. For any damn thing you did. Or didn't do!' He replied, 'She is angry with you, and I am the one getting screwed. You better fix it.' He warned me.

'Have you noticed?' Ada said to me one day, 'Vani is always the first one to be in the class.'

'Really? I hadn't!' I replied, feigning surprise. Though I knew it and the reasons why.

'Is it about that seat?' She asked, 'Is it like a throne or something to her.'

'I don't know,' I replied, 'Why don't you ask her?'

'Maybe I will,' she said, 'You guys not hanging out these days? Break up or what?'

'I told you she is not my girlfriend' I protested, 'And no. We didn't break up.'

'Don't get worked-up.' Ada replied with a smile, 'I enjoy pulling your leg.'

'I know.'

'Yes. Yes. You know,' she teased me, 'Be nice to your GF, Mr.!'

So, I had to be nice to Vani.

During the break, I accosted Vani in the canteen. She was drinking her milkshake and chatting with a visibly frustrated Aheesh. I couldn't help but pity him. He was just nodding his head to everything she was saying.

'Vani, give me a break!' I said to her. 'You cannot keep ignoring me like this. I am sorry. What else do you want me to do?'

And finally, she broke her silence and said, 'You know, Vasillor, it wasn't such a big thing. There was no need to be rude. I don't like rude people.'

'I am sorry,' I said, 'I was a jerk.'

'You are a jerk,' Aheesh butted in.

'Yes, you are a jerk,' Vani repeated.

'Okay. I am,' I said, 'Are we good now?'

'No,' She replied.

'No?' Aheesh said, puzzled, 'But he has already apologized.'

'No', Vani reiterated.

'Come on! What do you want me to do?' I asked, 'Take me to an art gallery if you want. It will kill me and make you happy.'

She laughed hysterically upon hearing this.

'If I had to kill you, there are other, more convenient ways.' Vani quipped.

'Psychopath,' Aheesh muttered.

'Seriously? I said to Vani. 'I don't think you are that bad.'

'You don't know me,' She replied, sipping her milkshake.

'Really?' I said, 'Okay, tell me, what are those other convenient ways.'

'Wait,' Aheesh chimed in, 'Are you guys burying the hatchet, or are we discussing the ways to finish Vasillor off?'

'Shut up!' Vani told him, and turning towards me said, 'I am not done with you yet.'

You should have seen how Aheesh's face lit up. It was as if that "Shut up" was music to his ears. It was the beginning of the end of the misery he had been in over the past week. I could see a big "Thank You" plastered across his face.

'Okay. How do I make it up to you?' I asked.

'I don't know.' She replied.

'Let me take you out for dinner this Saturday.'

'I don't know,' She repeated.

'Come on!'

'I have some other engagements.'

'Really. Like what?'

'Why should I tell you?'

'You are over doing it now.'

'Okay. Now that you are on your knees, I will consider it,' She replied finally, with a smug smile.

'That would be so gracious of you. Thank you,' I said.

'So, you are taking Vani out on a date?' Aheesh asked me after Vani had left to order another milkshake.

'It is not a date, you idiot.' I replied in a hushed tone, 'I am doing all of this for you'.

And here's how it unraveled.

By the next lecture, the entire class had received the news of my purported date and the 'talk' had started. I could hear things like, "The First Couple going out on a Date. Lucky Bastard," and so on. The boys looked at me and gave me a wink and a thumbs-up, while the girls gave me a look of amazement and disdain.

But Ada, somehow, seemed quite indifferent to all of this. She had taken a seat at the other end of the class and seemed quite busy with her phone. I watched her, hoping that she would give me a look. And after a long wait, for a brief moment, our eyes did meet, but she quickly turned her gaze back to her phone. I thought maybe she would text me, as she usually did, so I kept checking my phone, but there was nothing. *Who was she busy with?* I started feeling uneasy, and throughout the class, she gave me the cold shoulder like never before. This was unusual. Very unusual.

'Atleast buy me some beer,' Aheesh whispered, 'for all the donkey work I have done for you.'

'Sure, why not? But first, I will break your neck,' I replied, 'What have you told them? Everybody thinks we are a Couple now.'

'And you care about everybody?' he asked me quizzically.

He had caught me right. I didn't care about everybody. I cared only about Ada. And I was upset. Quite upset that she was upset. Okay, I didn't really know whether she was or wasn't. But I, somehow, felt that she was.

Chapter 7

Vani called and asked me to pick her up at 6 pm. *6 pm!* I thought. *Wasn't it too early for dinner?* 'Okay. I will be there,' I said. What else could I say? So, at exactly 6 pm, I was near her hostel. Not exactly at the gate, but some good hundred meters away from it, near the bus stop. Why? Because I really didn't want the girls from my class to see me there. Well, you understand what I mean. I called her up and told her that I was waiting at the bus stop. I was fearful that she would ask me to come to the gate, and I didn't have any solid excuse to say no to her. But luckily for me, she just said alright.

How nice it would be, had it been Ada? My Mind asked me. *I don't know,* I replied. *How would you? You asked Vani out instead of her.* It said. *Maybe, someday I will ask her out,* I replied. *Huh! May be someday, you will. What if Ada walks by and sees you here, waiting for Vani? She will understand,* I said. *Oh, ho! Now, will she?* It questioned. *She won't even talk to you now. She already thinks that Vani and you are a couple. Forget her already. You don't stand a chance…* This thought upset me. Why would my Nemesis No.1 create such demoralizing scenarios for me?

Let me ask you a question, before we move ahead: Name that one inanimate thing that has always fascinated you. Yes? Now, some of you might say a train or a JCB earthmover; some simpletons amongst you might even say a glass paperweight or a stapler. For me, it has always been a Bus. Maybe because, where I come from, a bus was the first big badass thing I laid my eyes on as a child. You could see how badass it was when everyone would scurry off the road when it moved. And that one honk from it, and you knew who the boss on the road was. And I was so awed in its mere presence. And one day, when its doors opened for me, and I got into it.…

Why am I talking Buses here? Because, they have always been my true friends. They make me happy, and I can just watch them all day long as they wheel on the roads. I don't know why not like Thomas the Engine, they don't have Babloo the Bus series. I would have loved that, and the Buses would have loved that, too!

This time, my true friend rescued me. You know, how my Mind can become an albatross around my neck, weigh me down, and try to crush me. But not today! My friend- the Bus- honked so loudly that my body fell aside the road, and my Nemesis No.1 lost all its controlling power over me. In trembling voice, it said: *You want to kill me!*

After the bus had moved, and I had gotten up and brushed the dust off my clothes, I saw Vani coming towards me. She waved at me, and I waved back. While she was approaching me, I couldn't help but notice how cheerful and beautiful she looked. She had put on a cute black dress and accessorized it well. She had a fashion sense! Who would say she was a painter? She had left her curly hair loose, and I could smell her perfume even from a distance.

Well, I was completely out of place! I hadn't even cared to change my clothes. I was still wearing the same set of clothes - loose grey T-shirt and blue denims that I had worn to the college for the day, and even they were dusty now.

'I have to compliment you,' I said, 'you are looking nice'.

'Thank you.' She replied. 'You look great too.'

'Really Vani?' I said, 'Don't be so charitable with your words. At best, I look like a pauper. And you, on the other hand, look like a princess.'

She laughed and said, 'For that compliment alone, I forgive you for dressing up so shabbily.'

'Now, that's the truth,' I said, 'So, where to, princess?'

'I thought you were taking me out. You had plans,' she said.

'Well, I just wanted your opinion. If you don't have one, then we are going to Anna's Hotel there,' I replied jokingly.

'My opinion? Let's go to Marine Drive,' she said.

Heck! Why's it always Marine Drive? And Bandra? And SRK's house? Why? Is there nothing else in this city? In my short stay thus far, I had been to Marine Drive atleast a thousand times! Ferrying my friends and my cousins, and their cousins, up and down to Marine Lines like a taxi. And now, here I was at it again.

Once in town, she insisted we get into a black and yellow fiat cab. I suggested we get into a Santro or any other car, but she rejected my suggestion and hunted down the oldest looking fiat car that was plying by, and we got into it. The cab was so old and crabby; it looked like it would break down anytime. The seats were worn out, the glass windows didn't work, and a clacking sound came every time the driver changed the gears. I was getting highly uncomfortable and anxious in that car. The only consolation I had was that this ordeal would be over soon, and we would be in Marine drive within ten minutes. But Vani seemed to have other plans. In between, she instructed the driver to take us to a couple of places before going to Marine drive. She had become so lively and animated that I was really surprised. What was she enjoying?

'Vani, can I ask you why you chose this wretched car?' I asked her.

'I liked it,' She replied, looking out of the window.

'What is there to like in it?' I asked, surprised.

She took a long breath and turned towards me before answering.

'Hmmmm… Nostalgia.'

'Nostalgia?' I asked.

'Yes, it's the best feeling in the world.'

'Really?' I chided her, 'Seems you haven't had any other feelings then.'

'One day, you will know...' She said with a mysterious smile. 'Nostalgia is what produces the greatest art.'

'Thank God!' I said, sarcastically, 'I am better off without it.'

'You won't always be,' she said and looked out again.

I shut my mouth and didn't respond.

What? Of course, she was right. Now, I know. Absolutely!

As we spent more time in the cab, I started getting a little comfy as well. The seats started feeling cozy; and somehow, I started missing my old sofa in our house in Dehradun. The sofa I had spent my childhood jumping up and down upon. Even our driver seemed like an acquaintance now. He was a good old man, who went about his job quietly. He didn't poke his nose into our conversations and kept his eyes on the road. Our conversations didn't seem to interest him, which I liked.

When we passed the Jehangir Gallery, I remarked: 'So, when are you showcasing here?'

'Next month,' She replied, casually.

How could she be casual about it?

'How do you do it?' I asked her.

'Do what?'

'Do you realize the position you are in? And still, you are like I don't give a damn.'

'What would you have done in my *so-called* position?'

Wow! I had never thought about it.

'I don't know. Maybe become bombastic.'

'For how long?' she asked.

'For long enough,' I said.

'And after that long enough, you would just want to be you.'

Well, Vani wasn't easy to answer to. Some of her remarks were ballistic. It was better for me to keep my mouth shut.

We rolled through other landmarks- The Asiatic Library, The Fountain, The Taj, The Gateway etc. I could notice that she was observing all these landmarks with an artist's eye. I was sure they would all become a part of her canvas one day. I wondered how she would draw them. Perhaps she would put wings on The Gateway, and a trunk on the Taj. I chuckled at the thought.

'What's so funny?' she asked.

'Nothing,' I replied.

'You chuckled. It must be something. Tell me.'

I didn't want to joke about her drawings, so I had to quickly come up with a lie.

'The last time I was here, a person slipped and fell down. It was funny,' I blurted out the lamest of the jokes.

She gave me a look which said- *Do I look like an idiot?*

I cleared my throat and thought hard to come up with another good lie.

'Have you been here before?' She asked.

'Yes,' I replied enthusiastically.

'With whom?'

'With my cousins.'

'Okay.'

Vani had so many topics to talk about. From the history of the Taj, she had suddenly moved on to the Art Deco, which, for your information, I had never heard of before. From Art Deco the conversation veered towards the Parsi Fire Temples and the Towers of Silence. Moments later, she was talking Ban Maska and Vada Pav.

'Wow!' I said, 'Vani, I think you are in love with this city.'

'Aren't you?' She asked.

'Well. I don't know.'

'Why?'

'Maybe I don't know this city that well,' I said.

'You don't fall in love after making acquaintances first. You just fall in love. Like this.' She said, as she clicked her fingers.

Of course, she was right. Wasn't it all too familiar?

We reached the restaurant she had chosen by around eight o'clock. It was one of those dimly lit restaurants where suited-booted managers stand near the glass door, waiting for people to come in. As soon as we entered, the manger immediately greeted us with a big smile. 'How many people, sir?' He asked. 'Two', Vani replied before I could. He signaled to a waiter who came rushing over. The manager whispered something to him, and the waiter nodded his head before looking at us. 'Please come with me.'

We followed him to the end of the restaurant. This part was slightly barricaded from the rest of the restaurant with a false wall. There were multiple two-seater tables placed in that area. It seemed as if this part had been specifically created for "couples". And the waiter left no doubts about it when he seated us at one of the tables and said, 'Enjoy your privacy.'

The false barricades were awkward, to say the least. People like me, who are somewhat tall could easily gaze over the barricades and have a grand view of all the restaurant, including the front entrance, and observe people coming in and going out. It was the shorter people who were at a disadvantage and had no access to such a view. Another awkward thing was that the walls were covered with paintings, and there was one large mirror on the side wall to my right.

'Some of them are fakes, you know.' Vani said as she saw me checking the paintings.

'Really!' I asked with genuine surprise, 'they seem so real.'

'Nah. Just knock-offs,' She replied with an air of authority.

'Hmm. You know better,'.

For dinner, I was craving dal makhani and some butter naan. But she ordered the Thai food. My mistake. I had told her earlier in the cab that I hadn't ever had Thai food. Now she insisted that I have it. And to ensure that I tasted the authentic Thai, she discussed and dissected the order with the waiter to its last ingredients. I kept watching them stupidly, as they conversed about what ingredients *I might like or dislike!* They spoke in an alien language about the different herbs and sauces to be used. Finally, when the waiter walked away after a lengthy discussion, I had a chance to say what I had been holding up inside me for the entire evening.

'Hey Vani, I am sorry Aheesh is such an idiot. He made it sound as if we are… you know. I could see how embarrassed you were.'

'No. I wasn't.' She replied casually, flipping through the menu card. 'What will you have for dessert?'

Her answer left me squirming.

'Ah! Well, we just ordered the main course. Let us order the dessert later.' I replied.

'We can order it now. It's not like they are going to bring it before the main course, anyway.' She said.

'Butterscotch…. Butterscotch ice cream, then.' I replied without using my brain.

'Okay,' she said, 'I will also have Butterscotch.'

She called out the waiter and placed the order for the ice-creams. It was funny how the waiter reacted. 'Do you want me to bring it to you right now?' He asked.

'No, after the main course.' Vani said.

'Okay.' He replied and left, scratching his head.

I continued the conversation.

'Please don't get Aheesh wrong,' I said, 'He didn't mean it. You don't have to worry.'

'I don't worry about such things,' she said succinctly.

What could I say after that? Nothing. I picked up the glass from the table and started drinking the water, one sip at a time, for as long as I could. I just wanted to keep my mouth busy, so that it wouldn't utter anything else.

Vani too fell silent. She engrossed herself with the menu card, reading aloud the names of the dishes. I took out my phone and began to read all my text messages, including the spam. I smiled as I went through Ada's texts. I wondered what she would be doing at this exact moment, where she would be? What… The clinks of the spoons that the waiter was setting on the table brought me back from my thoughts.

'Do you know? She said, immediately after, 'The painting over there is Van Goggh's Starry Nights. Ever heard of him?

'No. But I have heard of MF Hussain,' I replied.

She raised her brows and continued, 'He made this one during one of his fits.'

'Was he crazy?' I asked.

'No. He wasn't.' She replied, 'but he didn't have an ear.'

'Oh! so he was crazy and half deaf.'

'And you are a complete moron,' She said and continued, 'You know the beauty of this painting…'

I had already zoned out of the topic. My eyes were fixed on the front entrance, and I started counting the people coming in. And I thought of Ada, again. I wondered whether she also spoke of paintings and artists I had never heard of. What did she talk about? Hmm… People, mostly. And the juicy gossip about them. All that interesting stuff!

WAIT! I shook myself. Was that Ada at the door? I rubbed my eyes and looked again. She had just entered the restaurant with some guy. A shiver ran through my spine. While the manager was talking to them, she threw a look in my direction. I was so spooked! I didn't want her to see me. So, I did the unthinkable. I quickly went under the table. 'What happened?' Vani asked me. 'Oh! I think I dropped my phone.' I lied.

You know how you feel in these situations. It was as if I had been caught red-handed carrying out some sort of crime! I hadn't wanted anyone, and especially Ada, to find out about the dinner. But here I was. Everything blown up in my face. *Hmm! Whatever!* I finally reassessed and gathered some courage; I couldn't, anyway, hide under the table forever. *Man up!* I said to myself. I rose and claimed, 'Here it is!' and put my phone on the table. I sat upright in my seat and spoke with Vani for some minutes. And then slowly, turned my eyes towards the front door again. I didn't want to look, but how could I not? She wasn't at the front door. I tried to check whatever area of the restaurant I could. Couldn't find her. My mind dismissed her as hallucination, but somehow, I knew she was there in the restaurant.

Vani had moved on from Van Gogh to MF Hussain and then Raja Ravi Verma. 'Yeah, I have heard of them,' I said. I had hardly any interest left in the conversation. I nodded at whatever Vani was saying and sometimes replied without an affirmative "Yes Yes."

I was sure that Ada was somewhere in the restaurant. I kept looking for her. I couldn't find her in my part of the restaurant (barricaded by the low wall), so I assumed she had taken a seat in the other part. A great urge rose inside me to go up to the other side and check out, but I continuously fought it. It was during this commotion that I caught a glimpse of her in the side-mirror running across the wall. I looked at her laid-back hair, the chocolate-brown eyes, the luminescent cheeks, and the effervescent smile. Yes, it was her! *But who was that guy with her?* I asked myself. *Must be her boyfriend!* My Nemesis No1 answered. My stomach turned at this. This thought that she had a boyfriend, scorched me real hard.

I HAD TO see this guy! But he was seated with his back towards the mirror, and I couldn't see his face. *Could it be somebody from our college? Do I know the guy?* I asked myself. I kept looking at Ada for a while as she chatted and laughed.

'Excuse me,' Vani said suddenly and loudly, calling for the waiter, 'How much more time?'

I saw Ada stop in the middle of her laugh as she tried to pick up the voice. Before I could turn away my eyes, she had caught me looking at her in the mirror. I could see the bewilderment on her face, and I reciprocated, acting as startled, baffled, and puzzled as she seemed! Moments later, she turned her eyes away and moved her chair slightly to get out of my line of sight. It killed me! And I felt insulted- Very insulted.

The food arrived, and it looked sumptuous, but I had lost my appetite. I just wanted to get over with the dinner and get going. Ada's rebuff and the fact that she was hanging out with some guy was already too much for me. I just wanted to run away from that place, as fast as I could! *Wait a minute, you coward!* My Nemesis No.1, my mind said. *You want to run away? Why? Obviously, Ada is having a good time. What is stopping you from having one? And mind you, you came here with Vani! At least show her some respect!* For the first time, my Nemesis No.1 sounded reasonable, and I listened to it.

Vani started talking about the food, and how well it looked. She took out her phone, clicked some pictures of the food and expressed her satisfaction with the presentation.. Then she tasted the food, and a warm smile crossed her face. 'Perfect!' She said. I picked up a spoon and tasted the food as well. It tasted like heaven. I had never had anything like this before. 'Vani, I will never forget this taste,' I said exuberantly.

I could sense her pride as she had given instructions about the preparation.

We got busy with eating when suddenly my cellphone beeped. I picked up the phone from the table. It was a text message, and it was from Ada. It read: *The First Official Couple of the Class out on their First Date... Congrats!!*

This was interesting! Ada felt that Vani and I were out on a date and texted me. I read the message again. The words carried a whiff of tease and jealousy, and I couldn't be happier or more satisfied! I re-read the message a couple of times, thinking of how to respond.

I typed in a few words and then deleted them, then typed again and deleted again. I couldn't come up with a proper response.

'Your food is getting cold,' Vani said, matter-of-factly.

'Oh, yeah. Thanks.' I replied and kept the phone back on the table.

Let's keep Ada waiting! My Nemesis No1 said.

After a moment, my phone beeped again. There was another text, and it read: *No Reply!*

'Sorry.' I said to Vani, 'It's a friend. I have to reply,' and quickly typed in my response: *Come On! It's not like that. It's just a friendly dinner. I owed her.*

I put the phone down on the table again and continued with my dinner. Vani asked me how my food was, and I said I hadn't eaten anything so nice. 'Don't you see how happy I am!' I said.

Soon, there was another message: *Wasn't expecting to catch you people here!*

Neither was I !!!! What are you doing here? Following us? I texted back.

Oh Please! She replied.

I smiled at her reply. Vani looked at me, and asked 'What is it?'

'The food,' I replied.

I looked in the side- mirror and was surprised to see Ada looking at me. I smiled at her, and she smiled back. I saw her go back to her phone. And when she looked up at me again, my phone beeped, and she gesticulated with her eyes to read the text.

I read the message: *Pay attention to Ur DATE. Stop chatting! That's rude!*

No.1- She is not my Date, I replied, *No.2 - Aren't you doing the exact same thing? BTW who is the GUY?????*

I looked at her through the mirror as she read the message. She didn't react or reply; she simply placed her phone on the table. I waited for her response and kept looking at her in the mirror. She didn't look back and went on with her conversation with the guy. I felt agitated. *What is all this drama? Why's she acting so weird?* I thought. I put the phone in my jeans pocket and started talking to Vani. I saw Ada peep at me twice- once when I was having my ice-cream, and again when she rose to leave.

After our dinner was over and we were ready to leave, Vani proposed a walk on the Marine Drive promenade. She loved its yellow-colored ambience and the breeze that swept across it. Left sour by Ada's behavior, I wanted to head straight home, but Vani insisted, and I had to give in. While walking on the promenade, she thanked me for the dinner and said it had been a really good time for her. I thanked her for forgiving me and said that I hoped we would remain friends forever. She rested her head on my arm as we walked slowly on the promenade.

'Did you see her? Vani said suddenly, as if she had woken up from a slumber.

'Who?' I asked. I knew very well who that could be!

'Ada. She was sitting over there with some guy.'

'Really!' I replied with a tinge of despair in my voice and turned to have a look.

There was a "sea of couples" sitting over there on the bund- holding hands, stealing sneaky kisses, removing the breeze from each other's locks, and doing all that romantic stuff the couples usually do.

'Where?' I asked.

'Over there,' Vani replied, 'Let's go say Hi to her.'

'No. Let's respect her privacy and not do that.' I replied.

'What privacy? She's here on the Marine drive. People bump into each other here.' Vani said.

'Vani, you realize she might be with her boyfriend and she might not like our bumping into each other thing.'

'Oh! Yeah. You are right. Let's not do it. Must be with her BF.' Vani replied. Her tone sounded chirpy as she said this.

Next day, for the first time, Vani went up to Ada and spoke to her. She even walked out of the class with her during the recess, much to the bewilderment of Aheesh.

'What? Are they BFFs now?' Aheesh asked me, 'What are they bonding over?' And then with a look of suspicion added, 'Is it You?'

'Well, my friend,' I replied teasingly, 'In that case, I wouldn't be stuck with you over here.'

'You are not double dating them, are you?' Aheesh asked me in a serious tone.

I made a gun gesture with my hand and shot two rounds at Aheesh.

Chapter 8

I remember a few weeks after the restaurant episode, all of us- Ada, Aheesh, Sushant and others - were seated in the canteen, having food when Vani came running in and announced, 'Ada, your boyfriend is here.'

'What?' Ada said, blushing.

'You have a boyfriend?' Aheesh asked.

Although this announcement had already made me lose my appetite, I kept shoving the food into my mouth to keep quiet and not to show any evident reaction.

'No.' She replied, 'I don't have a….'

'There,' Vani interrupted her and pointed out through the window, 'There he is. He was asking about you, and I directed him here.'

All of us looked out through the window, I somewhat hesitantly. Here was a guy who had gone full-on charm: clean-shaven, hair spiked up; dressed in navy blue blazer, white shirt, red tie, and grey trousers. From looks, you could classify him as handsome; and from his attire, you could say he was somewhat formal and studious. And I could reckon that he was *that* restaurant guy. *A Good match for Ada,* I thought. *But what is he doing here?*

'You guys wait here.' Ada said, as she rushed out of the canteen to meet and greet him.

We kept watching through the window. He smiled and waved at her as she approached him and opened his arms SRK style to hug her. My heart sank, obviously, and my stomach wrenched. My mind rebuked me. *You are a moron Visheesh Vasu. You should have known better. Stupid! Stupid! Okay. Keep your distance now. She is taken. Someone else's. Keep away from her!*

Did she go running into his arms? You ask. It's a shameless question! But I will still answer. And the answer is - I don't know. I had stopped looking as soon as he opened his arms. I couldn't take any more of that pseud!

'Aww. Don't they make a cute pair?' someone from the group said, 'What do you think Vasillor?'

Really? Am I being teased now? I thought. *And who was this girl asking me, anyway?*

I chose not to answer.

'Aren't they a cute couple, Vasillor?'

This time Vani asked me.

Not again!

I took my time to chew all the extra food I had in my mouth and then replied sarcastically: 'Yes. I think they are the best couple in the whole world.'

My reply had its effect. It shut down further questions; and surprisingly (*or not so much!*) upset Vani. 'They are cute! But I wouldn't say the best couple in the whole world.' She said, wearily.

Moments later, Ada brought the guy inside the canteen. She had placed her arm in his arm, and they strode past the tables and the people sitting around these tables. Their steps were so synchronized it looked as if they were participating in the Republic Day parade. While for others their parade was a great spectacle, for me it was just a pompous show.

Talking of parades, have you seen the "Failed Parades" videos on the internet? They all start with great openings- clockwork coordination and organic cohesion. And then, in a microsecond, some odd thing happens- somebody goofs up, and the whole spectacle goes to debris. You don't remember it for the grand sight it was, you just remember it for that one goofy thing that undid it all.

That goofy thing was about to happen!

'Okay everyone, meet Harsh,' Ada said, and even before he could open his mouth to say Hi, she added, 'And tell them you are not my boyfriend.'

Ouch! It was so unexpected and awkward. Poor Harsh blushed left, right, and center. Somehow, he managed an awkward smile and shook hands with all of us, repeating every time: 'I am Harsh, and I am not her boyfriend.' Frankly, I felt bad for the guy. He had just met us for the first time, and this was how he had to introduce himself! Minutes earlier, I didn't even want to look at his face, and now he had all my sympathy. I was amazed with what Ada could do and the position she could put you in. She was brute!

Turned out, Harsh was a sorted guy. He was in IIT, looked like a model, and had cool stories to tell. He had a very impressive way of narrating things, and I could see how girls fell for his charm. How could Ada not have fallen for him? It was mind-boggling. I still couldn't believe that he wasn't her boyfriend. With the type of guy he was, I would say Ada had a deal. I couldn't understand why she wasn't grabbing it.

Harsh kept regaling his audience. He spoke about the fun adventures he and Ada have had together. They were childhood friends and had been inseparable since class one. 'That makes us as thick as thieves. BFFs', he said. Now! Though a sorted guy, he was still Ada's BFF. So, his talks -howsoever interesting and enthralling- just made me more envious. Human nature, you see! I tried to wriggle out of that mental space but couldn't find a way out. I decided- *Okay, why not play along.* When Harsh ended one of his stories, I said sarcastically, 'What a great story!' and then, looking at Ada added, 'how come you never told us these fantastic tales?'

Ada caught the hang of my sarcasm. She understood how uncomfortable I was with the stories of their camaraderie. While Harsh continued telling the tales, she looked down and fiddled with her phone. During one of these narrations, my phone beeped. I took it out from my pocket and checked the message. It was from Ada, and it read: *I know U r getting bored. Sorry! Harsh is a bit talkative.*

A bit talkative! Really! He had been raving non-stop for hours now. I turned towards her, but she was still looking down at her phone and fiddling with it. I wanted to draw her attention, so I put down my phone on the table with a thud. The entire gang, including Harsh, looked at me before continuing their chatter, but Ada didn't. She was too embarrassed to look at me. I felt sorry for her, but I still wanted to chide her. I picked up my phone and texted her: *Bored? Not at all. Who doesn't like adventure stories? That too from your BF.*

She replied instantaneously: He *is NOT my BF.*

I looked at her again. She was getting uneasy and angry now. She leaned towards Harsh and whispered something in his ear. Seconds later, Harsh said he had to leave and got up. He bid us quick farewells, and Ada escorted him out.

'They look so fab together.' Vani said as soon as they had left.

'Truly, the best couple in the world.' I repeated.

~

I vividly remember a weird (and, I should add, quite filmy) daydream I had later during one of our boring lectures.

I was seated on a bench on a railway platform. I didn't know why I was there. Was I coming or going? Or was I waiting for someone? I watched as the trains came by and stopped for a while. And the people got into and out of them, pushing each other frantically. There was dust and commotion all around.

And in that din, I felt a hand on my left shoulder. 'Ticket?' I was asked. I trembled and searched for the ticket in my pockets. It was nowhere to be found. The hand on my shoulder tightened its grip. I shuddered under its pressure. 'You don't have a ticket?' the man asked me authoritatively. 'I think I have it somewhere,' I replied meekly and continued my desperate search. 'I know people like you. You fucking freeloaders!' He replied sternly. 'Look sir...' I said and turned to face the man.

The man was none other than Harsh! He still had his hair spiked up and wore the same attire. But something about his face had changed. It wasn't the old cheerful face I had seen. It was a sad face- elongated with droopy eyes and hanging ears. A shiver ran down my spine. I felt guilty towards this man. He took hold of my hand and started to drag me away. 'Please Harsh!' I said. He gave me a stern look and kept dragging me.

While I was pleading with him, I saw Ada running towards us from the end of the platform. She looked like a flower - beautiful and dewy; and her hair flew like wild leaves in a breeze. My heart palpitated. I was ashamed and embarrassed. I would rather die than watch her see me being dragged away like a petty criminal.

But! But she didn't notice me. She ran past me towards the train. And as the train moved, she increased her pace. She wanted to get on that train. She was trying hard to reach for the handle of the last door but was falling short. I could see the desperation, the fright in her eyes. She was about to let go, when suddenly a hand pulled her inside the train. She leaned out of the door, looked at me with those fierce brown eyes and blew a goodbye kiss.

I was brought back into the real world by Aheesh, who shrieked in my ear: 'It is utter confusion out there.'

'What?' I replied, afraid that Aheesh had somehow read my mind.

'I mean look at this. So many signals. So much chaos. Doesn't make any sense,' he said.

'Cut the crap and come straight to the point. Not a good time for your wise-ass talks,' I said peevishly.

'Look bro,' Aheesh replied, 'Look around you. What do you see? So many intertwining stories floating around. Linkups and cross linkups. But four months, maybe five months down the line what do you think is gonna happen? All these stories, these linkups would be dead and buried. And the new ones will arise.'

'You enjoy this. This commentary. Don't you?' I said.

'Immensely.'

'Why?'

'I don't know. I am like Harsha Bhogle. I am not a player. But I am a damn good commentator. It is fun.'

Chapter 9

Days later, while we were as usual whiling away our time in the canteen, Ada asked me, 'So, what do you think of Harsh?'

I was caught off guard by the question. Why was she asking me this? Did she really want my opinion? Or was she just looking for some endorsement?

'He is cool and smart. Apt for you. You should marry him.' I said coldly.

'Shut up. I didn't mean it that way.' Ada replied crossly.

'What way did you mean then? Why in the world would I care or think about Harsh?' I retorted.

She showed no reaction to my outburst. I guess she knew the reasons behind it. She kept quiet for a moment. But being Ada, she couldn't let it go so easily. She started to chide me.

'You know a lot of girls from our class drool over him.' She said and waited for my reaction.

'Really?' I replied casually, 'Didn't know that.'

I understood what she was doing, and I wasn't going to let it go her way.

'Yes. Some are even asking for his number.' She said.

'Give it to them.'

'No way.'

'Why not? You want to keep him all for yourself?'

'What?' She replied, taken aback, 'What do you mean by that?'

I was in no mood to budge. 'What about you?' Don't you drool over him?' I asked.

'No' She replied, getting angry now. 'I don't.'

'You two have always been together? Such good friends. Comfy and all. Shouldn't you two…?'

'No,' She interjected me mid-sentence. 'Why are you fixated on me and him? What is your problem?'

What exactly was my problem? How could I explain this? How could I answer this? And if you can't answer a question, you do the next best thing- you turn the question around. And so, that's what I did! 'Why should I have a problem?' I asked.

But immediately after saying this, I regretted it. What if she said, 'Exactly, it's none of your concern'? What would I say after that? I gulped down a glass of water, came back to my senses, and apologized to her. 'I am sorry for my tone. I overstepped.'

She responded to my apology with a smile and continued, 'Do you know he asked me out?'

'When?' I asked with trepidation.

'Long back. In school actually. When we were in 10th Class.'

'Really?'

'Yeah.'

'So… you and he…'

'He was my best friend. So, I went out with him once. For a meal at McDonald's. Imagine! But that wasn't the fun part. The fun part was this. There was this girl who had a crush on him. Coincidently, she was there as well. She got so angry seeing him with me that she poured her cold drink over him. Poor Harsh! He was a sight to see. He looked like a wet frightened kitten! I had to wipe off the cold drink from his face and drop him home. He hasn't gone on any dates ever since!'

'So, you two are not in a relationship.' I asked again.

'My God! For the umpteenth time -NO,' she said. 'What about you? Do you have a girlfriend?'

'Why do you ask?' I replied, 'Are you interested?'

'No way,' She blushed.

'Then it shouldn't matter,' I said, giving her a smug smile.

'What are you so secretive about? It could be a simple yes or no.'

You know me by now. I am a drama queen. How could my answer be a simple Yes or No? Where is the drama in it? And I wanted some. So, I kept quiet and grinned.

'I take it for a Yes,' she said, 'Such a waste. There are many girls I know who would be interested in you.'

This piqued my interest. Really? I had underestimated myself then. I was in demand, and I didn't know! *Play it cool. Play it cool. Don't get overexcited.* My mind said. I acted disinterested, as if such things were routine in my life, and gave another of my magnanimous smiles. Girls! Whatever.

'Tell me.' She asked, 'Who is the girl? You always seem busy on your phone.'

So, she notices me! My chest puffed up a little. What a moment for me! I continued the drama.

'If I answer you, would you stop bothering me?'

She nodded her head.

'Yessss.' I said slowly, accentuating on "sss" sound. I watched her intently as I said it. Her reaction would give me the answer I wanted.

'I thought so.' she said, shrugging her shoulders. She saw me watching her and quickly turned her eyes away, looking out of the window. Something was running in her mind. I could sense that by the way she played with her hair- turning and twisting it with her fingers. Honestly, her reaction was giving me the goosebumps! I just hoped that I hadn't pushed her away by my superfluous acting. I was about to tell her that it was all false when she turned back towards me and asked, 'So, who is she? Is she from college or from school?' I heaved a sigh of relief and continued.

'What? Do you know about all the affairs in the college?' I asked.

'Try me,' She replied, 'I have my sources.'

'Sources? Who are you? CIA?' I said, 'And to answer your question, she is from my school.'

'Show me her picture,' She said excitedly, 'Let me see if she is good enough for you.'

'Are you serious?' I asked. 'Are you my grandma?'

'Ok. Chill. What's her name? I will Facebook her,' she said.

'Seriously, man! Are you interested in me or the girl? I thought you were interested in me,' I said, laughing.

'None,' she replied and got up from her seat, 'And both. I will find her!'

After she walked out of the canteen, I made myself comfortable in the chair, picked up the glass of water from the table, and gulped it down like a mafia boss - the boss of the entire world! There was a smug smile on my face for everyone to see. All the acting and the drama had been worth it. It helped me come to three valuable deductions:

Harsh wasn't her boyfriend. In fact, she didn't have a boyfriend.

My made-up girlfriend bothered her. She had some level of interest in me.

There was abundant hope for me.

Now, those were my deductions. Her interest levels had yet to be verified. So, I hatched a plan. I knew sooner or later Ada would check with Aheesh. So, Aheesh had to be roped in. I had to make him my wingman.

At the first opportunity, I took Aheesh by my side and revealed my plan to him - well, only a part of the plan where I needed him. I told him that I was playing a prank on Ada and gave him the context.

'But you don't have a girl.' Aheesh asked, in all sincerity.

'No. Of course not.' I replied.

'And you want Ada to believe you have one?' He asked.

'Yes.' I said.

'Why?'

He is going to catch me! I thought. *He has got brains. He will understand in seconds what my real intentions are.* But I needed him. I had to give it a try.

'Because', I said slowly and deeply, 'It will be fun. In or out?'

Aheesh thought for a while and then, nodding his head said, 'In. Anything for fun, man.'

~

'Who is RAR?' Ada asked me the next day.

'What?' I replied, acting surprised. 'I don't know. Who is that?'

'Don't lie,' She said, 'I saw it in your phone.'

'You checked my phone?' I asked, pretending to get angry.

'No. I didn't check your phone that way.' She replied, 'I... I saw the name while you were in the queue for the food. You had left your phone on the table.'

'So, you checked my call records?'

'No. I didn't. I just happened to look at the screen when your phone buzzed. Who's this RAR? Is that her?'

I was happy with my plan. It was working. I had left the phone intentionally on the table, with the display side up. I had walked away and made sure that RAR calls at the exact time and Ada can have a look at the phone.

'I am not going to tell you. Somethings are personal.' I replied.

As I said this, my phone buzzed again. She could see the Display name: RAR

'I have to take this.' I said, acting cheerful.

'Of course!' She said and went away.

I disconnected the call and followed her quietly. She went straight to Aheesh, who was standing some distance away and asked him, 'Who is this RAR?'

'Who?' Aheesh replied.

'The girl Vasillor keeps talking to' she said.

'I don't know,' Aheesh replied.

'You do Mr.' She told him, 'Now tell me, who is she?'

'Are you threatening me?'

'Yes.' She replied, 'Now tell me.'

'I don't know much,' He replied, 'Only that she is hot!'

'Really,' she said. 'So Beautiful?'

'Yeah! I said hot.'

'What is her name? Is she from our college?' she asked.

'Check out his Insta. She is there. I will show you,' Aheesh said.

Part 2 of the plan executed successfully. A day earlier, Aheesh and I had created a fake profile with pictures of one of the hottest Brazilian models we could find on the net. And now was the time for the final part. I quickly turned towards the classroom, took my seat, and opened a book. Moments later, Ada came in and took the seat beside me.

'Is she really your GF?' She asked quizzically.

'Who?' I asked.

'Come on! I know. I have seen her pictures.' She replied.

'Who told you? – Aheesh.' I acted surprised.

'She is quite a looker,' She said, 'You are lucky. How long have you been together?'

'Not that long, actually. Since college started.' I replied.

'Oh!' She said, 'So you two connected after our college started?'

'Yes.' I replied.

She fell silent for a moment.

'Do you want to meet her?' I asked.

Ada wasn't expecting this, and I could see the surprise on her face.

'Really? When?' she asked.

'Right now.' I replied.

'She is from our college?' Ada asked absolutely stunned. She had completely forgotten the first lie I had told her- that she was from my school.

'Let me call her up,' I said and dialed RAR's number in front of her.

'Hi Sweetheart,' I said, 'Ada wants to meet you. Can you come to my class for a moment?'

'She knows about me!' Ada exclaimed in horror.

'Yes. She knows a lot about you,' I replied.

I could see the excitement and tension on her face. She hadn't seen it coming, and she hadn't prepared for a moment like this. She started preparing herself for the meeting- brushing her hair with her fingers, pulling out a lipstick from her bag. For all the confidence she had, I could feel her grappling for words in her head. She looked continuously at the door, waiting for the grand entry of my purported GF. She was so engrossed that she didn't see Aheesh entering and walking up to us.

'Here,' I said pointing to Aheesh, 'Meet RAR- My Superhot girlfriend.'

Aheesh burst out laughing as soon as I said this. I started laughing too. Ada looked at our faces in utter confusion. It took her some time to realize that we had made a fool out of her. And when the realization dawned, she turned red with embarrassment. But you know Ada. She couldn't just sit through it. And she did something unexpected! She took out her slipper, picked it up with her right hand and began hitting me with it. Yes, in the classroom! In front of all the dumbstruck people. I stood up from my seat and ran out of the class, still laughing aloud. And she, with the slipper in her hand, ran after me. All over the campus!

Chapter 10

Vani asked me to accompany her to Navi Mumbai creeks one day. Taking me to art exhibitions was one thing, but I wondered what this new thing was that she wanted me to explore now.

'Why? What is there in those creeks?' I asked her.

'Flamingos,' She replied.

'Flamingos?' I asked, surprised, 'Are you a birdwatcher as well?'

'Have you seen those birds?' She asked me.

'Yes, in pictures,' I replied.

'They are so beautiful, so majestic. We have to go and watch them.' she said excitedly.

Knowing how different Vani was from others, I wasn't surprised with this request. While the other girls in the college would be planning which movie to catch or which restaurants to go to on a Saturday, Vani was preparing for a field trip to see flamingos.

Perhaps, she sensed my hesitation and said, 'It's okay if you don't want to come.'

'No, I would love to come,' I replied, 'and see these birds in real.'

I was astonished to find that the entire wetland looked like a canvas of pink due to the flock of birds that had settled in it. I cannot express how beautiful they looked; you have to see them for yourself to know that. We walked slowly into the creeks and took our place at a distance from the flock in the mangroves. It was still early morning, but the birds seemed full of energy with their shrills and boisterous calls. In addition to us, there were a handful of other people who had come with their big DSLR cameras to take pictures.

Flamingos weren't just beautiful pink birds; they were kind of mysterious too- they kept standing on just one leg. I had never seen a bird standing on just one leg before and was amazed by this. I even wondered if they had only one leg. When I asked Vani about it, she laughed at my ignorance and explained that they have two legs, like all other birds, but they stand on one leg at a time. This peculiar behavior is apparently to conserve their body heat. She also mentioned that these birds are migratory and come to Mumbai only during winters.

'So, we cannot come back here in summers to see them?' I asked.

'No. They fly away to other countries' She replied.

'Peculiar birds,' I remarked.

'Do you know what's even more peculiar? They choose a mate for a lifetime and remain loyal to them.'

'Wow!'

'And they dance?'

'What?'

'Yes. Maybe, if we are lucky we may get to see that.'

'This is my best Saturday.' I remarked.

She smiled and took out her phone to click pictures of the birds. Then, she retrieved her drawing pad and brushes. Ah! Now, I understood. She was here to paint them.

'Like humans, they are social animals. Always together,' she said as she started drawing strokes on the pad.

'Then, why is that guy standing alone over there?' I said, pointing to a flamingo that was standing alone near a mangrove tree.

'Maybe, like me, some of them, want to remain aloof,' She replied.

'You don't like company?' I asked.

'I don't usually seek it,' she replied.

'Vani, can I ask you a question, if you don't mind?'

'Yes,' she said, still watching that lone bird.

'You are so talented. What are you doing here?'

'What am I doing here? Well, watching Flamingos with you. What else?' She replied.

'I mean, what are you doing in a commerce college? Shouldn't you be in an arts or whatever is your type of college?'

She remained silent and kept watching the bird. Suddenly, disturbed by a honking car, the bird flew away. A person who had been keenly clicking the pictures of the bird from his DSLR cursed the driver of the car. 'God damn these honking idiots. Scaring these innocent birds.'

'So, how long have you been painting? I asked.

'For as long as I remember,' She replied.

'Oh! You are a child prodigy. Such great luck!' I remarked.

'Or curse,' she replied, shrugging her shoulders.

I was taken aback by her statement. Who wouldn't want to be a child prodigy? Bask in the glory that God-given talent provides, and not slog like other mortals, not be worried about being average in the faculties of life.

She started drawing the outline of the bird that had just flown away on her pad. I watched her intently as she started putting colors to it. She didn't raise her head from her pad. She was drawing everything from her memory, from what she had observed, and to me, it was astounding!

'You know, I am thankful that you came alongwith me today,' she said, without raising her head.

'I am glad that I came. This is so wonderful just sitting here with you, watching the beautiful birds,' I replied.

'Isn't it wonderful?' she said, 'just sitting and talking with someone.'

'Yes,' I replied.

'I have never done anything like this before. Never chatted with a person like this.'

'Why?' I asked in surprise. 'What about your friends?'

'I don't have any friends.' She replied, 'Never had.'

It was hard to believe that a person cannot have friends. How is possible not to have friends in one's school or in one's colony?

'Why didn't you have any friends?' I asked.

'Child prodigy, as you said,' she remarked, 'The only thing my parents ever wanted, still want, from me is to excel in what I am doing, to reach for the moon and the stars, to leave my mark, my legacy. They raised me like that, build me up like that… Like a machine in pursuit of excellence. They never asked how I felt or what I wanted. They still don't. They just want me to achieve the dreams they have dreamed for me. I have always been on clock, from one class to another, from one competition to another, always caught up in perfection of my art. They don't understand that art isn't perfect, people aren't perfect.'

I could see how emotional she had become as she said this. Talent, if it meant this, truly was a burden. Vani, the perfect role model for all of us in college, didn't want to be perfect. I wondered how difficult and hard it must have been for her, growing up so lonely, driven just by the ambition of her parents.

'I agree, nothing in this world is perfect,' I said empathetically.

'Love is,' she replied.

'Hmm. So, what do you want to do in life?' I asked.

'Just sit here and watch the flamingos,'.

'That's a good way to spend one's life. But you said, they come here only in winters. What would you do in summers, then?'

'Fly away with them,' she said, smiling.

'And why did you say you don't have friends? I thought we were friends,' I said.

'Of course, we are. Do you know, flamingos have their own friend circles, and they remain loyal to them?'

'I am enamored by flamingos. They are really something.'

'Yes,' she replied.

'And you are still drawing? I thought, you wanted to just watch them and chat.'

'That's my curse. I can't help it,' she said.

'Hmm. But you still didn't answer me. Why are you in a commerce college, here in Mumbai?'

'One day, I walked out of my home. I wanted to live my own life, so I came to Mumbai. The college happened by chance, and I am glad it happened.'

'So, you don't talk to your parents?'

'I talk to them. But I don't listen to them,' she remarked.

'So, you are independent?'

'You can say that. Independent to watch flamingoes whenever I want,' she said, 'Do you know Picasso drew flamingo. Wait, I will show you.'

She took her phone and googled in it. 'Look,' she said as she showed me the painting.

'This is Picasso?' I asked in surprise. 'I had heard he was a great painter who created complex and modern art. This looks like a drawing by a four-year-old. Ha! You can do better than him. Much better!'

She gazed at me for some time, making me self-conscious.

'What are you looking at?' I asked, embarrassed.

'Where is your pendant? The bullet one,' she asked.

I was surprised that she remembered it.

'I had to remove it. Prof. Kasbekar said it was against the college rules.'

'I liked that,' she said, 'Give it me if you don't wear it anymore.'

'Okay,' I said hesitantly, 'In return, give me one of your paintings.'

'Okay.'

While we were talking, the bird that had flown away came back, and this time it wasn't alone; it had brought a friend with it.

'See, even he has found a friend,' I said, pointing towards the birds.

She looked at the couple and smiled. Surprisingly, the flamingos did an amazing thing. They touched each other's beaks and made a beautiful heart.

'We are in luck. Quick, let's take a selfie,' Vani said as she picked up her phone and clicked a picture. It was a beautiful shot with Vani, me and the two beautiful flamingos, making a heart in the background.

But I never got that picture. Unfortunately, as we were about to leave, Vani's phone fell in a pool of water and got damaged.

Chapter 11

An interesting thing happened one Friday. An idea was floated around- it was time for a night-out, time for clubbing and partying. A list was prepared, and we had to write 'In' or 'Out'. A few reluctant ones who wrote 'Out' had it coming. They were cajoled with phrases like 'This would be fun!' and ridiculed, saying 'Grow up! You Mamma's boy, Papa's girl!' The techniques worked, and by the end of the day, almost everyone was in. Finally, we were going to have a taste of the Mumbai nightlife. A club in Bandra was selected, and it had a weird name- Weed.

The departure time was set for 9 pm. The second bus stop from the Girls' Hostel was chosen as the meeting point. Boys were already there by 8:30. Nobody wanted to take the chance of missing the *Parade*. And when the girls finally came out of the hostel gates, one by one, dressed up in their iridescent party wear, all of us - including the local population of auto-wallahs, shopkeepers, old men on evening walks, officegoers on their way back home - had to collect our jaws with our hands and push our eyes back into their sockets! The girls looked so amazing! For some, the transformation was surreal. From the plain janes of the day, they had turned into the night blooming jasmines. It was truly a scene to remember!

The girls said they wouldn't travel by the local train, so we hired the cabs, which made the trip expensive and meant we would have less money for the drinks later. We formed groups with three boys and two girls in each cab to ensure company and safety. It was an opportunity I had been dying for. Here was my chance to travel with Ada! I looked out for her. Anxiously. Desperately. But, unbeknownst to me, she had already taken one of the cabs with her friends. The Romeo boys, Laurel and Hardy, were in that cab too. Surges of jealousy and anger rose within me, but what could I do!

From another fully occupied cab, Vani waved me an excited goodbye. I was feeling let down. With whom was I going to go now? I looked around; the only people left were Aheesh, Sakshi, Ankita, and me. I didn't know the girls that well. To add to my woes, no cabs were coming our way. It took us more than 30 minutes to hunt down one. Finally, we found an old, broken-down cab, but we had no choice. I jumped into the front seat as fast as I could, leaving a foaming Aheesh to share the rear seat with the girls.

Honestly, it was a damp ride. The girls were engrossed in their own chatter, and though we tried hard to be included in the conversation, they ignored us. For most of the ride, Aheesh and I sat quietly, waiting for the dreadful journey to end. I cursed my luck. Of all the days, I had missed out on being with Ada today- the day when she looked mesmerizing in her black sequined dress. How much I would have enjoyed her company! How interesting our conversation would have been!

How uneventful the evening was turning out to be!

When we reached, the party was already in full swing. People were dancing, drinking, and having fun. At one counter, some of our friends were taking shots, and bets were being placed on who would be the last man standing. There was lot of hooting and rooting. Amidst all of this, Vani came over and took me aside.

'How do I look?' she asked.

'Beautiful,' I replied. She looked pretty in the sea-green gown.

'Not sexy?' she asked.

I baulked.

'Beautiful and sexy,' I said after a moment.

'Thank you,' she said and smiled.

'Maybe you should do a self-portrait in this dress like that favorite painter of yours.. I forget her name,' I said.

'Frida Kahlo. And maybe I will,' she replied.

'I am upset with you, though,' I said.

'Why?'

'You didn't wait for me.'

'I got pushed into a cab before I could find you. Sorry. I promise I will leave with you.' She said.

'That's Ok. Enjoying it here?'

'Yes,' She replied, 'Have you done clubbing before?'

'Sort of,' I replied, 'What about you?'

'I wasn't allowed,' she said. 'Do you dance?'

'No. I suck,' I replied honestly.

'Me too.'

'Vasillor!' I heard Aheesh call me out from the counter.

'What?' I shouted back and signaled him to come over.

'I need to talk to you urgently,' he said on top of his voice as he approached us.

'What happened?' I asked.

'You have to come with me,' he said and started pulling me away.

'What's happening? Vani asked, puzzled by Aheesh's behavior.

'Nothing,' Aheesh replied. 'Enjoy the party. See you soon.'

Aheesh took me out of the club into the open street. A concoction of smelly, damp air hit me – a buzzkill. I hated it. I wanted to rush back in.

'It better be something very important, Aheesh, or I'm gonna kill you for bringing me out,' I said vehemently.

'Are you interested in Ada?' Aheesh asked in a serious tone.

'What? No!' I replied, caught completely off guard. *Where the hell did this come from? How did he know?*

'It's not time for denials,' Aheesh said earnestly, 'I am asking you again, are you interested?'

'What's your angle? Why are you asking?' I rebuffed him, 'Are you interested in her?'

'Hell No!' He replied, 'I am asking about you.'

'What does that even mean?' I asked.

'Okay. Let me shoot it straight.' Aheesh said, taking a deep breath. 'I just overheard. Hardy is going to propose to her tonight.'

(Of course, he didn't say Hardy. He said his real name. But you get to know him only as Hardy. My choice.)

'Romeo boy Hardy?'

'Yes. Romeo boy Hardy.'

I suppose there was too much salt in the air. A sharp pain arose when it touched the rough cracks on my lips. My hands went into my pockets, instinctively, searching for something fervently. My Vaseline bottle! It was the balm I needed. But it wasn't there. Of all days, I had forgotten it today. Its absence made me uneasy and anxious. The pain increased. I moved my tongue over my lips. Aheesh watched me intently, waiting for me to say something.

'Good for him,' I said finally.

'You have no qualms about it?' he asked, puzzled.

'Why should I?' I said, still sucking my lips.

Aheesh looked at me in disbelief.

'I think we should wish him luck,' I said.

'Are you sure about it?' He asked again.

'Absolutely,' I replied, 'Let's get back in.'

Hardy! Bloody Hardy. My enemy from the first day. There were thirty-two boys in the class, and HE was the ONE approaching Ada. What if Ada was interested in him and said yes? For me, it would be a tragedy bigger than the Titanic.

Once we were inside, we went straight up to Hardy and the gang. He was being buoyed by the boys – "You are the Man, Bro! You are the Man!" The glasses were raised, clinked, and emptied, and Hardy drank like a fish. I could understand. It was not easy to go up to Ada. Courage was needed. Lots of it. I had not been able to muster much myself, and sadly, liquor gave me no courage. So, I was pretty sure I would never be able to propose to her. Anyway, I held out my hand to Hardy- one bro to another- and wished him luck. Weirdly, as I shook his hand, it felt as if Ada was watching me.

I don't know what it is -premonition or something else- but women generally know what's about to happen. And they knew even before Hardy had started. They knew he was drunk. They knew he would do something crazy. They knew it was Ada he was going to approach. And they started forming concentric circles around her. Hardy, even in his inebriated state, even with all the built-up courage, saw the battle formation taking place and got terrified. He lost control as soon as he got near the first defense, fell flat on his stomach, and puked all over. *'Eww!'* The girls cried in one voice and ran helter-skelter.

The boys hung their heads in shame. Our pumped-up brother had failed in his pursuit, lying down on the floor, covered in his own vomit. It wasn't just his failure; It was a collective failure. Failure of all bros here and anywhere. For some strange reason despite envy, I felt this failure too. A part of me had rooted for him!

'This is why I don't drink,' someone whispered in my ear.

'It's not about the drink,' I replied sagely, 'It's about the man.'

Moments later, Hardy stood up and shook his body like an animal. He scanned the area and headed straight towards Ada, who was standing in a corner, watching the happenings in horror! There were no girls around her now. No one had expected that he would get up. It was happening so fast, so suddenly. Everyone just watched, transfixed in their places, wondering what would happen next.

Amidst all the commotion, our gazes met. It lasted just for a second, but it was enough to send a chill down my spine. Ada's probing eyes held me guilty. The lips cracked again, and the pain intensified.

I saw him approach her, and I knew what he was going to say. Part of me wanted to pull away from there, but I stood my ground.

I couldn't resist the urge to see her response. They were at the other end of the pub, and the music was still loud, making it impossible to hear them. So, I tried to read their lips. I followed the movement of his shaky lips until I comprehended parts of his speech. And as soon as he uttered those words, gloom and fear engulfed me. The loud music faded, replaced by the pounding of my heart - *Thud Thud*. I feared my heart would jump out of my body. Now, here is the irony: somehow, my Nemesis No1, my mind replaced Hardy with myself. I felt as if it was me proposing to Ada with those pukey, wavering lips, and deep inside, I already knew her answer. That was it. The end of my story.

It all ended in a matter of seconds. She said 'No'. Shocked, he asked 'Why'. She didn't reply and started to move away. He caught hold of her arm, and she turned around, warning him that she would slap him if he didn't let her go. Drunk as he was, he didn't budge. The situation was becoming tense, and all of us watched frantically. Sensing the potential trouble that could brew, Laurel and a few guys quickly ran towards Hardy and coaxed him to let go of Ada.

'Sorry. Sorry,' Laurel uttered, 'Let's get back to party. Let's have fun! It is over.'

'It's not over,' Hardy shouted as he was being dragged away. 'It's never over.'

Pubs are messed up. Everything is forgotten soon. If a murder were to happen there at 11:45, they would be singing 'Happy Birthday' at 12! For the guy who has been murdered! That messed up.

The party returned to normal so quickly, as if nothing had happened. Everyone got busy with drinking, frolicking, and dancing. But Ada…I watched her from the opposite corner. She was no longer her usual self. She had turned pale and somber. All her glow and chirpiness had vanished. I had never seen her like this. Minutes later, I saw her walk out of the pub, leaving the party all alone in the middle of the night. I jumped out of my inertia and ran after her.

She had already hailed a taxi by the time I came out. I ran towards her as fast as I could. The taxi had already started moving when I opened its door and got in.

'Have you gone crazy?' I yelled at her, trying to catch my breath. 'Where the hell are you going?'

'Leave me alone,' She replied and started crying.

The driver turned his head and looked at us. 'What happened, madam? Is he with you?' He asked.

I didn't wait for Ada to reply. 'Bhaiyya, keep your eyes on the road. We are together.'

'What happened?' Why are you so upset?' I asked her.

'You are pretending as if you don't know.' She replied.

'I know. In bits and pieces. Why don't you tell me? I asked.

She wiped her eyes with her palms and said, 'Hardy proposed to me.'

(Of course, she didn't say Hardy. But, as you know, you get to know him only as Hardy.)

'Oh!' I said, 'So what did you say?'

'What did you say?' She said mocking me, 'Would I be sitting here had I said Yes. You know, you are a moron.'

I smiled. She was back! And I loved the moron compliment.

'So, he proposed, and you said no. Pretty straightforward. Why the tears then?' I asked.

'You don't understand.' She said, rolling down the window, and looking out. The air outside was still smelly and damp, and it played mischievously with her hair - raising it up and dropping it in waves. I watched in envy, wishing I could be that air!

'What's there to understand? Tell me.' I asked her.

She didn't reply and continued to look out. In the yellow of the streetlights, I could still see the tears glistening on her cheeks.

The silence persisted, and I was growing restless. There was something wrong, and she wasn't telling me. I had to know. I needed to know.

'Did he misbehave?' I asked. 'Did he say something wrong?'

'Do you know what he said?' She replied, without looking at me.

'What?'

'It's never over.'

'Don't feel threatened.' I said, 'There are ways to deal with him.'

She turned towards me and said, 'I know how to deal with him. I deal with...' She stopped abruptly, her voice trailing off, and looking out again.

What did she mean by that? What was she dealing with?

'You know I considered him a friend,' she said. 'Now that friendship is ruined. Completely ruined. Friends should never be lovers.'

Damn that salty air! My lips hurt again.

What could I say now? Well, that bastard Romeo boy Hardy ruined it for me as well! I weighed on her last words - slowly, one by one, till my mind registered them. I wanted no hope to be left alive in me! It was over. Even before it had started. Sayonara to it!

'You are right,' I replied, 'Friends should never be lovers. Why complicate?'

The rest of the journey was passed in complete silence. And I wondered the whole time - what did she mean by what she had said? That she was dealing with it... Who or what was she dealing with? Was she in some trouble? Was she being harassed? Something was wrong. She wasn't her usual self. She wasn't forthcoming. She just stopped talking. I wanted to help her. With all my might. But would she let me?

We got out of the cab near her hostel. I said goodbye. She hugged me and said, 'Sorry. I ruined your night.'

I looked at her and said in all earnestness, 'I am sorry. For all that you must endure.'

Her beautiful brown eyes welled up with tears, and she held me tightly again. She was in pain, and her pain pierced through my soul.

After seeing her off, I walked towards my hostel. My Nemesis No1, my mind filled me with horrid thoughts about her, and I shuddered. I wanted them to go away, but my freaking mind didn't stop, making me endure them. There was no one in my hostel wing when I reached there. I entered my room, switched on the lights, changed my clothes, then switched off the lights and lay down in the dark, gazing at the ceiling fan. I tried to sleep, but I couldn't. My horrid thoughts made a train in my head and kept mowing me down.

My phone rang, and I picked up the call without looking at the number.

'Are you fucking involved with Ada?' Hardy hollered.

'No,' I replied calmly.

'Keep your hands off her. She is mine,' He shouted.

Now, this tone I couldn't take! And the audacity of him considering her his property. No fucking way!

'Listen you bastard.' I threatened him. 'You had your chance, and you blew it. You better stay away now. Else, I am gonna stomp you.'

I heard him rumble something before he disconnected.

It took me a long time after that to fall asleep. And when I finally did, I dreamed of white jasmines, blood, and broken bones.

Chapter 12

Next morning, I saw Hardy leaning by the banister outside the classroom. I decided to confront him right away. I was sure some action would happen. I would throw some punches, and some would come my way. I started preparing for both – a sucker punch with my right fist for attack, and a quick duck for defense. But was he a leftie or a righty? My plans would change accordingly. What if he simply apologized? What would I do then? Let it go and be cool or confront him? I got so muddled up that I didn't notice Vani.

'Where did you vanish yesterday?' She asked, 'I kept looking for you. We were supposed to leave together.'

'Sorry,' I said, 'I had to leave on an emergency.'

'Was Ada your emergency?' She yelled.

I stopped in my tracks. Her comment was unacceptable to me.

'None of your business.' I yelled back.

My retort shocked her. She turned red in anger and clenched her fists. I had never seen her so angry; and hurt, maybe. I thought she was going to punch me. But she didn't. She said, 'I am sorry,' and walked away from me.

I was left mad by her. How could she yell at me? Who was she to ask me about my whereabouts? So, what if I had left without her? Hadn't she gone to the club without me? I hadn't yelled at her for that. What was her problem with Ada?

By the time I picked myself up, Hardy was already gone.

'Thank God you are here.' Ada said to me as I took my seat in the classroom, 'I was getting bored.'

'How are you feeling today?' I asked.

'As fresh as ever,' She replied.

'Good,' I said and turned around to look for Hardy. He was seated in his usual place, talking to Laurel.

'By the way, Hardy apologized to me,' Ada said, 'Said he was too drunk.'

'Great!' I said, 'See, I told you there was nothing to worry about.'

'Thank you for being with me,' Ada said, 'And don't dare telling anyone I cried. I will KILL you.'

I laughed.

'Can I tell, after you have killed me? You know, I am going to haunt you, Ada Khanna.'

She laughed. 'I won't mind that. You are good company.'

'Ah! After yesterday, I am sure you won't get other company, anyway. Poor boys are terrified of you now.'

'Guys! Guys!' Aheesh screamed as he entered the class. 'The professor hasn't come today. Go. Go. Go to the canteen. Go to your homes. Go anywhere. Just don't stay here!'

The class leapt in joy and hurried to pick up the bags and rush out.

'Not you,' Aheesh said to me, 'You carry on Ada. We will see you in the canteen, okay?

'What happened yesterday?' Aheesh asked me after everybody had left.

'You were there. You saw everything,' I replied.

'Dude! After you left with Ada?'

'Nothing. She was upset. We didn't talk much.'

'And?'

'And what?'

'You didn't ask her out?' He asked.

'Are you mad?' I replied, aghast with his question.

'Ok. Ok. Is she cool with Hardy, now?' He asked.

'I think so. He apologized to her. But I have things to settle with him.'

'What?'

'He threatened me yesterday.'

'Really?'

'Yes. And I am going to have a word with him now.'

It was like déjà vu. I saw Hardy leaning by the banister outside the class, and I started making plans- punch and duck! I was expecting Vani to show up anytime now, but she didn't, and I walked straight up to him.

'What were you saying yesterday?' I confronted him.

He snorted and looked at me with his brows raised up. 'I don't know. I was drunk.'

'Say sorry and let this be over,' Aheesh butted in.

'Fuck off!' Hardy said and pushed Aheesh. 'And you!' He said, turning towards me, 'Keep your hands off that bitch.'

I still can't believe how fast it happened! But as soon as he had finished his sentence, there was a tooth on the floor, blood dribbling from his nose, and a sharp sensation of pain in my right hand. I had sucker-punched him! There was no counterpunch. He just lay on the floor, writhing in pain.

Half an hour later, I was suspended.

~

'Why did you punch him?' Ada asked me while we were walking out of the college, 'Have you lost your mind?'

'Why are you so upset about it? Is it because he proposed to you, and now you have feelings for him?' I teased her.

'Yes.' She replied, 'You are a pig, you know.'

'Stop insulting the poor animals,' I said and smiled.

She gave me her trademark laugh and said, 'What are you going to do for a week now?'

'I don't know. But first I need to pop a painkiller. My hand still hurts,' I replied.

'That's what you get when you try to be a hero!' She ridiculed me. 'Now, Wait here.'

She went to a chemist's and came back with Moov and some bandages.

'Moov is fine. What are the bandages for?' I asked inquisitively.

'Stop talking.'

'No really! But I don't need bandages. I haven't been hit by a bullet,' I protested.

Bandages would make me look weak. People would think I had broken my hand while punching. I would be laughed at.

'Just shut up!' She said and went ahead with the bandaging.

I kept quiet and let her do her work. I would remove the bandages later.

'So, what are you going to do for a week?' She asked again.

We had walked some distance and were approaching a bus stop.

'I don't know. Watch movies,' I replied.

'Or we can just board the bus and go,' she said, pointing towards an incoming bus.

'And go where?' I asked, puzzled.

'To… Panjim,' she said as she read the name board on the bus.

'Panjim? Goa? Are you mad?' I was stupefied by her offer. 'I am not going.'

'Okay,' She said, 'I will walk the beaches alone.'

She stopped the bus and got in.

'I am not coming,' I shouted after her.

She looked down from the window and said, 'Well, Enjoy your movies.'

Like a dog, I chased the bus for at least a hundred meters before the driver took mercy and hit the brakes. And I got in, huffing and panting, and wiped the sweat off my forehead with my bandaged hand.

Chapter 13

Whatever was happening, I had never dreamt of it. Here she was, sleeping beside me, her head resting on my shoulder, her arm draped over my chest, her long dark hair flying in the wind that came through the open window, gently caressing my cheeks. I looked at her beautiful sleeping face and wondered, 'what could she be dreaming of?' Occasionally, a smile curved her lips. And I thought - was it possible that I was there in her dreams? Had I kissed her when that smile curved her lips?

I recalled with pride how she placed her hands in mine, when I took the seat after getting into the bus. 'I can't see you sulk.' She had said. How awe-struck I was! How astonishing she was!

I looked out of the window into the darkness of the night. The streetlights, the trees, the hills- all so cheerful. Soon, small silvery droplets of rain started coming down from the sky. Under the yellow lights of the road, it looked as if they were dancing. A few droplets found their way to Ada's cheeks. They sat there, curling into themselves like the newborn babies. They looked so beautiful and so innocent. Just watching them gave me joy.

Moments later, Ada - still asleep- wiped them off her face. Cautiously, I closed the glass window. I didn't want to wake her up. Soon enough, the rain gathered full force and rumbled against the glass. It seemed like a fight. Intruding rain against the gritty glass. I watched this fight for some time before I drifted into sleep.

The rains relentlessly slashed the glass windows of the cab I was in. I was also overwhelmed by a strange feeling- the fear of bumping into someone I didn't want to meet. I flinched in my seat and tried to shake off this feeling.

The cab did not stop at any signal and zigzagged through the traffic. It dropped me off at a place which seemed peculiarly familiar. It was a club, and I had been here before. I tried to remember its name. It started with W… Weed? Yes. Weed. The club hadn't changed a bit. It had the same colors, the same sign boards, the same bald and beefy bouncers. Even the air I breathed was same- putrid and salty. I went inside and looked around. The club was empty, except for a man at a table in the opposite corner.

I walked towards the table with trepidation and found a man - in a sparkling white uniform- mixing his drinks. I tried to see his face, but it was hidden behind a black cloud.

'My friend, I have been waiting for you,' The uniformed man said to me.

'Do I know you?' I asked, surprised.

'Yes, very well my friend,' He said, 'Come closer.'

As I moved closer to him, he stuck out his face through the cloud, and pointing to his nose said, 'Now do you remember me?'

I looked at his nose. It was broken in the middle, and a bubble of blood hung at its tip. The bubble looked as if it would fall, and I waited anxiously for it to fall. However, it defied the laws of gravity and continued hanging.

'Hardy?' I asked in surprise.

'Oh, yes. You remember my name.'

'I am sorry' I said sincerely.

'Really?' He replied, sipping a drink from his glass, 'Now, are you?'

Just then, a waiter passing by tripped over and spilled the drinks over Hardy.

'You bastard!' Hardy yelled at him, got up from his chair, and caught the waiter by his collar, 'Do you know what you have done?'

The waiter looked at him timidly.

'Do you know what you have done?' Hardy yelled at him again, 'Answer me.'

'Sorry, sir, I spilled the drinks on your clothes.'

'Not any clothes!' Hardy thundered, 'On my white Uniform. You have ruined it, you bastard!'

The poor waiter apologized again, wanting to escape his ordeal and get back to his work.

'You piece of shit.' Hardy said and started trashing him. 'You have ruined my reputation.'

Moments later, the scene changed. We were in a bus now.

'You shouldn't have punched me,' Hardy said, while driving the bus. 'Inside that club, you shouldn't have punched me.'

When did I punch him? I tried to recall. Oh yes! I remembered. I was sitting there - all by myself - mixing my drinks. And he came and tripped over me. Ruined my favorite white shirt! He deserved to be thrashed.

'You shouldn't have done that,' Hardy said faintly and skewed the car towards an incoming truck.

'Look out!' I shouted as a volley of bright lights flashed in front of my eyes. The truck hit our bus. I lay bloodied on the road, a bubble of blood sticking from my nose. I tried to wipe it off but couldn't. I shuddered and trembled......

'What happened?' She asked, half asleep.

'Nothing,' I replied, as I regained my senses. 'Go back to your dreams.'

She smiled and nestled her head back into my chest.

I tried to sleep but couldn't. My mind continuously took me back to the scene where I lay bloodied on the road, waiting to die....

We reached Goa the next morning. The bus dropped us at a place called Mapusa. We had decided to stay in Panjim, the capital city, and came to know that it was some 15 kms away. We had to hire a taxi.

'Can you take us to some nice hotel?' I asked the driver. 'Nice and a little inexpensive.'

'Why not? Everything available in Goa,' he said joyfully.

'You boyfriend girlfriend?' the driver asked as soon as we got into his car.

It was an awkward question, and we were embarrassed! He looked at us in the rearview mirror. 'Why I ask sir is because nice hotels ask for ID? Some people don't like to give ID. But no worries. I will take you to the place where no need of ID. No worry. Goa is merry, after all.'

'Okay.' I replied apprehensively. I was on the edge for the rest of our journey, but there wasn't much I could do.

The Goa I had seen on hoardings and in newspaper ads was only about beaches and sand. But the Goa I was seeing now was much more than that. It was green, pristine, and laidback. It reminded me of my ancestral village, where my grandparents lived. I felt nostalgic, and I loved it.

It was unlike the rest of the country I had seen. It seemed like a place on a holiday. There were tourists and revelers everywhere, people in colorful clothes and funny hats zooming around on scooters and in open gypsies. Lining the roads and streets were beautiful houses painted in bursts of bright colors: Orange, Pink, Yellow.

'Finally, I am here!' Ada exclaimed. She had already put on the get-up of a tourist, wearing a big white straw hat with a neat pink ribbon on one side. The hat, along with the sunglasses and the sunscreen, had been bought as soon as we got off the bus at Mapusa. I looked curiously at her hat; it was so big that it had hidden the upper half of her face.

'Do you realize how utterly insane you are?' I asked her.

She adjusted her hat and pushed its rim up, her brows furrowing in question.

'I mean, who does something like this?' I continued. 'You dragged me to Goa, just as you drag me to the canteen! Here I am with you in yesterday's clothes. Don't even have a toothbrush. In a way, you know, if I think of it- you kidnapped me.'

'Kidnapped you? Huh? In your dreams,' she replied, 'And why are you fretting over your clothes? Boys are used to wearing the same smelly old clothes for days on end! I should be the one fretting and fuming.'

'Ok. Madam Queen,' I said. 'I hereby abdicate my right to fret and fuss.'

'Thank you,' She replied, 'and I reserve this right for myself alone.'

'Oh! Thank you. And don't worry. I will buy us some clothes,' I replied.

'How chivalrous of you?' She teased.

'And some beer,' I added, as I looked at the liquor shops dotting the road.

Contrary to my apprehensions, the driver dropped us off at a nice place. It appeared small, but it was decent. The hotel was occupied by a young crowd, mostly collegians like us, and I felt relieved seeing them.

While we were in the queue at the front desk, I told Ada that I will ask for two adjacent rooms.

'We can share a room,' She replied, 'I won't eat you up as long as you sleep on the floor.'

'Okay, Madam Queen,' I replied, 'I will keep that in mind'.

The room we were assigned had twin beds. 'Thank God! I get a bed too,' I exclaimed in joy. Ada looked at me and laughed. 'You are getting luckier,' she said. I grinned. She went ahead and inspected the room, checking the pillows, sheets, bathrooms, and the wardrobes.

Then, she went up to the window and pulled open the curtains. The window opened directly onto the terrace of the adjacent hotel. She seemed disgusted with that and quickly closed the curtains. 'I am not going to stay here,' She declared, 'Where is the view?'

I was thankful enough for getting a bed, and here she was, complaining about the view!

'I don't think they have any other room,' I said, 'Or they would have given it.'

'This won't do,' she said and clicked her tongue. 'Wait here. I will get it changed.'

'Wait? What? Where are you going?' I asked.

She had already rushed out.

By the time I reached the lobby (the lift took ages to come!), she had already "talked" to the manager. Five minutes later, we were in a bigger and better room with a view of the glistening Mandovi river. And yes, I still had my bed.

How astonishing she was!

Two chairs and a round table were placed by the window. We sat in the chairs, perched our feet on the table, and watched the boats sailing in the river. Boats- that wouldn't be there if Mandovi weren't. Mandovi- that would look forlorn and sad without those boats. Together, what a marvelous view they made!

Moments later, I realized that this was the first time I had looked at her feet so up-close. And I remembered the first time I had seen them. How spellbound I had been! The green-pistachio nail polish had now been replaced by the teal-blue shade. I can't express how beautiful her feet looked. Petite and cute. Her toes so orderly- the big toe followed by others in decreasing order of size. I came to know later they are called Egyptian toes. Well, she had the feet of the Egyptian queens!

I was so lost in my thoughts that I didn't realize when Ada got up, brought a kettle and two cups, and placed them on the table. She poured the hot water into the cups and opened a teabag. She dipped the teabag in my cup first; and then used the same teabag for herself. We lifted our cups simultaneously and sipped our tea in complete silence, looking at the beauty that was the Mandovi river.

We were pulled out of our trance by the shrill ringtone of her phone. She looked at the number and cut the call. The phone rang again, and she disconnected the call again. I could see a feeling of unease overcoming her. *It must be from her home.* I thought. *And, of course, what would she say if they asked her where she was?* When the phone rang for the third time, she looked at me and said that she had to answer it and rushed out of the room.

While she was gone, a wave of anxiety engulfed me. *What if my parents called? What would I tell them? Of course, I would have to lie. I could not tell them that I had been suspended and was in Goa with a girl! They would kill me. But what if I was caught? I had read news like this in papers. Maybe it was time for me to be the news. I imagined the headlines: "Vishesh Vasillor Vasu, caught in a Goa hotel room with a girl named Ada." I saw myself being arrested by the Police and put behind the bars; and getting beaten up by a fat, pan-chewing Havaldar.*

She shook me out of my thoughts. 'Are these goosebumps!' She said, as she looked at my arms, 'Are you terrified that we would get caught?'

'No... No...' I said, trying to act manly, 'I am not.' *How could she read my mind?*

'Well,' She said coolly, 'you should be. If we do get caught, I am going to say you forced me to come here!'

'You are so mean,' I said, giving her a look.

'Well! What can I say? It is one of my many fine qualities,' She said 'Now, get up and get ready. We are going out.'

'Ladies first,' I said.

'Okay.' She said, 'I am taking a shower.'

I walked to my bed and jumped into it. I knew Ada would take time. I turned on the TV and fiddled with the remote for some time. I checked out the movie channels; they were showing the same old stuff. Then I checked out the music channels and watched a few songs. After that I moved on to the sports channel, where they were showing the highlights of an old India- Australia match. I put the pillow at the end of the bed towards the TV, lay flat on my stomach with my chin firmly in the pillow, and watched the highlights keenly.

Her phone, which she had kept on the round table by the window, rang. I ignored it and continued watching the highlights. Minutes later, the phone rang again and continued ringing until I couldn't bear it anymore. I called Ada, but she was showering and couldn't hear me. Left with no choice, I stood up, went to the table, and switched her phone to the silent mode. Inadvertently, I saw her phone screen. All the calls were from the same number, which hadn't been saved. It seemed as if someone was trying desperately to reach out to her. It worried me a little, as I feared the worst. Maybe something bad had happened in her family, and someone wanted to talk to her urgently.

'Can you hand me my brush?' Ada shouted from the bathroom.

'Yeah, sure,' I said, and added, 'Your phone was ringing.'

'Let it ring. Not important,' She said, 'Give me the brush.'

I picked up the brush from the polyethene bag, which was placed on the TV table. I went towards the bathroom and knocked on the door. She opened the door a little and held out her hand. I placed the brush in her hand and then took it back. She thought she had dropped it and started searching for it on the floor.

'Pick it up,' I said.

'Where is it?'

'To your left. No, a little towards right. What are you doing?' I said, teasing her.

It took her a few moments to realize that I was messing with her. And finally, she said, 'I will kill you as soon as I come out!'

It was fun. Messing with her. I wouldn't have stopped had my phone not rung. It was Vani.

'Hel….'

'Where are you?' she yelled, cutting me short.

'I…. I am out of town,' I said.

'Out of town? You didn't tell me. Are you okay? I heard about your fight.'

'Yea. I am fine,' I replied.

'Why did you punch him?'

'I will tell you when I get back.'

'When are you getting back? Where are you?'

'I will be back after some days…'

'I spoke to the HOD. He said he will revoke your suspension if you apologize…'

'No,' I replied, 'I am not doing that.'

'Please hand me some shampoo,' Ada shouted from the bathroom again.

'Don't be crazy. I told the HOD that you will apologize…' Vani said, 'Are you with someone?'

'No.' I said, 'It's TV. And I won't apologize.'

Reflexively, I grabbed the remote, switched to a random Hindi channel, and raised the volume.

'Why not?' she asked.

'I did nothing wrong,' I replied.

'Yes. You did. You wronged yourself. You don't deserve to be suspended.'

What logic could I give to that statement? So, I tried to do something different.

'Vani, Listen. I know you care but…'

'No. you don't know.' She interjected and disconnected the phone.

I tossed my phone aside and stared at the TV screen for a while. In addition to the colorful people in it, the TV screen showed me Ada as well!

'You done?' I asked, turning around.

She walked over to the TV table, draped in the bath gown, and picked up the shampoo bottle from the polyethene bag. 'Not yet,' she said, without looking at me.

~

She hadn't uttered a word to me since she appeared as a reflection on the TV. She had spent the last two hours getting ready in silence. It was really getting on my nerves. Every time I tried to talk to her, she avoided me. She would start playing stupid games on her mobile. At the door, as we were about to leave, I caught hold of her arm and said, 'What's going on? This is not happening. What's up with you.'

'Nothing,' she said vaguely.

'Why are you so cross?'

'None of your business.'

'You are being rude, Ada.'

She didn't answer and looked away.

'Did you bring me here for all this?' I asked angrily.

'I didn't force you,' she said.

'Fine,' I yelled, 'Have fun. I am going back.'

I released her arm, went up to the window, and sat in the chair. I wanted to leave immediately. I was so angry! But I had to cool down. I poured some water from the kettle into my cup and gulped it down. I looked out of the window and watched Mandovi. It was flowing calmly, undisturbed by the sound of the boats and the roar of the engines. *No. I cannot leave her alone. Not here. Not like this!*

Moments later, Ada came and sat in the chair beside me.

'Sorry,' she said.

I turned towards her and looked at her poignant face. 'I don't understand you,' I said.

'I hear that a lot,' She replied, 'But don't worry, we are cool. It isn't about you.'

'What's it about then?' I asked her.

'I...,' She started and then stopped abruptly, 'Why was she calling you?' She asked, after a while.

'Who?' I replied.

'Vani.'

'Is this about her?'

'Are you so stupid?'

'Yes.'

'Really? What's going on between you two?'

'Nothing,' I said.

'Then why does she keep calling you,' Ada asked.

'I don't know. Why don't you go and ask her?'

'Why should I?' She replied with a shrug.

We looked out at Mandovi again. The sun had turned the river crimson, creating a beautiful and charming view outside. And here we were acting so stupid- holed up inside the room, and within ourselves. As we exchanged glances, we knew instantly, it was not the time to be foolish or angry. It was time for fun and revelry. In unison, we got up and dashed towards the door, leaving behind our frustrations and misunderstandings.

'Let's rent an Activa,' She said to me at the bike shop, 'I want to ride one.'

'You will have to do it, anyway,' I replied, 'I don't know how to ride.'

'What?' She yelled in shock, 'You really don't know?'

'No,' I replied.

'Why?'

'Long story. For some other time.'

'Do you ever intend to have a girlfriend?' She asked me, with her brows raised.

'I can still have a girlfriend,' I replied, coyly.

'Yeah, sure,' She replied, 'In your dreams.'

While I was discussing the payment terms with the bike guy, she interjected 'And I want a Pink Helmet.'

'Pink?' Really?' I asked.

'Yeah, to match my clothes.' She replied.

~

The first beach we went to was Morjim, as suggested by the bike shop guy. 'Less crowded. Better privacy,' he said. The view of the open inviting sea, with the red setting sun in the backdrop and the waves crashing against my feet, was surreal. I wanted to go deep into the sea and play with the waves. The coast guards, however, cautioned against it on the loudspeakers. "High tides". "Danger". They kept announcing. 'Tomorrow, then,' I said to myself. I looked at Ada. She looked stunningly beautiful in her big hat, pink top and white shorts. Despite the warnings, she wanted to go deep into the sea. But I kept pulling her back. 'You are an obedient child!' She chided me.

'Always have been,' I replied.

I picked up a shell and gave it to her. She placed it on her palm. Suddenly, a small insect crawled out of it. She shrieked and threw the shell back into the water. I laughed. 'You are not as brave as you show!' I chided her. We continued walking along the length of the beach, holding each other's hands.

'Keep your eyes off her. You are embarrassing me,' she said to me, suddenly.

'What?' I gushed.

'Why are you ogling that girl?' she asked.

I looked at *that* girl. She was a foreigner, in a bikini, lying flat on the beach.

I swear, I wasn't even aware of her presence until Ada spoke of her. I was already a happy man. I had Ada by my side, walking hand in hand with me. Why did I even need to look at that girl? Or maybe, I had looked at her. Involuntarily. Briefly. It happens to all of us. Right? Sometimes, we are just absorbed in our own thoughts that we fail to notice that we might be ogling someone.

'She seems lonely,' I joked.

'Hear me, Kido,' Ada said, 'You are not going to get a girl like that.'

'Whoa! Whoa!' I said, 'You are insulting me.'

'Oh. I see!' She said, 'I dare you. Go ask for her number.'

'Don't dare me!' I replied.

'No. Seriously. Let's see your guts.'

'You can't be serious,' I said, perplexed.

'No… I am.'

Damn! What a mess I have put myself in? I thought. There was no way I could get out of this situation now. Ada pushed me, and I started walking towards the girl. It was going to be so embarrassing. How I wished the Coast Guards' warning would come true - a big tide would flow in and take me with it! Or better, take *that* girl with it. Ahhhhh! It wasn't going to happen, and I prepared for the possibility of my permanent debasement in Ada's eyes!

'What did you say to her?' a bedazzled Ada asked me when I returned triumphantly.

'The truth.'

'What truth?'

'That my girlfriend over there says I don't stand a chance with you.'

'And what did she say?'

'Nothing,' I replied, 'She just smiled and gave me her number.'

'What?' Ada exclaimed, 'She gave you her number, just like that!'

'Yes,' I replied.

Of course, I was grinning from ear to ear! It took Ada some time to ask me the question I had already readied my answer for.

'And since when did I become your girlfriend?' She asked, her cheeks turning pink.

'Say you aren't, and I am going to give Svetlana a call!' I said, smugly.

Chapter 14

The following couple of days were some of the best in my life. We went beach hopping, crisscrossing North to South- from Morjim to Pallolem. She enjoyed riding the scooter, and her pink helmet stood out prominently, drawing adulation from other travelers.

On the beaches, we played - in turns - with the sea and sand. She made beautiful patterns on the sand (I was left awe-stuck! She had never shown her artistic side before). She lamented that her name was too short to make big elaborate patterns. Mine, she said, was perfect and she made at least ten different patterns of it. She didn't like sandcastles. Castles, she said, were over-rated and for *damsels in distress* type of girls. She hated that stereotyping.

I remember in Cavelossim, a little girl who was making a castle asked for her help. And Ada helped her eagerly. But at the end of it, the little girl looked at her in shock and anger. The structure built looked more like an ugly Mumbai tower. I had to pull Ada away quickly before the little girl started crying over that monstrosity!

'She doesn't understand.' Ada said in her defense. 'That building is going to be her reality. Not the castle. Sooner she knows, the better.'

I just have a recollection of all those things that we did. We had set some ground rules after that first day's fight:

Rule No 1: No calls, except to and from family.

Rule No 2: No Pictures. (Unbeknownst to her, I had a picture of us taken by a photographer on the beach. A single hardcopy, which I collected secretly from him later. I don't have that picture now.)

Rule No.3: Not a word about this trip to anyone.

It was in Goa – in Colva - that we first played the Game of Gazing (She named it!), which became a part of *Our Thing*. We were seated in an empty shack and had ordered food and drinks. She was facing the sea, and I sat opposite her, watching her intently as she looked at the waves crashing on the beach.

'What?' She asked me as she realized that I was gazing at her.

'Do you know there is something wrong with your eyes?'

'What is wrong with them?' She said and started rubbing her eyes.

'Don't do that,' I said and pulled her hand away.

'What's it?'

'Your right eye is bigger than your left?'

'What non-sense?' she said.

Looking perplexed, she closed her eyes. I waited for her to open them.

'Stop gazing at me.' She yelled.

'I didn't say they aren't beautiful.'

'First you find the defects. Then you start admiring?'

'They really are.'

'Stop doing it,' She said again, 'You are making me uncomfortable.'

'Making you uncomfortable? How? Why don't you look back into my eyes and make me uncomfortable too? Fair?'

'I can't do that,' she said, turning her eyes away.

'Why not?' I asked, 'You chickening out?'

'Don't dare me.' She replied.

'Oh! I dare you!'

'Okay! Bring it on then.'

'Whoever blinks first loses,' I declared, 'and pays the bill'.

'Then be ready to lose.' She replied, locking her gaze with mine.

Oh! How I lost myself in her eyes! It was as if I were in a dream-watching myself, watching her. Everything else had lost its presence. There was no shack, no beach, no sea. Nothing but calmness and tranquility. And that calmness was overpowering. I wanted to close my eyes and let it prevail.

What are you doing, you loser? My Nemesis No.1, my Mind shouted and flung into action. Using its authoritative powers, it forced my eyes to remain open. But you know the problem with authoritarianism, right? Rebellion happens! And sometimes rebellion gets misdirected. And that's what happened! My face had moved towards hers, and my lips had touched her lips. She pulled her face away quickly, in a snap. Her mouth wide open, her cheeks blood red, her eyes clouded. I didn't know what it meant, and I felt shit scared! I feared it was the end. And I prepared myself for a tight slap and a wretched, remorseful life. But! But something else happened. Something magical. She closed her eyes and leaned in towards me, her lips yearning for mine.

After an hour of awkward silence, I finally said to her, 'Just for the record, you lost.' She smiled, called the waiter, and paid the bill.

Chapter 15

'Where the hell have you been, dude? Didn't even know if you are dead or alive?' Aheesh burst on me the day I joined back.

I knew he would be upset. I hadn't answered any of his calls. Rule No. 1. Remember? No calls except for family.

'I wanted to be alone for some time,' I replied, 'to ponder over my life.'

'Ponder over your life? My ass,' He said, 'Tell me exactly what you have been up to?'

'I was in Pune,' I said, 'Went to see my cousin there.'

'Wow! What a coincidence?', he said mockingly. 'Ada said the same thing- that she was with her cousin.'

'What?' I replied sheepishly. Had she really said that! I had told her that it was going to be my alibi, she had to find a different one. Now, there was no way I could shake it off. She had given us away!

'Don't act smart with me, okay?' Aheesh continued. 'You think I am stupid? You two were together. I know it.'

'I really don't...'

'Don't fool me!' Aheesh interjected.

'Okay' I said, exasperated. 'We were together. Happy?'

'Yes!' He said excitedly and hugged me.

Aheesh was bro. He could be trusted. I could tell him the truth. But! The next in line was Vani. I didn't know what to tell her. I couldn't tell her the truth as she was already upset with me. I had only one option: to avoid her for some days until everything settled down. I was sure she would try to seek me out and question me. I just had to save myself from those questions. Matter of days, and she would let it go. And everything would be back to normal. To my surprise though, she gave me a snub. She avoided me as if I were a disease! She would go straight to the last row and sit beside Hardy. Would you believe that?

'What the hell is happening?' a shocked Ada asked me, as she saw Vani seated with Hardy.

'Good to see you, too,' I replied, 'How are you feeling today?'

'Confused! What the heck is Vani doing with him?'

'Maybe you should ask her,' I replied.

'I will,' She said, 'She isn't talking to you?'

'Nah! Not today.' I replied, 'She will.'

'Ah! I miss Goa.' Ada said, as she couched in her seat.

'Thank you for the trip, btw.'

'Well, what can I say?' She said, 'I am your Man.'

I chuckled.

The Accounts professor came in and started talking about the balance sheets- the assets and the liabilities... And I wandered off.

This is not good. Vani shouldn't be with him. He is good-for-nothing.

'And why am I good-for-nothing?' Hardy popped up in my thoughts and asked.

'Because you are an embarrassment.' I replied indignantly.

'Yet Vani is with me.' He said mockingly.

'Vani!' I shouted.

He laughed.

'Look around. She isn't even here.' He said.

He was right. She wasn't there.

'Where is she?' I asked.

'To know that you have to come with me.' he replied.

The setting changed. The classroom vanished! I was in car with Hardy. He was back in his stained white uniform. He pushed the accelerator, and the car raced away. I recalled - we had rammed into a truck, and I lay bloodied on the road. It was frightening. I was petrified, that it was going to get repeated. But this time, the car didn't hit a truck; instead, it stopped in front of a white castle! As I came out of the car, he held my arm and walked me up to a huge door. He knocked on the door, and a loud bell rang inside. The door opened, and a silhouette started to emerge. I watched as the silhouette transformed into a person. A person I knew very closely. Vani? Yes, it was her!

'Come in,' Vani said and walked away. We followed her as she led us across multiple rooms into a huge hall.

'Where is the liquor?' Hardy thundered. 'We have a guest in the house.'

Vani vanished and came back carrying a bottle of Old Monk and two glasses. I looked at her and wondered. She showed no expressions and moved like a robot. I wasn't even sure whether she had recognized me or not.

'Vani' I said to her meekly, 'Do you remember me?'

'Yes,' She said without batting an eyelid, 'I remember you. Always do'.

A loud sneeze from the professor snapped me out of my thoughts.

'Any doubts? Are we clear?' he asked and sneezed again.

'No, sir. Yes, sir.' The class replied in unison.

'Very well then,' he said after blowing his nose into his hanky. 'Test tomorrow. come prepared.'

The class began to disperse soon after the professor left. I caught a glimpse of Vani at the door. I had to talk to her.

'Gotta go.' I said to Ada and hurried towards the door.

'Where?' She asked, surprised.

'Tell you later.' I shouted.

I caught up with Vani in the corridor, near the banister where I had punched Hardy.

'Hey Vani, are you avoiding me?' I asked her.

'Yes,' She replied without mincing her words.

You know, it's hard to prepare yourself for a straightforward answer. I fumbled and asked meekly, 'why?'

'Because you have been avoiding me! How many times have I called you? And did you bother to talk to me once?'

'Sorry about that,' I said sheepishly.

'How could you just vanish like that?' she asked.

'I said, I am sorry.'

'Don't apologize to me,' She said, 'Apologize to Hardy. You shouldn't have hit him.'

'I told you, I won't! You don't even know why I hit him.'

'And you never bothered to tell me,' She said angrily, 'I am sure he did nothing wrong.'

Now, this got my goat! You know, I had all the intentions to make amends with Hardy earlier. But the way Vani was taking his side and admonishing me, I decided to throw all my good intentions into the wastebin.

'I don't care about what you think,' I said furiously and stomped away. 'And keep him away from me, now that you are good friends with him.'

'Are you okay?' Ada asked me later in the canteen. 'You look a little off-color.'

'Yes. I am fine.' I replied.

'Sure?' She asked again, 'Come on, tell me what happened?'

'I had an altercation with Vani,' I replied.

'Oh! Then I am not getting into the details. But if it cheers you up, I can take you out for dinner tonight.'

'What?' I said, smiling. 'Is this a date?'

'I am your man, you know.' She replied, 'And besides, I don't think you will ever have the guts to ask me out.'

I chuckled at her remarks.

'And no need to pick me up. I would be there by myself,' She added.

'I can pick you up,' I said meekly, realizing that I should have offered earlier.

'No need to be a gentleman,' She replied, 'I have to go out with Riya first. She wants to buy a shirt for her BF. See you at the Spices at 8?'

'Sure,' I said, 'See you.'

I reached the restaurant, Spices, at around 7:45. Ada had messaged me that she would be fifteen minutes late and had asked me to go in and order food. However, I didn't want to go in without her and decided to wait outside. I gazed at the brightly lit signboard, at all the capital letters- S.P.I.C.E.S. *What a boring and uninspiring name!* I thought. There must be hundreds of SPICES in Mumbai alone! I checked the time. It was around 8 now. I still had some time. I could talk to someone. But who? Mom. No. She would inquire about my whereabouts, and I didn't want to lie. Aheesh? No, he would invite himself in. Vani? Forget her!

Suddenly, an auto approached me, and I saw a hand come out of it and wave at me. I waved back. The auto stopped, and Ada got out. She haggled with the auto driver for a while and then ran towards me and gave me a warm hug.

'I hope I am not late,' She said, 'Riya...'

'You look sexy,' I said interrupting her.

She blushed and said cheekily, 'Now, don't I? I knew it. That's why the auto driver couldn't keep his eyes off me!'

I laughed at her remark and said, 'Thank God! He didn't kidnap you.'

'What would you have done then?'

'I don't know. Maybe prayed for him!'

She laughed.

'Shall we?' I said, offering her my arm.

'Of course, my man!' She replied and put her arm in mine as we entered the restaurant.

'What a poor name for a restaurant?' She said while flipping through the menu card, 'It is so commonplace. Isn't it?

I looked at her and smiled.

'What?' she asked.

'You know, I had the exact same thought.'

'See. Great minds think alike,' she said with a smile.

'How's the food here?' I asked.

'I don't know,' She replied.

'Haven't you been here earlier?'

'No. Riya said it's a nice place. So here I am, with you.'

I prayed for the food to be good, especially after seeing the prices. Even though Ada had asked me out, I had decided to man up and pay for the dinner. On any other day, I would have been okay with the prices, but that day, I was running low on money. The Goa trip had left a big hole in my pocket.

I waited for Ada to order first. Depending on her order, I would have to adjust mine. And when she ordered spaghetti pasta and virgin mojito, I knew I had to settle for curd rice.

'Would that be all, sir?' the waiter asked.

'Yes.' I replied.

I could see the dismissive look in the waiter's eyes, but I ignored him.

'I wanted to tell you something,' Ada said hesitantly, after the waiter was gone.

I took my eyes off the menu (I was still checking the prices!) and looked at her. The way she said it, I got a little nervous.

'What?' I asked.

'I think Vani really likes you.'

I raised my eyebrows and said, 'Ha! I think we already discussed this in Goa.'

'No, It's different this time.' Ada said.

'What do you mean?' I asked, surprised. 'How is it different this time?'

'She caught hold of me today when I was leaving'.

I looked at her in disbelief.

'And?'

'I think she knows we were together last week.'

'Big deal!' I replied, 'Everybody knows.'

She looked at me in bewilderment. 'Really?'

'Do you think they are fools?' I replied.

'Hmm. Makes sense,' she said after a pause. "Don't you have any feelings for her?'

'No,' I said, 'And I have already told you that.'

'I think you two would make a cute couple.'

Ha! Here she goes again! Same old game!

'Yeah. That's true,' I replied, sarcastically. 'We do look cute together.'

The waiter approached our table and placed the dishes in front of us. Ada's plate was adorned with hot red-saucy pasta, while mine contained the cold and plain white curd rice. Oh, how I longed to taste that pasta! But I had no choice, after all, I hadn't ordered it. Quietly, I dipped my spoon into the rice and began to eat it.

'Really?' She said angrily, 'Is that what you are going to eat?'

'Yes,' I replied, 'I like curd rice. It is plain and simple.'

'Well, I don't,' she replied, and pushed some pasta onto my plate.

'What are you doing?' I asked, bewildered. She made a mishmash of the red pasta and the curd rice on my plate - it looked horrendous!

'Now eat this!' She thundered.

Hmm… I knew why she was angry!

I kept calm and took a spoonful of that horrendous- looking food. It tasted awful! But I kept eating it.

'It's nice,' I commented.

'Everything is nice and cute to you.' She replied mockingly.

I smiled.

'And…. I didn't say you have to be…', She said while making spaghetti loops on her fork.

'Excuse me?'

'You know, I didn't say you two have to be a couple.'

'Really?' I asked. *I was winning the game!* 'I thought you wanted us to be a couple.'

'I didn't say that.'

'So, who do you think I should be with?' I asked.

She didn't answer. She scooped a spoonful of my mishmash dish and tasted it. 'Yuccck! It is disgusting!'

'Isn't it?' I said and laughed.

'And you were eating it so coolly?'

'Yeah! I am a good actor.' I replied.

'I know that. You won't believe what she said.'

'What?' I asked.

'She said, "I would get out of your way for Vasillor's sake",' Ada replied.

'What?' I almost shouted in bewilderment. 'What are you guys' cooking? Do I have a vote in all of this?'

'No', Ada replied with a smile, 'You don't.'

Chapter 16

Vani had changed; I could sense that. She started keeping a distance from me and hardly spoke with me. And whenever we talked, it was very short. She even stopped sitting beside me in the class. I wasn't the only one to notice the changes. Aheesh had noticed them too. In fact, she didn't talk much with him as well. Aheesh asked me what the issue was. 'I don't know,' I remarked, 'Maybe she doesn't want us to be friends anymore.' 'That's absurd,' Aheesh replied, 'Who wouldn't want to be friends with us.'

Yes, I missed her. I missed watching her doodle in her book. I missed teasing her about her drawings. I missed our conversations. I missed the intriguing new world she had introduced me to- the world of art, and the famous painters and their many quirks. With her, I knew that I was in the company of someone destined for greatness. Sometimes, I would turn my head to observe her and see what she was up to. As always, she would be engrossed in her drawings and wouldn't even look up.

I remembered the Saturday when we had gone bird watching. She had told me we would always be friends, but I guess things change with time. More often than not, all relationships come to an end in due course of time. Or maybe, the reason was something else. Perhaps my proximity with Ada was the reason why she kept a distance. I wanted to go up to Vani, and assure her that no matter what, she would always be close to me.

In between, she went missing for a week. I asked Aheesh if he was aware of her whereabouts, but he didn't know where she was either. I started getting worried and called and texted her many times. There was no response for a couple of days, and when she finally called back, she spoke to me normally, as she used to, much to my relief.

'Nothing to worry about. I am traveling for my art exhibition,' she said.

'You didn't tell me anything. You cannot go like this.'

'It was very last minute,' she replied. 'And if I ever leave, I will do proper goodbyes.'

'Vani, why were you ignoring me?' I asked her once she was back.

'Oh! I wasn't. I was in my own world, busy finishing a project.'

'So, you are not upset with me.'

'No,' she replied, 'Why should I be upset with my best friend.'

I was happy to hear her words. Everything seemed to be back to normal.

I wanted to ask her about the conversation that she had with Ada. But I couldn't bring myself to speak about it. She sensed that I was struggling with something in my head, and looking straight into my eyes said, 'I know, and I am happy for you. You are the best couple in the world.'

Chapter 17

For all the frankness that Ada brought in, there was an excruciatingly mysterious side to her as well. And quite honestly, if I must confess, it had only added to my craziness for her. Once, I lovingly called her my Monalisa, and when she asked me why, I replied, 'You have smile on your lips and sorrow in your eyes. I know what makes you laugh but I don't know what makes you sad'. Her eyes welled up when she heard this.

And that was exactly my issue with her as well! I had seen her in tears so many times, but I didn't know why, and she wouldn't tell. Do you know what's the most painful thing in this world? - to helplessly watch your beloved suffer. And in their suffering, you burn. You feel like you are in hell, being roasted alive. No. Not a good feeling! I tried talking to her, but she would always brush me aside and quickly morph herself into the ever-effervescent Ada. It was as if she had some mysterious on-off switch.

One day, I found her in one of the desolate corners of the library, crying inconsolably.

'What's wrong, Ada?' I asked her. I was concerned that something terrible had happened.

'Nothing,' She replied wiping away her tears.

'Come on, tell me. What is bothering you?' I asked.

'Nothing.' She repeated herself.

'I can help,' I said.

'It's really nothing.'

'Really?' I said, angrily, 'then, why are you crying?'

'It's nothing,' She repeated meekly.

I took a deep breath, realizing that anger was of no use. She was clearly in bad shape, and my yelling and shouting wouldn't help. I decided to be calm and resolved to get to the root of whatever was bothering her.

'Are you missing your home?' I asked, calmly.

'No.'

'Mom?'

'No.'

'Dad?'

'No.'

'Then who is it?'

She didn't reply and continued sobbing.

'Some guy?' I asked her with dread in my heart.

She didn't reply. She got up, wiped her eyes again, untied and tied her hair; and turned her switch ON and smiled.

'Let's go and join others,' she said.

I pulled her back by her arm and said, 'No, Ada. This is not done. Today, either you tell me what it is, or we don't talk ever again'.

'Don't…'

'No,' I said vehemently, 'This cannot be.'

She sat down. The tears were back in her eyes. She lowered her gaze, watched her hands, and fell silent.

'Ada?' I said after a moment.

She took a deep breath, and said in a wavering voice, 'I don't know what to say?'

'Just tell me whatever it is.'

'I have never told this to anyone.'

'Trust me, Ada. Let it out,' I said calmly.

She fidgeted continuously, as if she were on hot coals, and with shaky fingers made circles out of her hair. I could feel her struggle. I was struggling too! She had to open up and share. And I had to be receptive, regardless of how damaging her words could be for me!

She continued to remain silent, and after a while, I decided to take the matter into my hands again.

'Who do you always talk to on the phone? I saw it in Goa too. After every call, your mood changes? Boyfriend? Ex?'

'No.'

'Come on Ada. Tell me the truth. Please…'

'There is this guy… I don't know what to do?'

'Which guy?'

She hid her face in her hands, took a deep breath, and said, 'My school friend…'

'Okay,' I said, my heart pounding hard.

'I went out with him once.'

'So, you guys are in a relationship?' I asked her, shocked at this revelation.

'No!' she replied.

'What's the problem then?'

'It's complicated.' She sighed.

What a cliché! I thought. *Always complicated.*

Okay, my friend! My gullible idiot! My mind jumped in. *This is the end of the road for you. How could you not see the signs? They were always there. All over the place. Whenever he calls, she speaks with him privately. Even in Goa, when she was 'supposedly' with you. She is in a relationship with him. You have been played, you moron!*

'We are family friends. Our Moms are very close. And he was my friend in school. We went out once. Just once. And he keeps bothering me. I don't want anything with him,' She said and broke down 'I want him to go away! But he keeps calling me. He doesn't understand.'

I was zapped when I heard this. And angry! This was unexpected, and I felt sorry for her. She was going through something terrible, and I had judged her unfairly! I was ashamed of myself. I didn't stop her from crying. I waited patiently until she composed herself.

'Sorry,' She said, 'I am a mess today.'

'No, you are not,' I replied, comforting her.

'Okay! So, you know now.'

'Hmmm. Just tell him, you aren't interested in him and not to bother you.'

'It's so easy for you guys.' She said, looking straight into my eyes.

'Why is it difficult for you?'

'You won't understand. It is complicated.'

'What's so complicated, Ada?'

'I have tried telling him, but he won't listen.'

'Ignore him. Don't pick up his calls.'

'Okay,' she said after a pause. 'Let's ignore him right away and talk about something else. Where's all this noise coming from? What's happening out there?'

'They are rehearsing on the stage. Some music festival today. You forgot?'

'Oh yeah. Let's go and check it out,' she said and pulled me by my arm.

Did I tell you that sometimes I felt she was crazy? I will tell you why. Before I knew it - and just a few minutes after our dramatic conversation- she had already jumped onto the stage. With a mike in her hands and cheered on by the people, she sang out aloud the latest Punjabi songs!

How could you not orbit around a girl like that?

Chapter 18

The college break was a couple of days away, and there was a lot of excitement. People were looking forward to going back to their homes. I had no such excitement. I wanted to spend more time with Ada. But she wanted to be in Delhi with her family. So, I booked our train tickets together. That way, at least, I could spend some more time with her. On the day of our departure, the first thing that caught my eye when we met to leave for Mumbai Central was her big pink trolley. I laughed out on seeing it.

'What?' she asked.

'Pink Trolley? Seriously? How old are you? Six?'

'What is your problem with pink? She asked me.

'Nothing. Just keep it away from me.'

That journey- I will never forget. It is kind of bittersweet for me. Sweet because on day one of our journey, in that confined space, we somehow understood the infinite attraction that we had towards each other. We nearly scandalized the elderly *Uncle-Aunty* seated opposite us by what you could describe as the PDA. I still remember the way that poor *Aunty* looked at us from the corner of her eyes every time I took Ada's hands in mine, or how that smart *Uncle* smarted in his berth and kept lighting up his mobile just to check what we were doing in the darkness of the night.

We hardly slept that night. (FYI… We didn't do anything fishy for our elderly *Uncle-Aunty* to be ashamed of us). We just had so much to talk about. It was as if I was knowing Ada for the first time. She had so many layers to her. Ada in college was so different from Ada in Goa, and Ada in Goa was so different from Ada in the train.

For the first time, she spoke about her family- particularly about her mom. She was so respectful and loving of her mom. 'I will never say no to anything she asks of me,' she said. She spoke of her younger sister - who was in school, and how worried she was about her. 'She has to stay away from the boys, you know how it is.'

It is such an exuberant feeling, you know, when the person you love opens up to you and talks about their family; when they make you privy of their small family secrets, jokes, and talks. By the end of that night, I had known so much about her family it felt as if they were my own kin. I knew what her mom aspired for her and what haircut her sister wanted to have.

When I finally slept, which was around 5 in the morning, I dreamt of being in her house, chatting with her mother, and teasing her sister on her new haircut. And strangely, I responded when her mom called out Ada's name. Strangely, I had morphed into Ada!

Day two was when we had one hell of a fight. By the time I woke up, she was already talking on her phone. The talk was upsetting her, and tears had already welled up in her eyes. I knew who was at the other end of the call. I got so furious. I had told her to ignore him. But here she was, talking to him again! And it got me angry. She was letting him abuse her! After she had finished her call, I yelled at her. I said things that I shouldn't have. I behaved as if I had some right on her life. At that moment, I felt I was doing it all for her well-being but now, in hindsight, I know how wrongly I behaved. She kept quiet and listened to all my nonsense.

'Stay away from me, please.' She said finally, tearfully.

'With pleasure.' I replied, haughtily.

We didn't talk for the entire day. Even the Uncle-Aunty looked worried. They tried to strike a conversation with us and offered homemade food and sweets. Sweet Uncle-Aunty! They tried their best to keep the mood in our compartment light. They shared embarrassing stories of their grandchildren and joked about their own marriage. They even went ahead and did a little show of their own PDA. I really felt for them. They were trying so hard to help us patch up. But we were in no mood to relent and sat quietly till we reached Delhi.

I got off the train first, and without any care, started walking towards the station exit. I was so mad at Ada that I didn't even wait for her. When you are upset and the anger overtakes you, you don't realize what a brute you become! And at that moment - one of my worst- I had become one.

Fortunately for me, I remembered that one thing my dad used to say: Always drink a glass of cold water whenever you get angry. There was a small railway shop on the platform, and I bought a bottle of ice-cold water. I sat down on a bench nearby and drank the water. Some of the water I splashed over my face. Slowly, the good sense crawled back into me and calmed me down. I realized the mistake I had made. I just shouldn't have left like that.

I quickly gathered my wits and my bag, then ran back towards the bogey. I got onto the train and checked our compartment. It was empty. I got down and started running towards the second station exit, pushing and cutting through the crowd. I won't be able to describe to you the relief I felt when I finally saw her. No, the sighting wasn't perchance as they show you in those bullshit movies. I could spot her only because she had that big, protuberant pink trolley bag! Otherwise, trust me, there is no way you could spot anyone in the Delhi station crowd. I followed her quietly as she jostled through the crowd.

It was only when she reached the stairs and struggled with her luggage that I paced up and approached her. She shrieked in shock and yelled (mistaking me for a thief!) when I quietly relieved her of her luggage and started pulling it up. I had moved in so suddenly that it took her a moment to realize what was happening, and in that one moment, I could see a sea of expressions overwhelm her. Once we reached the foot over bridge, she, surprisingly, charged at me and pushed me with her full strength. I lost my balance and fell, bleeding from my left arm. The pink bag slipped from my hand and slid down the stairs.

Seeing my bloodied arm, Ada was dazed and broke down. 'What have I done? I am sorry,' she said. For me, it was just karma, and in a way, I felt good. I put my right arm around her, sat her down on the bridge, gave her some water and calmed her down. 'It's OK Ada. It's just a scratch.' But she wouldn't move. I stood up and pulled her with my left hand. 'See, It's all good.'

Thankfully, the bag hadn't hit the people on stairs and had rolled down and settled nicely on the platform. I ran down the stairs, picked up the bag with my left hand, and climbed up. It hurt, but I wanted to show Ada that I was alright. It took us ten minutes to come out of the station onto the road.

She was still guilt ridden with what had happened. She kept looking at my arm, asking me whether it was fine. 'It's OK, really' I said, 'It is nothing. Just a scratch. Have had worse on the Cricket field.'

'I am so stupid' She said, 'See, what I did. You shouldn't have come back.'

'Really?' I said, 'This is what I get after all this. Let me leave, then.'

'Shut up,' She said, 'And stay here.'

She went away and left me to watch her pink bag. You should have seen the way people kept looking at me. What was their problem with pink! Had they never seen a guy with a pink trolley? She came back after fifteen minutes, carrying a medical kit with her. Cautiously, she cleaned my left arm, put on some betadine on the wound, and bandaged it. This was the second time she was nursing me, and I had started loving it.

'What are you going to tell your parents when they see this?' she asked.

'The truth: That a crazy girl pushed me down at New Delhi Railway station.'

'Huh? And won't they ask which girl and why?'

'I will say Ada did it because she likes to beat up handsome boys.'

'Ha!' She replied, 'I like to give a thrashing, yes. What time is your bus?'

'Don't know. I will get into any that's leaving immediately.'

'Where do you get the bus from?'

'From the Paharganj side, I guess… I think I must leave.'

'Yeah sure.' she said, 'have a safe journey!'

'Yeah. See you,' I said, 'Is anyone coming to get you?'

'Yes,' She replied.

'Do you want me to wait?'

'Oh no. You better get going. You have a long road ahead.'

'Yeah, that's true. Bye then,' I said to her as we shook our hands.

'Bye.'

I had just crossed the railway station to the Paharganj side when my cell phone beeped. I took out the phone from my jeans pocket and read the message: *Sorry for all that happened. Will miss you.*

Will miss you. I read this sentence a hundred times. And a hundred times I smiled.

'Don't miss me too much,' I messaged back, 'don't want the pimples!'

It was a thing we said in school- that you get pimples when you are missed!

'LOL.' She replied.

I felt so lucky when the guy at the ticket counter told me I was just in time for the bus. 'Hurry up! The bus is leaving. There isn't another one for two hours.'

I got onto the moving bus and took my seat at the back. I had just settled down when my phone beeped again. I took out the phone from my pocket to read the message.

Missing you already. Want to give you a Hug and a Kiss.

What the heck! I got up from my seat, collected my bag, and yelled at the driver to stop. The conductor yelled back at me – 'Be seated'. I continued with my protestations. 'I am in the wrong bus,' I said, 'I am in the wrong bus. I need to get out.'

'What an Idiot!' People in the bus moaned loudly. I ignored them. They didn't know what I was striving for. They were idiots. The driver slowed down slightly and asked me to jump out, and I did so happily. I just wanted to get off the bus, anyhow!

On the road again, a thought came to my mind. What if Ada had already left? It meant I had just stranded myself for two hours and made a jackass of myself. *You fool! It's time to run. Not over-think.* My Nemesis No1 woke up from its slumber and spoke up.

Okay! I started running towards the railway station. I pushed the people out of my way, ignoring the profanities and slurs they yelled at me. On the foot over bridge, the TCs were stopping people and checking their tickets. One of the TCs saw me running and asked me to stop. I had no time to waste, so I ignored him and continued running. I hadn't realized, but a couple of TCs were on my tail. I was just two feet away from the exit when one of them pounced on me and pinned me down to the ground.

'You are going to pay for this, you bastard,' One of them said, still panting from the chase.

He took out a register from his bag and began to write in it.

'Wait! Wait! I have a ticket,' I said, 'and here is my I card!'

They couldn't believe it! 'What?' One of them said, 'Are you crazy? Why the heck did you run?'

'I am an athlete. I always run,' I replied jokingly.

'Get the hell out of here!' they bellowed.

I rushed out of the station, as fast as I could, and there she was, still waiting.

I picked up my phone and showed the pictures to her. 'This one is from the temple there.'

'Nice,' Mom said with folded hands.

Dad also joined in and looked at the pictures keenly.

'Let me guess the people in the picture,' Mom said to me.

'Okay,' I replied.

'This here is the love of my life. My beta.' She said, beaming with joy.

'Ha! Mom. Well done.'

'I am just warming up.'

'The girl with curly hair. This is easy. Vani. Right?

'Yes.'

'The boy with the mischief in his eyes. Aheesh?'

'Wow! You are good at it, Mom.'

Dad was quite bewildered at what was happening. 'How?' his eyes seemed to ask.

'I told you. I know all his friends,' My mom said.

'Colored hair, colorful shirt… Sushant.'

'Yes.'

'This girl', 'She said as she put her finger on the screen, 'this girl I don't know.'

I could feel the lump forming in my throat, and my lips dried.

'Who is this girl?' She asked me.

'Ada,' I replied awkwardly.

'Ada. Hmm. You never told me about her.'

'Might have missed,' I replied meekly.

'Ada,' my mom repeated the name.

You fool. You just gave yourself away! My mind said. *They know now. About you and Ada. They know.* I could feel the heat of a thousand suns inside me. I blushed. Mom placed her hand over my forehead and asked me if I was okay. 'You look feverish.'

'I am fine, mom.'

'okay'.

She was still checking the pictures when my phone rang. It was Ada. What perfect timing! I blushed more. I don't know why, but I was embarrassed. So, so embarrassed.

'Talk to her,' Mom said and handed me the phone.

I walked away quietly and went into my room, carrying with me the ten thousand tons of embarrassment.

'Hello,' I said.

'I did it,' she said, exuberantly.

'Did what?' I asked.

'I told him to get lost.'

'And?'

'And what... I told him if he didn't stop bothering me, I would tell his parents and lodge a police complaint.'

'And what did he say?' I asked anxiously.

'He sounded terrified and said he would never call me again.'

'That's great! Told you, you are worrying over nothing.'

'Besides, if he still bothers me, it's your job to take care of him.'

'What? Why is it my job?' I asked, surprised.

'It is. I did what you told me to do. Now, he's your problem,' she said teasingly.

'Wow! I am learning so many things from you.'

'Yes sir! You are,' she said.

~

Dad was right. I hardly spent any time with my parents. Physically I was there, but mentally my thoughts were elsewhere. Mostly I could be found with my phone, either talking or texting.

During visits to my relatives, I would sit in the most obscure place in the room and take out my phone and chat. Most of my chats, obviously, were with Ada. I knew what time she woke up, what her plans for the day were, who she was going out with, the shopping she had done, the food she had eaten, in short- everything about her daily routine. And she knew about mine. Our nights usually ended with a *good night, sleep tight* message, except for one night when she didn't respond, and things changed completely between us.

I think it was a Friday night. I sent her the usual *Good Night* message at around 11 pm. I know you would ask, "Isn't 11 pm too early for a *Good Night* message?" What can I say? I was at home in Dehradun, and the entire city is in bed before 10 pm. My Dad had already checked upon me twice. He wanted me to put the phone aside and give my eyes some rest. I had told him earlier that my eyes were hurting, and he had blamed my phone for that. My eyes were still hurting, and I was feeling sleepy as well. 'Five minutes more, please,' I pleaded with him. He nodded, turned the lights off, and left.

She usually replied within two minutes. I wanted to see her reply, and then off I would go to my dream world! But… She didn't reply. 2 mins. 3 mins. 5 mins. 15 mins. 40 mins… Nothing. No reply. The sleep which was beseeching me earlier started to avoid me now. I started getting worried and kept checking my phone every five minutes. *Was she alright?* This had never happened before. *Maybe she had already slept.* I thought. *But she doesn't sleep so early. Delhi doesn't sleep so early. Delhi… Delhi isn't safe. Is she safe?* My Nemesis No1 started creating all the unpleasant scenarios. I shuddered at my thoughts and shook my head vehemently to throw them off. *Should I call?* I checked the time. It was already 12:10. *It's late. She is not in the hostel. She is with her family. Cannot call…. should not call!*

I called. My call was cut. I called up again. Disconnected again. *Why is she cutting my calls?* I thought. *Must be with her mom. That's why?* It was a reassuring thought. And I closed my eyes. They were hurting so much! It was already 2 am when I opened my eyes, and I felt guilty. How could I doze off! My damn eyes. I shouldn't have shut them. I quickly searched for my phone. The small LED was blinking. It was the blink of hope and excitement! Thank you, H.J. Round, Oleg Losev, James R. Baird, Nick Holonyakon- the great gods, the inventors of LED! You guys saved my life that day. I quickly unlocked my phone. There was a message. It was from Ada and it read: *Sorry couldn't reply earlier. I was out.*

The first feeling I had was of relief. *Thank God! She is safe.* But that feeling immediately led to another one- that of envy and anxiety. *Who was she out with?*

Should I ask her that? I thought. *Wouldn't I look nosy? But I had to know!* I looked at the time again. I was 2:05 am. Any other day, it would have been too late for me to strike a conversation, but today I didn't care.

I replied: *It's Ok. Hope you had fun!*

I received the reply immediately: *U still up?*

Yes. On a call. I lied.

I wanted some buildup. She would ask me, "Who have you been talking to?" I would counter-ask "Who have you been out with?"

Continue ur call. GN. She replied.

GN? How cold! Not even a proper, fully typed out Good Night. Just *GN! Was she upset? Should I get angry?* These two letters- G & N had dispatched all my buildup to dogs. It was time to make quick amends. I wouldn't get anything out like this.

Finished the call already. Howz your day? I wrote.

Was OK. You had called? She replied.

I didn't want to tell her that I had been sick-worried about her. I didn't know how she would react.

Yes. Any idea when college is opening? I asked.

U r asking the wrng person! I don't know. I am extending my stay. She replied.

It pinched me hard. Here I was, waiting for the vacations to end, desperate to be with her. And there she was, extending her stay! It just made me angry. Why was I feeling desperate? Why wasn't she feeling the same way?

When are you coming back? I asked.

Not sure yet. What about U?

I will be there on the first day. Must focus on studies, this time.

Okay!!!!! U will miss me then. She messaged.

I won't. I replied curtly.

There was no response from her.

I lay awake in my bed for more than an hour, tormenting myself. *I shouldn't have said that. Why did I get so pissed off?* I loathed myself for having texted '*I won't*'. That wasn't true at all. I knew, I would be miserable in college without her. I knew I would miss her laughter, her pranks, her presence! *Why didn't I just tell her the truth? Why did I hold back? Why do I always hold back?*

In those moments of self- flagellation, I sent out a message to her: *I WILL MISS U.* And topped it up with another one: *I LOVE U.*

Ah! The sound of silence. Have you ever heard it? Do something as crazy as I had just done, and you will certainly hear it. Suddenly, everything became so calm. I could hear nothing, not even my breath! I felt at peace with myself. I had just accepted the truth. Even my Nemesis No1 patted me on my shoulders and said Well done, brave boy! And it made me so joyous, for a moment. Yes.

And then I realized what the heck I had done! The folly. The biggest blunder of my life. I had just drawn curtains on my relationship with Ada. And my heart began to beat fast, till it blew my ear drums apart. I had gone too far. And there was no coming back now. I remembered what Ada had told me in the car that Friday night, after that fiasco in the club: Friends should never be lovers.

Of course, I couldn't sleep. Now, I was even scared to look at my phone. The same LED which was a lifesaver earlier had become a terrorist now! The disquiet was overbearing. I had to switch off my mind. So, I went into our living room and switched on the TV. A Jackie Chan movie was running, and it was relaxing to watch him do his silly village buffoon antics. I dozed off before he became the Kungfu master in the movie.

When I woke up, it was already 9 am, and I was curled on the sofa. Someone had put a blanket over me. I tried to snuggle back into the warm blanket when the night's happenings rushed back into my mind, and my eyes popped open. I didn't have the heart to go into my bedroom to check my phone, but it couldn't be avoided. I started preparing myself. What is the worst that could happen? I think it was too early for my brain to function properly. I couldn't fathom an answer to this question. I got up from the sofa and walked towards my room. From a distance, I could see the LED blinking. I had received the reply.

With shaky hands, I typed in my password. There were two messages:

First one at 5:14 am: *Have you gone crazy? How could you?*

And the second one at 5:33 am: *I Luv u 2.*

Chapter 20

Okay! You know how awesome technology is. It makes everything so simple. Even something like confessing your love! It took me seconds to text 'I love u'. Do you think I would have ever gathered the courage to say this in person? No. Never. I am way too timid for that. Anyway, you know Ada had decided to extend her stay. And she had taken this decision like a dictator without caring for my emotions! College, without her was miserable. I counted the days till her return. Sure, I had people for company but hers was the one I pined for!

What do you think happened when Ada finally came? The first day I saw her walking in front of me (unbeknownst to her), my heart swung like a circus monkey on a trapeze, and my knees got wobbly. By confessing my love, I had shared something deeply personal, a super-secret with her. And now it was too embarrassing for me to face her! Eventually, we spoke, but I kept it short. And thereafter, for several days, despite my yearning to spend hours with her, I kept away. I didn't have the courage to go up to her, look her in the eyes, hold her hands, kiss her. Not yet.

She was patient. Or maybe uncomfortable too. She too kept her distance. She would go and chat with her girl gang, hardly talking to me. The people around us did notice the change and assumed that our relationship had turned bad. Little did the poor people know about the beautiful thing birthing inside us, waiting for its time to come out and blossom. They would see us standing in the opposite corners avoiding one another, but they missed the surreptitious exchange of our sweet smiles and the meeting of our sideways glances. It was ironic, our hide and seek, but it had a thrill of its own!

This drama finally ended on Aheesh's birthday. We were all in the canteen, and in between the cake cutting and the subsequent clapping session, our eyes locked. And I realized how foolish I had been, wasting precious time! *That's it!* I resolved. And when everyone had eaten up their piece of cake and two samosas and drank their Fantas and left the canteen, I messaged Ada to come back. I sat at a table and ordered two Thumps up.

What are you going to say? My Nemesis No.1, my mind, asked me.

I don't know. I replied.

Ask her if she really meant it? It asked.

Meant what?

That she loves you…

No! that would be idiotic. I replied.

Okay. Okay. Kiss her then. On Lips.

No!

While I was busy dueling with my Nemesis, I had failed to notice that Ada and the canteen boy were standing in front of me. The canteen boy put two glasses and the cold drinks on the table and left. Ada slid into the chair opposite me and smiled. I smiled back and started pouring the cold drink into her glass.

'Have you forgotten? I drink straight from the bottle,' she said, smiling.

'Sorry,' I replied, 'you want straw.'

'Since when did I use straw?'

'Sorry,' I repeated.

I passed her a bottle, and she raised it up to her lips. I watched as she took a sip from it, playing with the cola in her mouth for a while before gulping it down. I loved the way she savored the taste of every molecule in that drink. It was a sight I could pay millions for! When she finally caught me watching her, she put the bottle back on the table and straightened herself up in the chair.

'What?' she asked.

'Nothing,' I replied, smiling.

'I know this game. Take your eyes off me.'

'I can't,' I said helplessly.

She laughed.

I took her hand in my hands and said the most bizarre thing, now that I think of it!

'I am sorry,' I said.

'What for?' she asked.

'For that message….'

'What?' She interrupted me. 'You didn't mean it.'

'No... No…,' I said.

'No?' She turned red in her face.

I kissed her hands. (Yes, I did that!)

'Ada. Listen to me,' I said, 'You never hear me out completely. Please be quiet and listen. I said sorry that I messaged you. I shouldn't have...'

She sat quietly and listened carefully to every word I uttered, her face getting redder and redder with every passing moment.

'I shouldn't have messaged you,' I said, 'I should have held your hands like this, looked into your beautiful, mesmerizing eyes, and said, "Ada, I love you. I have loved you from the day I first heard your voice. You remember? The day, you first whispered in my ear. Your silky voice! You don't know for how many days it didn't let me sleep. I have loved you from the day I first caught a glimpse of your eyes. How many days did I spend searching for them? You don't know. I have loved you from the day I first saw your pistachio-polished toenails," And I should have told you all this, poured out my heart to you while looking at your beautiful face, holding your hands. I took an easy route. I just messaged you. And that's why I am sorry.'

Her response?

Well, I will come to that. First, let me tell you how my spirit and my body responded. My spirit was quenched. I had told her the truth, the truth I didn't know would ever come to my lips. My body was dehydrated. My throat was parched, my lips dry, and - don't judge and laugh at me- my stupid eyes were wet.

As for Ada, well, I think she was frozen! She didn't say a word for a very long time, and the color of her cheeks didn't get back to normal. Her eyes opened like a tap, and tears rolled down her cheeks. Her hands- which were still in mine- turned cold. Very cold! And when she finally opened her mouth, her voice trembled, and the only words she said were – I love you too.

Chapter 21

You must have seen in the Bollywood movies how, as the love story progresses, the ensemble cast of the friends (and the frenemies!) of the Hero slowly fades out of the story line. I had always felt this sort of storytelling to be a farce. I mean, where the hell do other people - that mattered - go? But from my own experience now, let me admit that a part of this progression is true. Over the months that followed, everyone else (well, mostly!) zoomed out of my life. I was hardly interested in other people's lives. I was too occupied with my love life. I believe it had a reciprocal effect as well. The other people also started caring less about my life and, after a while, even started to keep a distance. 'We will leave you alone, you are a couple', they would comment.

Days turned to nights and nights turned to days, just like that. Time flew! At the end of every day, it felt we hadn't spent enough time with one another. And at the end of every night, we knew the phone calls were incomplete, there was so much left unsaid. I remember one peculiar thing from those days, which I will tell you. Our attendance in the library increased exponentially. Yes! That's true. If you had seen the library register, you would have found our names in it on most of the days. You would have deduced that we had suddenly become the studious types. The fact, however, was that we went to the library to doze off! We couldn't afford to waste our nights in the useless sleep.

Ada was a different beast, though. While I was completely cut off from the rest of the world, she still managed her social bridges well. She always knew the things and had the juiciest gossip. I am still bewildered. How did she manage it all so well? During one of our nightly calls, the discussion veered towards the linkups in the class, and she told me that we weren't the only *Couple*. There were a few more.

'Really?' I said, 'I thought it was just us.'

'You thought wrong.'

'Who else is there?' I asked, quite intrigued.

'Guess who?'

I pondered for a while.

'Jaswant and Ruchi for sure.'

'Well done! That's ten points for you,' She said cheerily, 'Who else?'

'I don't know. Maybe Sameer and Roshni.'

'Wrong,' She said, 'Deducting twenty points.'

'Twenty points! Isn't that too much? How's that fair?' I protested.

'That's fair in my world. Don't you know my philosophy.'

'Oh! Didn't know I was dating a philosopher. What is your philosophy, by the way!'

'Reward lightly, punish severely,' she said.

'Wow! That's your philosophy. I will have to be careful, then,' I said.

'You better be!' She said, 'And don't try to wrong me.'

I laughed and said, 'I am already terrified of you and your philosophy.'

'They are planning a couples' night-out.' She continued. 'I have said Yes.'

'What?' I replied, 'I don't even know who the couples are! And who is this They?'

'The girls.'

'Of course,' I said.

'We talk.'

'Oh! I get it. What else do you talk about?'

'I can't tell you all,' She replied.

'Come on!'

'No.'

'You shouldn't have brought up the topic then.'

'Can't tell.'

'Okay,' I said, sullenly.

Do you know what's the most important thing that all the guys of this world want to know? No, it's not how gravity or the internet works. Really. The real thing they want to know is what exactly is this "girl talk". What do girls talk about in their privacy? What topics are included and discussed in this talk? Guys know nothing about it. You would have seen the girls talking amongst themselves - those subtle lip movements and not-so-subtle sniggers, slight eye contacts, and touches of hands on their ear lobes, the hair-brushings, and all other morse-codes; and then - in between their talk- they throw a sudden glance at you, and you wonder- Am I looking like an idiot today? Oh God! Is it my smell again? And in seconds, you see yourself morph into a cockroach, ready to hide in the darkest crevice. That's the power of the girl talk! That's the power I want to understand, one day.

'Listen,' I said, 'I need to hang up.'

'Why? What happened?'

'Just feeling sleepy.'

'Feeling sleepy? Didn't you sleep in the library today?'

I didn't answer.

'I know what's wrong,' she continued. 'My poor baby. Ok, I will tell you one thing! Just one thing.'

I smiled at my conquest. 'Okay,' I said happily.

'Promise you won't tell anybody a thing,'

'I promise.'

'Mira is sleeping with Sanjay.'

'What?' I blurted in disbelief. I was about to fall off the ledge that I was sitting on.

'Yes,' she said, 'I will kill you if you tell this to anyone.'

'Sanjay is a lucky bastard.'

'And you are a dog,' She replied.

'Why? Did I say something wrong?'

'I know what you mean,' she said.

'I mean nothing wrong. Besides, you have threatened to kill me if I ever wrong you.'

'I know you, sweetheart,' she said lovingly, 'You are a meek soul.'

'Now, you are insulting me!' I replied.

'Cheer up, my baby,' She said, 'By the way, there is news about your ex.'

'Ha! My ex?' I asked.

'Yes, Vani.'

'What about her?' I asked curiously.

'There is gossip about her and Hardy.'

Hardy and Vani? She is making a mistake. Man, I need to caution her!

'Hello?' Ada said, 'All, Okay?'

'Yes.'

'You still have feelings for her?' Ada teased me.

'Really? When are you going to stop this?' I replied.

'Never,' She said, 'Don't tell me you are planning their break-up?'

'What? No. Why should I? It's her life.'

'Okay! And before I forget, keep an eye on Aheesh.'

'What did he do now?' I asked, surprised.

'He is going to get beaten up.' she said.

'Why?'

'Because he is chasing a girl from the final year and her boyfriend is a bodybuilder.'

'What? Are you sure? He never told me.'

'Yes. Pretty sure.'

The fact that I was hearing this from Ada instead of Aheesh made me sad and angry. Why hadn't Aheesh told me about it? He was my closest friend, and yet he had ignored me. Why? Had he been with me at that time, I would have killed him! Yes, for sure. I would have killed him.

'What about the girl? She has a problem with him too.' I asked.

'Just keep an eye on him. Okay,' she said without answering my question.

'I will talk to him.'

'If you talk to him, he will understand that I told you this. Just watch out for him.'

'Okay.'

'What time is it?'

'4:35,' I said, looking at my wristwatch.

'Need to sleep, then. See you tomorrow at the Orientation.'

'What Orientation?'

'You forgot! I am on the committee. You better be in college by 9 am.'

'Okay, madam,' I replied.

'Good night, Baby,' she said.

'Good night.'

I was back into the house where Hardy had taken me. I was sitting there in the living room, drinking my tea, when suddenly the elephant-trees and the winged-trains sprung out of the walls. They started dancing around me in concentric circles. After a while, my head started spinning, and I closed my eyes.

When I opened them again, I was in the classroom and saw Hardy and Vani there, making out on my chair! I yelled, "Vani don't do this. He is not a good guy." But she ignored my protestations and kept going on! I fumed. I wanted to close my eyes again but couldn't. I felt as if someone was forcing me to keep my eyes open and watch. I felt so helpless.

After they were done, she stood up in all her nakedness, looked at me, smiled, and then went back and slapped Hardy. Hardy, enraged, picked up the chair and threw it at Vani. Vani fell on the floor. The elephant-trees and the winged-trains stopped their dance and ran towards her like puppies. They licked her feet, her face, her naked body. But she made no movement. There was blood everywhere- on the floor of the class, on Vani's naked body and on Hardy's white uniform. I couldn't bear to see the sight and my body shivered! Please wake me up! I begged my mind. Please! But it didn't. It forced me to see that horrible sight.

My phone, my savior, blared vociferously at 8 am, pulling me out from my nightmare. You cannot imagine how thankful I was to return to the world of sunshine!

At 8.10 am, Vani called. I was surprised. She hadn't spoken to me for days.

'Hello, Vani,' I said.

'Can you meet me at 9 am today?' she asked.

'Sure… Sure. All okay?'

'Yes.'

'See you in the canteen,' I said.

'No.' She replied, 'Not in the college.'

Though we had grown apart a little, Vani was still someone close to my heart. After all, she was the first friend I had made in college. She kept to herself (which others thought as weird), but I liked her. She had a heart of gold and held no malice towards anyone. Sometimes, I felt that she was too noble, too good to be true. I have already spoken of her talents. I had seen her paintings and was left awe-struck. And her doodles… How relaxing was it to watch her doddle in her notebook! Ah, how I enjoyed teasing her and making fun of those drawings!

'I have something to ask of you today, and please don't say no,' she said.

'What is it?' I asked, surprised by the unusual request.

'Promise me you won't say no,' she said.

There was something different about Vani today. This wasn't the way she usually spoke. She wasn't the one to make requests. And what did she want from me? Maybe it was true. She was seeing Hardy. And he had asked her to stay away from me. And today, she wanted to end our friendship. The thought sank me!

'Why are you saying this?' I asked her.

She sensed my discomfort and laughed, 'Don't worry. I am not dying.'

Her laugh calmed me. 'Okay. Whatever you want.' I said hesitantly.

~

When I met her, she hugged me and said, 'I want you to come with me today.'

'Where?' I asked.

'To my exhibition in the Jehangir Gallery.'

'Wow! Congratulations.' I said, happily, 'And you are telling me now?'

She smiled. 'I wanted to tell you about it earlier, but you are busy elsewhere.'

I understood what she meant.

'But I am not dressed properly,' I protested, 'Look at you, all dressed up. You should have told me in the morning.'

'Come as you are,' she said.

I stopped a taxi and put her luggage in the trunk. 'Let's go,' I said as we got into the taxi.

'What's with so many bags?' I asked after we sat inside the taxi. 'So heavy.'

'All my stuff…. For the exhibition.'

'I am very happy for you, Vani,' I said.

'Thank you.'

As we drove towards the Town, I suddenly remembered the terrible nightmare. It had left me shuddering! I turned around and looked at her. She had taken out her book and was scribbling. I watched her intently. 'What's this? Serpent or a large intestine.' I teased her. 'Shut up! What do you know?' She yelled back. I smiled. I wanted to ask her about Hardy, but I feared it might not be a good idea right now. So, I tried to stick to a safer topic. I asked her about her parents. 'Your Dad would be proud,' I said. 'Well, he is.' She replied, without looking at me.

I don't think I have told you about Vani's dad yet. I had the privilege of meeting him once. Let me remember the time… Ah, it was in the early days of our college. Vani had invited me to dinner. We used to go out for dinner sometimes. So, it was nothing unusual. However, when I reached the restaurant, I was in for a shock. She was accompanied by her dad, and she hadn't mentioned anything about him before. From her dad's reaction, it seemed he was surprised to see me as well. It was supposed to be a family dinner, and I had no business being there. Nevertheless, there I was, and I could see the disdain in his eyes.

Her dad had a daunting personality, and he interrogated me. He asked me about my family, my hobbies, and even my marks from Class 1 to Class 12, subject wise. I confidently told him my Class 12 marks, because those I remembered accurately. However, for everything else I had to conjure up answers on the spot. So, for class 9, I said 98 in math and 96 in science. If he had asked me to repeat the numbers, I'm sure I would have bungled up and said 78 in math and 87 in science.

He asked me where I saw myself after college. I replied, 'Uncle, in college'. He raised his brows, demanding an explanation. I explained that I wanted to go for an MBA from a top college. 'Okay,' he replied stiffly. Then he asked me if I liked art. I said I didn't know much about it until I met Vani. 'I like her drawing though', I said. 'She is very talented.' Vani blushed as I said this, and I think her father took note of it.

'How many girlfriends do you have?' he suddenly asked, changing the gears of the conversation. I almost choked on my Paneer Tikka. He didn't ask me if I had a girlfriend; he asked me straightaway how many. I couldn't understand whether I should take this as a compliment or get offended. Was I that charming? Or was I a Casanova? The Question was tricky, and my answer had to be deft. I paraphrased my dad's advice (something I had been hearing since class 8!) and said, 'No Uncle, I don't have a girlfriend. This is the time to focus on studies and build my career first.' I sounded sincere and authentic, and even he was impressed. I could tell because he finally smiled at me and offered me an extra piece of Paneer Tikka.

Done with me, he turned towards his daughter.

'That's what I have been telling Vani as well. Stay focused,' he said.

Vani ignored him and continued eating her roti and dal makhani.

'I think she is very focused,' I said.

'Is she?' Her dad said sarcastically, 'Tell me Vishesh, if she had been focused, wouldn't she be in an Arts College right now?'

'Yes, sir!' I replied without thinking much. 'That would be better for her.'

Okay guys! Here's what I learned that day: when you're in the middle of a family drama, it's best to keep your mouth shut. When her father commented, she ignored him. But when I commented, all hell broke loose. She got angry and pushed her plate away!

'I know what I am doing,' she said angrily, got up, and left.

I looked on with shock at the unfolding events. A raw nerve had been touched. The free food was turning out to be costly!

'See, that's the problem,' her father said to me, 'She doesn't listen. She can go places if she just listens to me. I am worried about her. She is throwing her talent away. What's she doing in a Commerce college? She has open invitations from the top Arts colleges, but she refuses. I wish I could knock some sense into her.'

I was in a dilemma. Should I go and sympathize with Vani, or should I just sit tight and sympathize with her dad instead? Well, I could feel that this wasn't the first time they were fighting, because his father just threw his arms in the air and then went back to eating his food. He made no effort to go after his daughter. I really started feeling bad for Vani and asked her dad's permission to go and check upon her. As I rose from my seat, he caught hold of my hand and said, 'I am tired now. Could you, please, talk to her on my behalf? I only want the best for her.'

'Sure Uncle,' I said and went out.

Vani was standing outside, under a lamp post, and charged at me as soon as she saw me.

'You shouldn't have...' She started, 'I am not angry with my dad. He has always been like that. But you... I am very, very angry with you. You are my friend and I told you everything... Still, you took his side.'

'I am sorry,' I said, 'I shouldn't have.'

'What gives you the right to say what's good or bad for me?' She retorted angrily, 'Nobody, including you, gets to decide what's good or bad for me.. Understand?'

'I am really sorry,' I said meekly, 'I didn't mean to offend you.'

She did not acknowledge my apology and walked away from me. That night, I couldn't sleep well. I kept wondering about Vani and her relationship with her dad. I cursed myself for having taken her dad's side. Another lesson that I learnt that day - at all costs, avoid meeting Uncles. Uncles of any kind or creed! They are injurious to your health and wellbeing!

You could see that she was the "Star". She was given such a grand welcome at the gallery, and the people spoke highly of her work. There were people from the press too, clicking her pictures every now and then. As for myself, I felt completely out of the place and searched for a quiet spot to hide. But she wouldn't let me go. Whenever I tried to wriggle out, she came looking for me. So, there I was, standing with her - in my loose T shirt and dirty jeans - getting clicked by the cameras.

Her art was truly amazing! I could see it in the eyes of the connoisseurs. Their eyes lit up when they saw her paintings and listened to her. Every piece of painting had a beautiful backstory to it, and she narrated the stories so wonderfully, at times pushing her curls back, or touching her nose. I felt privileged to be standing beside her in that great place. And I wondered whether I would ever be as great as she was! She was way above me, above all of us in college. Her dad's words echoed in my ears: "She can go places. She has the talent." Now, I could see what he really meant and wished for his daughter! And she wasn't failing him.

Towards the end of the day when everyone was gone, she gave me a separate audience. She walked me through all her paintings and asked me which one I liked the most.

'They are like children. I cannot pick a favorite,' I said.

She smiled.

'I am glad you came today. Thank you.'

'Thank you!' I said, 'You are a Star!'

'I am just Vani.' She replied.

'Should we go now? I will call the taxi,' I asked her.

'Let's sit on the stairs outside for a while,' she said.

'Sure,' I replied.

As we descended the majestic stairs, she stopped in the middle and sat down. I put aside her luggage and sat down beside her.

'Vani, you know,' I said, 'I don't think anyone from our college would ever achieve what you have. Our HOD is surely going to keep one function in your honor soon.'

She looked straight into my eyes and said, 'I am not going to be there for that honor, Vasillor.'

'What do you mean?' I asked, surprised.

She paused for a moment and said, 'I am transferring to an arts college.'

My heart sank.

'When?' I asked.

'Today was my last day...' She said in a faltering voice.

'You....' I choked and looked at her face.

For the first time I saw tears in her eyes.

'You wanted me to transfer. Are you happy now?' she asked.

'You made your father proud,' I replied after a moment and hugged her. 'I will miss you.'

'Not like me,' she replied. 'Not like me.'

For a few minutes, we sat in silence, looking at the traffic rushing by. How fast were the cars and the buses going? Why was everyone in a hurry to go somewhere? How fast does everything change? How fast does time fly?

I looked at Vani. She was wiping her tears, quietly. I shouldn't have asked her to transfer. Yes, she would go places, but I will miss her.

'Hey! Don't forget me when you become big and famous.' I commented after a while.

'I never will,' she said, 'I have a favor to ask.'

'Anything.'

'You know, you have been my only friend. Ever… Can we continue to be friends?'

'We will always be friends, Vani,' I said.

'Promise me, you will talk to me whenever I call.'

'I promise.'

While leaving, she handed me a box and said, 'It's a gift for you. Don't open it until I say so.'

'I won't,' I replied somberly.

Chapter 22

How about a small detour before we proceed? I told you about one Uncle- Vani's dad. Let me tell you about another now. And you will understand why I advise everyone to keep the distance from "Uncles".

It starts with the day when Ada had to move out of the hostel into private accommodation. Ada and a couple of her friends had found a decent one-bedroom flat. As a dutiful boyfriend, I had insisted on helping her with shifting. But on that morning, as I was readying myself, my dad called. This was quite unusual because my parents never called me in the morning, and I had already spoken with them the previous night.

'Hello dad,' I said.

'Hello beta. You are up early?'

'Yes, dad. I have a morning class,' I lied.

'Good. Good. Atleast you have started waking up early. How is college going?'

'Nothing changed since the last evening.' I joked.

Dad had asked me the same question the previous night. I could hear Mom laughing at the other end. Dad had put the phone on the speaker.

'Hello mom.'

'Hello beta,' she said.

'Okay. Dad, I am getting late for college. I will call in the evening.' I said.

'Yes. Yes.' Dad said hesitantly, 'Can you do something for me?'

'What's it, dad?'

'You remember Bhushan Uncle.'

'Yes.' I said, 'How is he?'

'He is in Mumbai for his daughter's admission. You remember Pammi.'

'Yes. Puma.' I said. When we were kids, she called me Vish Bhaiya and I called her Puma.

'Can you go and help him with the admission process?' Dad asked.

'Sure. No worries.' I replied.

'Great! I have given him your number. He will call you. Make sure you help him out in the best way. He is your guest.' My dad said in a relaxed tone.

'When is the admission?' I asked.

'Today, I think.' Dad replied.

'Today?' I asked startled.

'Yes. Today.'

'I have an important class today, Dad.' I said, 'I can't miss it.'

'Take a day off for me, please,' My dad said awkwardly, 'When he asked for help, I couldn't say no to him.'

'Okay, Dad,' I said, reluctantly, 'I will wait for his call.'

'Thank you, Beta,' Dad said, 'Keep me posted.'

I was ashamed. What should I tell Ada now? I had promised her I would be there, this one time when she needed me. Why Bhushan Uncle, why? What awkward position you had put me in? All these uncles, every time they say they have seen the world, that they know better, that we are just kids. But when it comes to facing real-world challenges like college admissions or changing the settings on their phones and TV sets, they come to us for help! What hypocrisy! *What would Ada think?* My Nemesis No1 said. *You wanted to be a Hero, but you failed. I will give you a solution. Switch off your phone!*

My Phone rang. It was Bhushan Uncle. Without much of a talk, he asked me to come to CST. 'How much time will you take?' he asked. 'An hour,' I replied. 'Okay. We will wait here.' He said gruffly. When I reached the designated place in CST, I saw Bhushan Uncle and Pammi eating Vadapav. Pammi jumped on seeing me and cried 'Vish Bhaiya'. 'Puma.' I replied. I was delighted to see her. We had so much fun as kids. But I hadn't met her for some time now, and I was really surprised to see her grown up! After exchanging pleasantries, Bhushan Uncle offered me a Vadapav which I took happily. I hadn't eaten anything.

'Is this station always so crowded?' Bhushan uncle asked me.

'Yes Uncle.' I replied.

He seemed to be disgruntled with the crowd.

'I had told Pammi to do her graduation in Dehradun. So many good colleges there. But she insisted on coming here.'

I looked at Puma. She was watching the crowd with awe. I could understand why she wanted to leave Dehradun. She wanted to live her life for a while. And what better place than Mumbai for that!

'Can you tell me the address of the college?' I asked.

Bhushan Uncle took out a small, torn diary from his shirt pocket, and turned some pages over. Finally, stopping at one of the pages, he said, 'DES College of Engineering, Dadar.'

'East or West?' I asked.

He looked at me with surprise. I could understand. This wasn't a question for someone coming to Mumbai for the first time. He wouldn't know how significant East or West in Mumbai was!

'We will have to take a cab,' I said.

Man! I hadn't noticed it until now. You should have seen the luggage they were carrying- five trolleys, a rolled- up mattress, even buckets! Yes, sound the bugle. Let Mumbai city know that you didn't expect to find mattresses and buckets here, so you brought them all the way from Dehradun. I had a hard time finding a taxi, and I couldn't blame the taxi drivers. I was sure the luggage made them switch to the fifth gear and swoosh away!

'What kind of city is this? Not a single taxi stops.' Bhushan Uncle moaned.

With great difficulty, I finally convinced one driver. Secretly, I offered him an extra hundred bucks for the luggage. I was sure if Bhushan Uncle knew of the extra charges, he would ask the driver to leave, and I would have to keep searching for the taxis.

'So, how long have you been in Mumbai now? Two years.' Bhushan Uncle asked once we were seated in the cab.

'Yes Uncle.' I replied.

'How far is Dadar from here? 10 kms.' He asked.

'Forty minutes with traffic. Twenty minutes without traffic.' The driver replied.

'Why is Mumbai so crowded? Too many people coming from outside.' Bhushan Uncle commented. All three of us – the driver, who was from UP, Puma and I - looked at each other in the rearview mirror at the same time. We are all from outside!

While Bhushan Uncle kept talking and commenting about Mumbai, its tall buildings and slums, its high-end showrooms and roadside stores, I observed that he had a very peculiar way of talking. He spoke in Questions and Answers. After a while, it felt so amusing that I played along.

'So, Uncle, how many days will you be staying here? A week.' I asked.

'How can I stay for a week? I have so much work at home. I will leave in 3 days.' He replied.

'What all do you want to see in these 3 days, uncle? Juhu Beach, Gateway.'

'Why should I go to Juhu Beach and Gateway? I don't have time. Pammi gets admission and I leave.'

'Okay.' I said and kept quiet.

'Where is Amitabh's bungalow? Juhu.' He asked our driver, after a while.

'Yes.' The driver replied, 'Do you want to go there?'

'Why should I go there? We will go to college.' Uncle replied.

'Yes, why should you go there?' the driver said, 'Nothing much to see. You just stand on the road, waiting for them to come out. All these film stars are arrogant.'

'Did I ask your opinion? What do you know about Bachchan Ji?' Uncle replied, miffed, 'I will go to see his house.'

I was amazed! Our driver had also entered the field now and was playing the game. He even told me to keep the extra hundred bucks with me. 'This is a fun ride. You don't get such people every day.' He told me in a low voice. I looked at Puma in the rearview mirror. She absolutely knew what was happening. I could bet that she also wanted to be in, play the game. But just out of respect for her old man, she didn't!

Ada, my dear Ada- What would she be doing right now? I had spoken to her before leaving for CST. Do you know the first thing she told me, 'You don't need to come so early. I am still packing my stuff.' It really broke my heart (and maybe her's too) when I said I wouldn't be coming. 'Oh!' she remarked without even asking me why? I explained my position and the urgency of the matter. 'Don't worry about me. I will manage,' she said. I must have said sorry a thousand times, and she finally laughed and said, 'Don't overdo it. I understand. You carry on.'

You don't get friends like Aheesh nowadays. What a gem of a person, my friend Aheesh. My second call went to him, and I explained the situation to him. 'Even if you would not have asked, I would still have been there to help Ada,' he said.

It took us the entire day to complete the admission formalities. The admin office and Bhushan Uncle made me a sprinter that day. Everything was urgent, and every document needed a thousand copies! So, here I was, running from the office to the xerox shop and back. I would have walked atleast 100 kms that day! My legs became sore, and I couldn't even stand properly. As for Bhushan Uncle, he made himself at home in a chair and did nothing. Even to get a document signed, I had to bring it to him and then go back to the admin.

With the admission process done, we went to check Pammi's hostel, and yes, I carried the mattress and the buckets to the hostel room. Bhushan Uncle was disappointed with the room and made some sniping comments before finally addressing Pammi, 'I told you Dehradun is better'. After that, I had to go shopping with them. They had to buy towels, curtains, and laundry items. By the time it was 8 pm, I was dead tired. I wanted to leave now, but Uncle insisted that we have dinner together. To my shock, after dinner, he proclaimed that they would be coming with me to spend the night at my place. I excused myself and called up my mom.

'Hello? Mom?'

'Yes, beta. How are you. All done.'

'Yes, Mom.' I replied, 'But there is a problem now. Bhushan Uncle wants to stay at my place. You know, we have a small flat. Where will my roommates go?

'What? He should have made his own arrangements.' My mom said, concerned at my situation.

'What do I do now, Mom? I am stuck.'

'Let me talk to your father.'

I overheard her talk with my dad. The discussion heated up, and for ten minutes, I anxiously waited for the outcome. You know how college boys live. Like animals, to say the least. My place was dirty, filled with all kinds of filth and empty beer bottles, and we lived in harmony with ants, spiders, cockroaches and other life forms. And I was sure, my roommates would kill me for bringing in any guests. This was against our house- policy! Finally, Dad came on the phone and said sternly, 'Do as he says. He is your guest. And make sure that you attend to him well.'

Dad's words ended the discussion.

I immediately called my roommates and updated them about the situation. Though I least expected their cooperation, I still begged them to ensure that the flat was cleaned, empty beer bottles thrown away and new bed sheets used. However, they laughed villainously at my situation and said it wasn't their problem. They wouldn't lift a damn thing except their own asses out of the flat as they didn't want to be stuck with my relatives for the night. It was my sin, and only I had to pay for it. I could only curse their insolence and say that Karma would soon bite them someday!

After fifteen minutes, we were in a cab. Bhushan Uncle had suddenly become animated and lively. He even began lavishing praise on how Mumbai was still alive despite it being so late. He talked with the driver in his question-answer style, but this driver got irritated. The more questions he asked, the faster our driver accelerated. He could do that. At least he had something under his foot to vent out his frustration. I had nothing. Where could I take out my frustration and irritation? My head was already spinning. I wished I had someone to massage my head. I wished I were with Ada. She would have gently caressed my head. Oh, what all I had planned for the day and how it ended!

To manage their expectations, I told Bhusan Uncle that our place was a bachelor's pad and might not meet their expectations. He just smirked and said nothing. Well, it sure was going to be embarrassing. Ironically, I was also relieved. Seeing the pathetic condition of the flat, I was sure they would refuse to stay there and opt for a hotel instead. And I would gladly help arrange it.

To my surprise, our flat looked like a five-star hotel room! My good-for-nothing roommates had magically turned our garbage can into a neat clean room. There was not a speck of dust anywhere, the kitchen sink was cleared, fresh curtains and sheets were used, bottles and magazines were gone and there was not a sign of any pest life. I could smell the deodorant in the air. I was sure they had emptied my deodorant, but I wouldn't complain. The place was lit. Puma complimented. Bhushan Uncle, though visibly impressed, remained silent.

It was well past 11 pm, and I set up their beds. I assumed they must be tired and would like to sleep immediately. Besides, I wanted my space. I hadn't spoken with Ada the entire day and I yearned for a soothing, loving conversation with her. However, Bhushan Uncle seemed to have other plans. He sat down in the living room and started the conversation.

'Do you know how long I have known your father?' he said.

The same old story! What satisfaction do they get by repeating their stories? I don't know. I wanted to tell him that I had heard it many times, both from him and my father. But I didn't want to come across as rude, so I kept quiet as he continued with his monologue. We were nearing midnight and he was still in no mood to stop! I realized I won't be able to talk with Ada, so I messaged her discreetly: I miss you.

After five minutes, my phone rang, interrupting Bhushan Uncle's monologue. He gave me a firm look. '*Who is calling you at this hour?*' - His eyes asked me. I ignored his gaze. He turned to his daughter and said, 'It's late. Let's go to sleep.' Once they were gone, I picked up her call.

'What took you so long? Where are you?' Ada asked.

'Thank you for saving me,' I said in low voice, 'I am with Bhushan uncle.'

'Still?' She asked surprised.

'Yes. They came to my place.'

'What? They are staying over. So, you are not meeting me tomorrow as well.' She sounded anguished.

'If they leave early, I might come to college.'

'I want to see you tomorrow!' She demanded, 'What kind of boyfriend are you?'

I smiled, as she said this.

'Did Aheesh help you today?'

'Yes. I think he will make a better boyfriend.'

'Go for it! You have my blessing.' I said and laughed.

Bhushan Uncle coughed from inside. It was a signal for me to keep it down.

'Good night sweetheart.' I whispered.

'Good night, baby,' she said.

Next morning, I was in for another shock! Bhushan Uncle didn't leave. Instead, he asked me to show him my college. He also insisted upon meeting my teachers and the HOD. That made me furious. *Why in the hell?* I wanted to call my dad and complain. All this was too much now! I had been a good host, spent a full day with them, helped them in all possible ways… but now, he was just imposing. However, I knew even if I complained, dad wouldn't understand. He might as well be happy that someone was meeting with my teachers and checking upon me.

As much as I loathed it, I had no choice but to take them to the college. I showed them the campus, the different departments, the grounds. I made him meet the teachers- the ones who liked me- and kept him away from those who didn't. Making him meet the HOD was out of the question. I had already arranged it with the office-boy. 'Sir is very busy. No meetings without appointments,' he said firmly.

'I hope you liked my college, Uncle?' I asked.

'Who wouldn't? Nice college. Nice college,' He replied.

'If I have your permission, can I take your leave now. I have an important lecture to attend.'

'Why not? Yes, of course.'

'Let me get an auto for you. He will drop you at my place,' I said. *Finally,* I thought, I *will be able to spend some time with Ada.*

As they were about to leave the college premises, Ada suddenly appeared out of nowhere and came running towards me. As she hugged me tightly, I stood frozen. Puma looked at me in awe, while Bhushan Uncle appeared scandalized with this unexpected event. Things were out of my hands now, and no explanation would suffice.

What happened afterwards, you ask? Well as soon as they left, I got a call from Dad. No 'Hello' or 'How are you, beta' this time. He shot straight – 'Who was that girl?'

Now you understand why I hate Uncles! What all had I done for him, and this is how he rewarded me? He didn't tell me anything and went behind my back to complain to my dad. He even got my mom worried. 'Your son has lost his way in Mumbai,' he told her.

'Mom, I have already told you about her. She is just a friend.'

'Do you hug all your friends…… Pammi was also there. Bhushan Ji was so embarrassed.'

'Mom, she is just a friend.' I said, 'If you don't trust me ask her. I will give you her number.'

'Okay.' Mom said, 'Give me her number.'

I froze! I hadn't expected it to come from my mom. A word of caution: don't ever push your luck with moms. I had done it, and now I was getting choked. I couldn't give mom Ada's number. She would call her, and it would be over.

'No' Dad interrupted, 'We don't want her number. We trust you.'

~

Hmm… TRUST. A five-letter word. Easy to spell. Easy to build. Easy to break. TRUST, an emotion I have difficulty dealing with now. You will get to know why. Be patient, we are getting there.

Chapter 23

One of the curiosities that every college boy has is to see a girl's room. You would have heard the stories of the boys dressing up as girls or wearing veils just to get a glimpse inside. Well, seeing a girl's room was on my college checklist too. I had never been inside one before. The hostel was out of bounds for us, and I wasn't adventurous enough to snuggle into a girl's outfit and sneak in. Plus, Ada hadn't ever offered to smuggle me either.

However, now that Ada had her own place, I finally had a chance. And one day, I decided to show up at her place. As I was going unannounced, I just couldn't go empty-handed. So, after a lot of thinking, I decided to buy a wall-clock, a box of chocolates and a bouquet. Wall-clock for the house, chocolates for everyone (My way to placate her roommates, if they got angry with me!) and bouquet for my sweetheart, Ada.

I had another reason to be in her room. I wanted to see her Teddy Bears. She had four of them, and they always featured in our conversations. She spoke of them as if they were her lovers. She had named them Bruno, Pronto, Shego and Sheru. Yes, I still remember their names! I hated it when she spoke about them with me. They received the good-night kisses and the good-morning hugs that should have been mine. How much I wanted to punch them in their faces!

I was all set to meet and impress. I wore my best black shirt and liberally sprayed the deodorant over my body. I took care to style my hair the way Ada liked it (She didn't like gelled hair) and used the aftershave that she had gifted me. I was confident that I looked nice and smelled nice.

All my deodorant vanished as soon as I finished the climb to the 10th floor (my bad luck, the lift was not working). 80% of my macho confidence vanished, just like that! So much for the Deo ads. They should really be sued for false advertising. The sweat trickled down my body in a free flow, dampening my clothes and causing my hair to become a disheveled mess, half wet, half dry. The only thing that helped me keep an iota of my confidence still intact was my black shirt. At least, my sweat stains wouldn't show. Anyway, I gave myself a moment and took a deep breath, wiped away my sweat with my handkerchief and styled my hair meticulously with my fingers. After five minutes, I rang her doorbell.

'Who's it?' I heard the voice from inside. Ada's voice. Music to my ears!

There was no peep hole in the door for her to see who was outside. So, I thought why not mess around for a while. I didn't answer and the door remained closed. After a few seconds, I pressed the doorbell again, this time ringing it twice.

'Who's it? She asked again.

Again, I didn't answer, and the door didn't open. I pressed the doorbell again, three times.

'I swear it's those kids. Let me show them this time.' She yelled from inside.

The door opened swiftly, and she shrieked in surprise on seeing me.

'What are you doing here?' She asked and hugged me tightly.

'I came to see you.' I said, as I soaked in the warmth of her hug.

'You can't come like that. Unannounced. This is a girls' flat. No entry for boys here.' She said and pushed me away softly.

'Should I go back, then?' I asked.

'No,' she said and slammed the door on me.

How cute she looked! This was the first time I was seeing her in house dress – a loose white T-shirt and pink shorts with small teddy bears printed all over. Her untied hair fell over her shoulders, and her face glowed like an evening moon.

I waited at the door for a good ten minutes. Something was transpiring inside the flat which I could just imagine. Maybe there was a conversation with her roommates, negotiating whether to allow me in, for the first and the last time. Perhaps there was a fight accompanied by a threat that she would move out. Maybe I would have to start looking for a new place where two of us could live together. Or maybe....

The door opened and a different Ada welcomed me in! She had gone through a complete make-over. Her hair was tied in a neat bun, and the eyeliner and the makeup had returned. Her face shone resplendently like the radiant sun. And the cute T-shirt and the shorts had made way for a yellow sunflower-patterned dress.

'Come on in,' she said, smiling.

I entered the living room, to the presence of her roomies. I uttered a nervous *Hi* to each one of them. And they reciprocated cheerfully. 'Here, this is for you.' I said and handed over the wall-clock and box of chocolates to them. Ada smiled as I did this.

'Thank you!' they said in unison.

'Wow! You have set up the place beautifully.' I said, as I looked around the room. The decor was impressive.

'Thank you for noticing,' one of the girls said merrily. 'We are not done yet. We must get curtains and matching wall papers. We are thinking of putting the wall papers...'

'Priya,' another girl interrupted her. 'We have to go.'

'Oh yes!' Priya replied, 'See you later. Bye.'

All three girls made their way out of the room while Ada bid them goodbye. I could see them giggling as they left.

'Sorry. Priya is a bit talkative,' Ada said after closing the door.

'Oh! is she? I didn't notice.' I replied.

Ada laughed.

'And she is the one who has set up this place.'

'Well, she has done a good job.' I replied.

Priya had really done a great job. She had fought with the owner to get the flat repainted from the hospital white to sky blue. Furthermore, she had adorned it with hand-painted cards, amazing picture props, and beautiful artifacts. The window boasted melodious wind chimes that produced soulful sounds at the slightest touch of the air. The entire setup exuded the ambiance of a faraway beach. They even had a sofa adorned with beautiful sea-green cushions! Can you imagine a sofa in a second-year college students' place? I couldn't help but contrast their way of living with ours. What a stark contrast to the filth I lived in?

By the way, that Priya girl is none other than Priya Ranjan, the famous decorator who now designs the rooms for the bigwigs. You can catch her interviews on various lifestyle channels. And you thought I was fibbing when I told you I know some famous people! For some strange reason, she doesn't mention graduating from our college. Instead, she insists that she studied in Milan. Strange girl!

'They didn't have to leave,' I told Ada.

'I asked them to stay, but they thought you would feel awkward.'

'I would have enjoyed their company. More the merrier' I quipped.

'Is that so? I can call them back right now.' Ada said.

'Poor girls! I shouldn't have barged in like this.' I said apologetically.

'You know, you are the first guy we have hosted here.' Ada said.

'Wow! They don't have BFs.' I asked.

'They have. But they haven't been allowed in yet.'

'Oh! Funny business.' I said laughing.

'What's funny?' Ada asked.

'So, if one guy comes in, three girls have to leave.'

'Shit! Yes, it seems so.' Ada said in low voice.

'So, don't let boys in here.'

'Ha! So, I let my boyfriend in but won't let their boyfriends in. How is that fair?' Ada exclaimed.

'At least, your boyfriend didn't come empty-handed.' I replied.

'What's in that packet?' Ada asked, pointing to the packet that was still in my left hand.

'This? That one is for my sweetheart.' I said and took out the bouquet from the polybag.

'Woah! You and Bouquets? I never expected one from you.' She said, mockingly.

'Expect the unexpected,' I replied.

'Thank you, they are so beautiful.' She said, as she collected the bouquet. 'And this is for my sweetheart,' she gave me a peck on my right cheek.

'Forgot to ask. Do you want tea?'

'Tea? Does Anna deliver here?'

'I can prepare. We got everything in the kitchen,' she said.

'Ah! How can I refuse then.'

'Okay! Let me give this bouquet to Pronto first.'

'Pronto!' I said, 'I want to punch him. Where are you hiding him?'

'In my bedroom.' She said, laughing.

'What's he doing in your bedroom? I am going to kill him.'

She went inside and returned carrying all the four bears in her arms. Well, I am too soft. I couldn't bring myself to punch them. They were just too cute!

Oh, you should have seen their kitchen! It had everything one would need: a gas stove, bowls and dishes, and an army of small, yellow-colored tea sets. I received the royal treatment – Tea in a yellow cup set, dry fruits (almonds and cashews!) and Good Day biscuits. Unfortunately, there wasn't a table we could place these things on (Priya hadn't finalized the table yet!). So, we spread an old newspaper on the floor and placed the items on it. We pushed the sofa aside and sat on the floor.

'Today is going to be a historic day!' I exclaimed.

'What?'

'Today, you made tea for me.'

'Ha! Today you came to my place for the first time' she said. 'UNANNOUNCED!'

'Ouch!' I said.

She smiled.

'How is your Bhusan uncle?'

'He left.' I said, 'You scandalized him.'

'What did I do?' she asked.

'You know what you did. His jaw dropped when he saw us hugging.'

'Shit! What would he be thinking of me now?'

'Forget him. Half of Dehradun is talking about you right now,' I said.

'What do mean?' she asked, puzzled.

'Bhushan Uncle called everyone he knows in Dehradun and told them that Mr. Vasu's son has lost his way.'

'Shit! What did your parents say?'

'They want to talk to you. I have given them your number.'

'No way!' She said, terrified, 'I am not going to talk to them'.

'Expect the call today.' I said jokingly.

I watched her petrified face as she fell silent. While I enjoyed tea and cookies, she seemed completely disconcerted. I could tell that in her mind, she was already talking with my mother, engaged in a tough conversation The unease on her face revealed everything. I savored this sight! What's that sassy difficult German word for this type of feeling? Ah yes, the one that doesn't roll off Indian tongues easily. Schadenfreude.

'I don't know how to face your parents.' She said finally, hiding her face in her hands.

'Relax, Ada.' I said, pulling her closer into a hug. 'I was just teasing you.'

'What?' She said, and pushed herself away from me, 'You lied! Your parents don't know.'

'They know. And I am sure half of Dehradun knows as well. I didn't lie about that. But I lied about the calling part. They won't call you. I didn't give them your number.'

'About us... What did you tell them?'

'I said we are friends.'

'That's it? They didn't ask anything else?'

'No. That was pretty much it,' I replied.

'Uff!' She said and threw herself on the floor.

'Do you know how tense I became?' She said in a broken voice.

I propped myself beside her and watched her mellow face.

'I am sorry,' I said. 'I pranked you.'

'Listen, can you hear how fast my heart is beating?' She said and closed her eyes.

I gently rested my head on her chest and listened to her heart beats. I could hear my name resounding within them.

'One day, my love, they will want to talk to you.' I said softly.

'I know,' She replied meekly, 'But today, I am not ready for that.'

Slowly, I inclined my head towards her face and gently kissed her closed eyes. A smile spread across her lips. As my stubbly cheeks rubbed against her soft cheeks, I worried I might scratch her. I attempted to move away, but she pulled me back towards her and placed her lips upon mine... And slowly, softly, kiss by kiss, we undressed each other and let our nude bodies dance and wriggle like snakes as we made passionate love.

Chapter 24

'I miss Vani.' Aheesh said to me one day as we were having lunch in the canteen. 'Do you remember our first-year days? She used to sit in this chair.' I gazed at the empty chair in front of me.

'I miss her too. We had good times,' I replied.

'Let's meet with her sometime,' Aheesh said, 'Have you talked to her recently?'

'No,' I replied.

I lied to Aheesh. I spoke with Vani every now and then. I had even met her a few times in her new college. That day, on the stairs of the Jehangir Gallery, she made me promise her two things: That no matter what, we would always remain friends, and that whenever she called, I would talk to her. 'You are my only friend.' She had said.

'I still wonder why she left?' Aheesh asked me.

'I don't know.' I replied.

'Why are you going like this, Vani?' I asked her that day.

'Because I don't want to lose you.' She replied.

'What do you mean?' I asked puzzled.

She gazed into my eyes and said, 'You know what I mean. I'm aware of the relationship between Ada and you. And I don't think she likes me around you.'

'She said that?' I asked startled.

'Not so much in words but I can infer. If I want to maintain our friendship, I must stay away.'

'I think there is some misunderstanding. I will talk to her,' I said.

'I already spoke with her.'

'About what?' I asked, surprised.

She paused for a moment and then said, 'You.'

'Me? What about me?'

'I asked her if there was anything between you two.'

'Why did you ask her that?'

'You weren't forthcoming.' She replied, 'I wanted clarity.'

'Hmm…And you got your clarity?'

'Yes.'

'What did she say?' I asked.

'She told me it was none of my business.'

'I am sorry she spoke to you that way,' I said. I believed Ada had spoken rudely.

'It's okay. I did feel bad for a moment. But she was right. It wasn't my business. I would have given the same answer, had I been in her place. Her reply gave me the clarity I sought.'

Now I could connect the dots. That's why Ada often teased me with Vani's name. In her own way, she too was seeking clarity.

'But you don't have to leave because of her,' I said.

'I am not leaving because of her,' Vani replied pensively, 'I am leaving for my own sake.'

'Your own sake?' I asked.

'Yes, you are my only friend. And I don't want to lose you.' She replied.

'Please stay. We will always be friends.' I pleaded.

'You are so naïve!' She said, 'What if Ada asks you not to talk to me? What would you do?'

'She wouldn't say such a thing!' I retorted.

'What if she did?'

I fell silent. I didn't know the answer.

She smiled and gently touched my face with her hands. 'Now you understand why I am doing this. I'm being selfish!'

'Why did Vani leave?' Aheesh asked me again.

'I don't know.' I repeated myself.

'How could you not know?'Aheesh yelled. 'She left because of you.'

'What the hell? I didn't tell her to go?' I replied angrily.

'You messed up the things.'

'What do you mean. What things?'

'What things?' He mimicked me, 'You think I am a fool.'

I was infuriated! He had no right to interrogate me.

'Don't meddle in my affairs, Aheesh!' I yelled at him. 'Handle yours properly.'

He looked at me in shock.

'What? You think I don't know about your things? You are being stupid, chasing that girl from the final year! Sooner or later, you will end up getting seriously hurt.'

He was taken aback by my outburst. 'Stop it.' He said meekly.

'Oh, come on! You think you deserve her? She doesn't even look at you. And you're lecturing me about my relationships?' I responded.

Aheesh stormed out of the canteen without uttering a word.

~

Sometimes, I felt I should tell Ada that Vani and I still talked over the phone and met occasionally. I thought she should know, but I hesitated because I was uncertain about her reaction. What if she really told me to break my friendship with Vani and stop talking to her? I had made a promise to Vani that we would always be friends, no matter what. So, I decided to stay silent and never mentioned anything to Ada. She asked me about Vani a couple of times, but I always managed to withhold the information. I would have confided in Aheesh, but that idiot stopped talking to me after our argument in the canteen.

Ada realized that Aheesh and I weren't talking and asked me about it. I told her that he got upset when I chided him about his stupid endeavor to woe that girl.

'Wow! What exactly did you tell him?' She asked me.

'The truth. That he was stupid, and that she was out of his league.'

'You shouldn't have told him that.' She said disparagingly.

'What wrong did I say? He has no chance with her.' I said, surprised by her response.

'You don't know that.'

'You know he will get hurt. She will stomp on his feelings.'

'Maybe.' Ada replied, 'but at least he will get to share his feelings.'

'It doesn't make sense!' I said, 'you want him to share his feelings, knowing well that he would be rebuffed?'

'Yes. It's better to be rejected than not to approach at all.' She said, somewhat philosophically.

'Huh!' I grumped, 'What about her boyfriend? He is going to beat the hell out of Aheesh.'

'That's why I said stay with him. What are you for?'

'Oh! So, I am there to take the blows for him.'

'Yes. That's what friends do.'

She waved at Aheesh, who was seated at the other end of the canteen and beckoned him to come over.

'What's wrong with you two?' She said to us, 'you are behaving like children. Who started it?'

'He did.' Aheesh and I both said simultaneously, pointing our fingers at each other.

'Come on! Patch up.' she spoke loudly, 'or else I am going to tell everyone your secret.'

'What secret?' Aheesh asked puzzled.

'Where you guys met for the first time? And how you…....'

'You told her?' Aheesh interrupted Ada, looked at me and shrieked.

'I might have.' I replied and laughed.

The promise of friendship also encompasses the promise of forgiveness. Despite your shortcomings, true friends forgive you. And that's exactly what Aheesh did. He forgave me and hugged me tightly, and shared laughter with me.

'So, you really like her.' I asked.

'Yes, I do.'

'What's her name?'

'Shreya.'

'Couldn't you find any from our batch? You know she is a senior and has a boyfriend.'

'I know.'

'You know, her boyfriend is going to come after you.'

'Hmm… yes. Worst case I get punched.'

I placed my arm around his shoulder and said, 'As if I am going to let him punch you?'

He looked at me and smiled.

'Yes, you are a pro and have a reputation when it comes to punches.' He said, laughing.

'Yes, that I do.' I replied.

'So, when are you proposing to her?' I asked.

'Soon.' He replied.

Chapter 25

Alright! Before I fast forward to the final days of our college, let me assure you that time flew by crazily. I was experiencing the best moments of my life with Ada. We were deeply and openly in love, holding hands, hugging, and kissing without any hesitation. We went on movie dates, enjoyed dinners together, indulged in shopping sprees, and explored various sights without care in the world.

Aheesh's Shreya had already graduated from college. Whenever I asked him when he was going to propose, he would always say 'Soon'. However, his 'soon' never came!

My friendship with Vani remained intact and concealed. I continued to talk to her and meet up with her. She was doing so well for herself! Her achievements were celebrated not only in her college but also in our college. She was regarded as a prestigious alumna of our college and received invitations for various functions. However, she consistently declined the invitations.

The final year of college was peculiarly different. Something in the general attitude of the people, including myself, changed. It felt as if a switch had been flipped, transporting us to an enlightened world. The usual conversations about cricket, films and opposite sex gave way to the conversations about the future, jobs and companies. It was a period of mixed emotions, a mashup of joy and trepidation. Joy because we would soon be graduating from college and trepidation because we didn't know how the world would treat us! People were also sad because everyone was going on their separate paths; and the familiar faces they were accustomed to seeing every day would no longer be there.

Resume writing had replaced 'proposing' as the latest fad. It was like a competition. Everyone was busy trying to outdo the other in terms of the colors, the fonts, and the use of jargon in their resumes.

However, it was exciting as hell! The college had managed to bring in some companies for the placements and we were expected to give our arms and limbs to get the job. The college's reputation hinged on the placement percentages. We were strongly encouraged (or rather pushed) to do mock interviews and group discussions in our free time. Professors transformed into counsellors, delivering lectures on how to excel in interviews, although I doubted if even one of these professors would make it past the first round of the corporate interview!

Ada had a clear goal in her mind. She wanted to go for an MBA. She had already given the exams and had been shortlisted by a college in Mumbai. I, on the other hand, wanted to get a job and have some experience. Additionally, I also wanted to make some money. Ada had once mentioned that Bali was on her bucket list, and I was determined to take her there.

I had been shortlisted for an interview with a reputable company for an executive role in their accounts department. I earnestly wanted to be selected. I practiced for days, holding mock interviews and group discussions with Aheesh, Ada and others. At night, I stood in front of the mirror and rehearsed, closely watching my expressions, hand movements, and body language. I critiqued and motivated myself, striving to do better.

On the evening before my interview, Ada and I went to our favorite Chinese joint for dinner. She ordered Chicken Fried rice for me and Hakka noodles for herself.

'Can't believe time flew so fast?' She said, as we waited for our food.

'Yeah…' I replied softly, a realization dawning upon me that in a couple of months, we won't be spending our days together anymore. 'Three years…'

'Three years!' She repeated with a sigh.

'Yes. Three years since you asked me out.' I teased her.

'What? I didn't ask you out.' She said, raising her brows.

'Yes Ma'am, you did. Remember the day of our first movie at the cinema? During the interval, you said, "I Love You" and kissed me. You looked like a puppy.'

'You know, Vasillor,' She said, picking up a fork and positioning it near my throat, 'One of these days, after the placements, I am going to kill you.'

'Ah! And I would die willingly and happily.'

'So cheesy.'

'Whatever you say.' I replied.

'And for the record, you proposed to me! In the middle of the night, through a text.' She asserted.

I took her hands in mine and kissed them.

'You are the best thing that has ever happened to me,' I said.

She looked at me like a puppy (Yes, true this time!) and gave me a peck on my left cheek.

'And you are my treasure, my love,' she said.

Our friend, the waiter, brought us mouth-watering food along with a variety of sauces, and we eagerly dug in.

'Hey, what's wrong? I asked her, as I saw tears in her eyes.

'Nothing.' She said and wiped her eyes.

'All okay?'

'Yes.' She said, 'The food is spicy.'

'Come on! You love spicy food. You gulp chili sauce like cold drink!' I remarked.

'It's too hot for me today,' she said.

'Are you thinking about our future?' I asked.

'No.'

'I have a solution,' I said.

'Okay. Let me hear out your nonsense.'

'Let's get married, as soon as you finish your MBA.'

'Ha.'

'I am serious. Will you marry me?'

'Ha. Is that it? Is this how you are going to ask for my hand. I was expecting flowers, chocolates, a bottle of wine and a very big ring.'

'You should stop watching those stupid romcoms,' I said.

'Look who is talking!' she hollered. 'You enjoy romcoms. I don't'.

I smiled; what she said was true. I was indeed a romcom buff. I enjoyed the buildup, the romantic elements, the lively characters, the heartwarming smiles, and some occasional tears. Ah, how I adored the happy endings!

But now, I find them over-the-top.

'Whose blazer is this?' Aheesh asked me the next morning as I arrived dressed up for the interview. I was wearing black pants, a white shirt, a blue tie and a navy-blue blazer.

'Did I ask you about yours?" I replied.

'Guys, you both look dapper. Best of luck!' Ada exclaimed.

We were divided into two groups, to be interviewed by a different team from the company. One team was led by a beautiful lady, while the other was led by a bald guy. I was riding my luck that day, as I got selected to be interviewed by the lady. Aheesh, on the other hand, found himself in the other group.

'Bastard! Aheesh exclaimed. 'You got lucky!'

'You shouldn't have teased me about my blazer.' I retorted.

She introduced herself as Natasha from the HR department. I can't describe to you how beautiful she was! She looked all corporate in her sharp cream-colored suit. Confident. Powerful. Awesome. For a moment, I envisioned Ada in her position and wondered how incredible she would look! Yes, I was awestruck in her presence, and when she asked me the first question I stuttered. Perhaps she was aware of the impact she had on people, as she offered me a reassuring smile and spoke in a warm voice, attempting to put me at ease.

Instead of the usual "tell me something about yourself, where do you see yourself in five years etc", she asked me about my college experience, the canteen food and even about my girlfriend. She spoke like a friend, and even laughed at some things I said. She said she missed her college life. I asked her the year she had graduated in. She simply smiled and said, 'it was long back.' My interview went beyond the scheduled 15 mins and lasted about 45 mins. I spoke from my heart, sharing my aspirations and career plans. 'I want to be in a position like yours in 5 years' I said. She smiled as I said this. Before concluding, she asked me if I would be open to relocation. 'Yes', I replied without hesitation.

As soon as I came out of the room, Ada came running towards me and asked, 'How did it go?'

'I don't know.' I replied honestly. It dawned upon me that I might have been too casual with Natasha. Interviews weren't supposed to be like that. Perhaps Natasha was testing my professional attitude, and I had mostly talked about personal matters. Surely, she would have marked me down for being low on confidence and professional demeanor.

Yes. You were pathetic. Low on confidence and yet flirty with her! My mind admonished me. *Tell Ada the truth. You think Natasha is hotter than Ada. You want….*

NO! I said aloud.

'No?' Ada asked.

'I mean…. I don't know. They are still shortlisting.' I said, fumbling for words.

'Okay. I hope you get through!'

'Fingers crossed.' I replied. 'Did you see Aheesh?'

'No. Where is he?' Ada replied and looked around.

'What about your girl gang?' I asked, 'Did anyone get placed?'

'Yes! Supriya, Shruti and Aanchal'.

'Wow! That's nice.'

'Let's go to canteen. You must be hungry,' she said.

'Yes. Starving. Let's go.'

It was nearly 7 in the evening, and I had interviewed with a few companies, even making it to the second rounds. However, my name was yet to appear on any final lists. I was getting anxious now. I sincerely hoped to get a job that day. Finally, around 7:30 pm, I was called in by Natasha.

'Mr. Vasu, Congratulations!' Natasha said to me, rising from her seat, 'We have decided to extend you an offer.'

'Thank you, ma'am.' I replied, unable to contain my happiness.

She extended her hand, and I eagerly shook it.

'Please have a seat,' she said.

'Thank you, ma' am.' I said as I sat down.

'Please call me Natasha.'

'Sure, Ma'am.'

She smiled. 'Sure Natasha! In our company, we address everyone by their first name.'

'Noted, Ma'am. Sorry, Natasha.' I replied.

'Great! So, you will be joining us in April in our Bangalore office.

Bangalore? My heart sank.

'Let me help you understand your annual package.' She started. 'So, this would be your gross and your net would be…'

Honestly, after hearing 'Bangalore' I lost all senses of comprehension. *So, I will be staying far away from Ada. Long distance relationships don't work. We will head towards a break-up. How will I live without her? Breakup…. Long distance… doesn't work.*

'All clear?' Natasha asked.

'Yes. All clear.' I replied softly.

'Congratulations, once again.'

'Thank you.' I said, rising from my seat.

Bangalore? Of all the places? I had never been there before. I had heard it was a beautiful city with nice weather and kind people. But I already started resenting it. Why? Because Bangalore was taking me away from Ada. And I also started resenting Natasha, despite her kind nature. She was taking me away from Ada too. 'You are a fool!' My Nemesis No1 roared. 'Don't you remember what your dad said: 'Focus. Build your career. Get a job'! If you mess around with this opportunity, you won't get another! How will you face your father?' But... how would I tell Ada that I was going away! 'Forget her! If you mess up with placements, the HOD will blacklist you from all other interviews. You won't get a job!' But... How will I live without her?

That walk, from the chair to the door, felt like the most arduous journey I had ever taken. It drained me, both mentally and physically. I was torn apart by the continuous battle raging inside my head. However, as I reached the door, something inside me cracked, and I turned back towards Natasha.

'I am sorry, Ma'am.' I said remorsefully, 'I don't think I would be able to accept this offer.'

She looked up from her papers, her expressions startled.

'Why Mr. Vasu? Do you have another offer in hand?' she asked, politely.

'No, Ma'am,' I replied, standing in front of her like a schoolboy with my eyes lowered.

'Please take a seat. Let's understand why you have changed your mind.' She said calmly.

I obediently sat back in the chair.

'Is there is a concern regarding your pay package, Mr. Vasu?'

'No Ma'am.'

'Any concerns about the job profile? I discussed that with you in detail,' She asked.

'No, Ma'am.'

'Okay. What is the concern then?'

I felt so overwhelmed that I was unable to talk.

'Come on, Mr. Vasu.' Natasha said warmly. 'Let us have a frank discussion here. I would like to understand why you changed your mind suddenly.'

'Ma'am, I don't want to go to Bangalore.' I replied meekly.

'I believe you were okay with relocation.' She responded.

'Sorry, Ma'am.' I said, 'I wasn't sure at that time.'

'Are you sure now?' she asked.

'Yes, Ma'am.'

'Is your family based out of here?' she inquired.

'No, Ma'am.'

'Okay.' She said, 'I respect your decision. But let me tell you this, it's a very good offer that you are letting go of.'

'Can I join your Mumbai office, Ma'am?' I asked nervously.

'We have already filled all the positions in our Mumbai office.' She replied, 'I am afraid I cannot do anything.'

'Thank you.' I said, 'And I am really very sorry.'

'All the best, Mr. Vasu,' she said.

'Thank you, ma'am.' I responded, standing up to take my leave.

'I hope you don't mind asking me, but is your girlfriend the reason?'

My heart rate quickened, and I felt my face turning red. She had understood the reason!

'Hmm. Commitment. I appreciate that,' she said. 'Best of luck, again!'

Ada, who had been waiting outside the room, pounced on me as soon as I came out. 'What happened? Why did it take so long?' She asked anxiously.

'I didn't get the job,' I said.

'But you were shortlisted.'

'I think I goofed up.' I replied.

'Oh! Don't lose heart.' Ada said, hugging me. 'The final list is still not out.'

'I am not waiting for the list.' I replied, 'Come on, let's go.'

'What's wrong?' She asked, confused, 'You always wait till the end.'

'I don't want to wait today. Let's go.' I insisted.

'But...'

'Let's go, please,' I pleaded.

I wanted to go straight to my place, but Ada wouldn't let me. She could sense my dejection, so she insisted to take me to the Chinese restaurant again. We had just settled down and ordered our food when Aheesh called me on my phone. 'Where are you?' He yelled.

'At the Chinese joint,' I replied, 'You still waiting for the list?'

'HOD and that beautiful lady are looking for you,' he said.

Oh Man! I was sure Natasha had complained about me and narrated the entire story to our HOD. I was convinced that I would be blacklisted now.

'Why? What happened?' I asked timidly.

'You are on the final list! They need your sign on the acceptance letter.'

'What?' I asked, 'Did you check the list yourself?'

'Yes. It's in front of me. You need to come fast.'

'Have they mentioned the joining location on the list?'

'Yes, yours is Mumbai.'

I couldn't believe it! And when I broke the news to Ada, she jumped up in joy and hugged me tightly. 'What are we waiting for?' She exclaimed, and we rushed out of the restaurant. Natasha, that sweet lady, had just made my day!

And on that day, for the first time in my life, I got incredibly cocky. Super cocky! I believed that I had the power to shape my own circumstances, to create my own destiny. I thought that if I could get a job, I could get anything. I was convinced that Ada and I would always stay together. ALWAYS! No matter what!

Chapter 26

When you start a job, you don't know how the first year passes. You are both an early bird and a night owl. You work on weekdays and extend your work into weekends as well. It's expected of you! You are asked to learn and absorb as much as you can, sort of politely saying- "work the hell like a mule". In short, life got super busy after I started working. Ada got busy too as she pursued her MBA. As a result, our calls became shorter and our meetings less frequent. It happens; it's not unusual. We still messaged each other whenever we found time, and we managed to speak on the phone every morning.

One Tuesday, during one of those calls while I was on a bus heading to the office, she casually mentioned that Akash would be staying with her for some days.

I was dumbstruck. Who was Akash? I had never heard this name before. What did she mean by saying that he would be staying with her?

'He is a very good friend of mine.' She replied when I asked her who he was.

'I have never heard of him,' I said.

'Now you have.'

'But!' I protested. 'Why is he staying with you?'

'He has been told to vacate his flat. Where else would he stay?'

Her last sentence felt like a dagger to my throat. What did she mean by "Where else?"

'How do you know him?' I asked.

'He is in my class.' She replied.

'Shouldn't I have known about him?' I asked.

'I don't ask you about your friends.' She replied, emphasizing the word "friends".

'What do you mean by that?' I asked furiously.

'Nothing.'

'I don't think he should be living with you.'

'That's not for you to decide.'

'Fine,' I said and disconnected the call.

That day, I missed my bus stop and went far ahead. I had to walk back 5 kms to reach my office. As I walked, the strange conversation we had kept playing in my head repeatedly. WHO IS AKASH? WHY IS SHE LETTING HIM STAY WITH HER? WHY? WHY? WHY?

Perhaps, I am overthinking. I tried to reassure myself. *Maybe he is just a friend. There is nothing wrong if a friend stays over. Didn't Pammi stay at my place?*

It was a satisfying thought, and it temporarily calmed my mind. I believed that a conversation with her would clear all my doubts. However, I was furious and not in the mood to call her. I was certain that she would call back and explain everything. I expected it! But she didn't call, and as I kept walking and thinking, I felt like going through the most painful and miserable time of my life.

I entered the office late and in a terrible mood. I skipped the morning meeting and sat in front of my computer, staring at the dark screen. The letters W, H, Y kept running through my mind in endless circles. Why did she do it? Why didn't she tell me about it? I was her boyfriend, and I deserved to know. But she chose to keep it from me. I felt shattered. The darkness of the screen seemed to engulf the entire office, and I lost consciousness. When I regained my senses, I could hear voices all around me. The entire office was gathered, discussing what had happened.

'Are you okay?' My boss asked me. 'What happened?'

It took me a moment to recognize him. 'Yes sir.' I replied, as I pulled myself up from the floor.

'Here, take another sip.' He said offering me a water bottle. I took a few sips to regain my composure.

'Better now?' He asked, concerned for me.

'Yes sir.'

'Okay, everybody back to work. He is fine now,' my boss announced to the rest of the office.

Once everyone had dispersed, the boss pulled up a chair and sat beside me.

'What happened?' He inquired.

'I don't know sir.' I replied.

'Does this happen frequently?'

'No sir. Happened for the first time.'

He fell silent for a moment and then asked, 'Why don't you go home and take rest today?'

'It's alright, sir. I am fine.'

He pondered for a moment and then said, 'You are young. This needs to be checked!'

'I think I know what happened,' I said, seeing that he was getting concerned.

'What?'

'I missed my bus stop today and walked back 5 kms. I think I got dehydrated.'

'What? You walked all that way in this humid weather. Why didn't you take an Auto?' He asked, clearly surprised.

I didn't respond. *Yes. Why hadn't I taken an auto?* I wondered about the decision I had taken.

'You think this is the right way of saving money?' He questioned. 'Remember my advice: Never be penny-wise, pound-foolish! Understood?'

'Yes, sir.' I replied, nodding.

'Good, ' He said, standing up and patting my shoulder, 'Now, let's get back to work.'

How do I tell you how I spent that day! How would you understand? How could I make you feel my emotions? Let's see. How do you feel when you are about to drown? How do you feel when you are about to puke? How do you feel when the hot tea burns your tongue? Helpless. Self-loathing. Scarred. Multiply the mixture of these emotions by ten billion, and you might get an idea!

I waited impatiently for her call, for her text, hoping that she would tell me that I was wrong, that I had misunderstood, that it was nothing, that she had been joking, pulling my leg. But nothing like that happened. That day, she didn't call or message. You cannot imagine how angry I was and how helpless I felt!

Putting all my anger aside, I called her up in the evening. I didn't say 'Hello', 'How are you doing, Love?' this time and went straight to the point.

'So, what have you decided?' I asked.

'About what?' She replied. I could hear music in the background. She was out somewhere, perhaps in a restaurant.

'About Akash.' I said. Even uttering his name burned my throat.

'He is staying.' She said assertively.

I had never ever heard such assertiveness in her voice before. *It's over buddy!* My Nemesis No.1 said to me.

'Fine,' I said, upping my ante, 'In that case you'll have to choose. Akash or Me?'

When Ada didn't immediately say "YOU" but waited for a while, my Nemesis No1's voice in my head grew stronger and yelled, WAKEUP! DAMN IT! IT'S OVER!

And her response reaffirmed it.

'He is staying.' She said, without giving me a straight answer.

'Goodbye, Ada. You won't be hearing from me anymore.' I said firmly and ended the call.

I felt betrayed. How could she do this to me? I would have been Ok, if she would have told me on my face that she wanted to break-up. I wouldn't have pleaded with her. No. I had my pride. I would have said "okay, be happy". But the way she turned the things on me. Why did she have to throw her new boyfriend's name at me? Why did she have to tell me that he would be staying with her? There was no need for it if not to tear my soul apart! How simple could it have been? She just had to say that she no longer loved me. And like mist in the air, I would have vanished forever from her life.

I was furious. How could I let her do this to me? How could I not know there was another guy in her life? How could I not see this coming? How could I be so blind? Yes, Love makes us blind. But still! Fuck Love, once and for ever. Never again, I said to myself, am I going to trust anyone. Never again, I repeated to myself, am I going to fall in Love. And never again am I going to think of her!

Chapter 27

They are not wrong when they say 'Love' is the biggest drug. It truly is. First, you get addicted to it. And then, when you want to break free from it, you become miserable and go mad in the head. You start fighting against it, which leaves you restless, and the cruel pangs of longing keep biting you in the heart. One moment you are consumed by anger, and in another, you are filled with self-loathing and pity. You think weirdly and you do the weirdest of things. I will come to the weirdest things shortly.

But before that, here's a billion-dollar idea for my entrepreneur friends: Open the de-addiction centers for the dumped and the broken-hearted. You would be surprised to know how large the customer base is! And they will buy anything that can alleviate their misery. The only catch is that it must be discreet. People don't want to show that they have been dumped. Wait! Would that be a de-addiction center? Hmm, no, I think it will be an addiction center for a new product to replace 'Love'. Well, anyways, you get the idea. Now it's your job to figure out a business plan.

Here are the things I did (in order of difficulty levels):

Entry Level (Basic ones):

Deleted her number- Took me 10 seconds. Fruitless though, because her number was the only one my stupid brain had memorized and etched into its millions of neurons.

Deleted her messages - Took me 10 days, as I read and re-read them millions of times before finally mustering the courage to delete them. I fought with my Nemesis No1 about which ones to save for posterity. There were so many beautiful and romantic lines we had exchanged. I ended up copying some of the messages in my notebook without providing any context. Maybe, forty or fifty years later, when my memory starts failing me, I would read those beautiful lines and wonder who had written them.

Medium Level:

Rationalize the pain: I started reading the materials on the philosophy of detachment. I delved into teachings of Buddha, the Bhagwad Geeta, and the omnipresent internet quotes. I started telling myself that in the greater scheme of the things, my pain didn't even matter. Afterall, at any point of time there would be millions of people going through the same thing as I was. So, I was just a speck in that universe of million break-ups!

Top Level:

Duel with my Nemesis No1: Undoubtedly the toughest one. The provocations from my Nemesis were relentless: *You must get her back! At any cost! You cannot be a loser. Confront her. Show her! Take your revenge.* And every time I resisted and said NO, it would browbeat me. *LOSER! No wonder, she left you. You don't deserve to live. Go, Kill yourself!*

This fight was wreaking havoc on me. I started feeling weak, pathetic, and deplorable. The world lost its meaning and the joy. It was a tough fight, really! The relentless convoy of thoughts were leaving me beyond repair and redemption. I couldn't find a way out. How do I control my mind, my thoughts? How do I let go of her? She had no business to be in my head anymore. But she refused to leave, and my Nemesis No1 provided her with sustenance, air, and all the luxuries she needed to stay put.

One day, under the shower, I had my enlightenment. I just needed to control my thoughts. It was so simple. I realized that I didn't have to leave any space in my mind for her to crop up! And the only way to do that was by overwhelming my mind with other thoughts.

So, I began slogging in the office. I would attend all the meetings, even if I wasn't really required to, and would actively participate in the discussions. To their questions that I wasn't required, I would assert that I was there to learn. My peers started hating me because I was setting the wrong precedents. They feared that their dedication and their performance would be benchmarked against mine. I worked and worked, from eight hours to twelve, from twelve to fourteen, until one day my boss called me aside. He handed me a promotion and a decent increment, but also cautioned me to slow down and avoid burning myself out.

Another step I took was to sever communication with anyone who could potentially remind me of her. That meant cutting off contact with my closest friend, Aheesh, and half of my classmates.

I would say my plan worked well for some time. Slowly, her thoughts began to recede until one day I didn't think of her at all. I was so happy with my victory that I ordered biryani to celebrate. But she had her ways, and my Nemesis No1 provided her full support. She made a back door entry. Now, she started appearing in my dreams; night after night, laughing, chirping, hugging, and kissing her new boyfriend. This became my new struggle. How do I control my dreams now? How do I control my subconscious that feeds those dreams? I had to stop it, somehow.

So, I started all over again. I read books on dream control, watched hundreds of documentaries and videos on Youtube, and even attempted to read Sigmund Freud. I tried to practice the techniques, but everything failed, and I despaired. Every morning, as soon as I woke up, I became aware of her and my reality, and it was terrible.

I had my Eureka moment again, in my shower. But it was an idea I loathed and was terrified of. It was something I wouldn't have done even if someone held a gun to my head. I hated it so much, so, so much. But right now, it was the only thing I could do to make her go away from my dreams. I had to duel with myself for many days. I was going to do something that was gut-wrenching and agonizing for me.

I don't think I hate anything more than watching horror movies. They give me creeps and torture my soul from earth to hell. I had watched one in my childhood and had nightmares for six months. I would wake up in the night crying and acting funny. Every night. For six months. It had worried my parents so much that they took me to both a Baba and a doctor. The Baba had impressed them by telling them what they wanted to hear – that I had been possessed. The doctor, in their eyes, was stupid as he couldn't diagnose what was wrong. After an excruciatingly painful six months, when everything else, including Baba's remedies, had failed, I was finally cured. It happened one night, when my dad slapped me hard for waking him up in the middle of the night and causing a scene.

This is what I had come to now. I was ready to face the ghosts, get possessed (again!) than to see Ada's face in my dreams. This is how desperate I had become! I watched them all, just name them. The Exorcist, The Ring, The Conjuring, Evil Dead- All versions of it! I even watched our own Ramsay brothers' movies- Veerana, Purani Haveli, Bandh Darwaza. After ghosts, zombies were next on my list. And I am proud to say for three days nonstop, I had zombie fiesta at my home! My experiment started to have its impact. Forget dreams, I couldn't even sleep. I started looking pallid and ill. I wouldn't have noticed my condition hadn't one of the girls in my office remarked, 'You look like a zombie!'

Zombie! Really, a Zombie! I was about to burst, but then I realized being called a zombie was not that bad. I could live with that. At least she didn't call me Devdas!

'Why a zombie?' I asked her.

'Because you look like mush!' she replied.

'Watch yourself.' I said, baring my teeth, 'I might bite you.'

Next day, I was called in by the HR. I received a stern warning and was required to take a course on Sexual Harassment. I tried to explain my side of the story, but they didn't have any policy regulations on situations where people are called zombies. After the HR, my boss called me into his office and gave me an earful. While he was at it, I recalled how only a few weeks earlier he had doled out a promotion and appreciated my hard work and sincerity.

'Get a shave and a haircut!' This is an office!' He thundered at me before asking me to leave.

Who was he to tell me to shave off the beard I had grown over the past few months now? I wanted to complain to the HR, but I knew I wouldn't be entertained. So, I dropped the idea. I would still have continued on my path and endured all the insults and insinuations, had this plan also not failed. A few days later, the cracks started appearing in my Horror-Spooking-Dream-control Plan. More than being scared, I started enjoying the genre, the misery of the ghosts, the mushiness of the zombies, the death of the expendable characters. I began to empathize with them. I started to see myself as a ghost and a zombie in my dreams. Besides, some of the witches and the female zombies started looking sexy to me. I ended this madness when one night, Ada came into my dreams as a witch, and we made mindless, freakish zombie-witch love!

Chapter 28

Seven months later, I went out on a date with one of the girls from the office. She had been dropping hints, asking about my work, seeking my help with the printer settings (every now and then), and lingering around my cubicle. We went out for dinners and watched movies together. She seemed alright to me, and I was ready to take it forward. But I bailed out after date no 3. I will tell you why. She told me straightforwardly that she didn't want to waste any more time with movies and dinners and wanted to get me into the bed. The way she spoke to me, I felt like a whore. I rejected her proposition and told her that I was looking for a deeper connection. She became upset and insulted me, calling me stupid and damaged. We never spoke again.

After that fiasco, I stopped dating and kept to myself. I didn't feel the need to have anyone around me. I still went out for movies and dinners, but all by myself. I started traveling too. Those solo trips, by the way, are amazing. There is no burden of expectations, no need to wait for people till they are done eating or pissing. You move around at your own pace, as you like it. I started to enjoy my company. It was so liberating. And yes, finally I was rediscovering my inner peace.

But… Fate has a habit of getting in your way and kicking you in the butt. It happened to me. It kicked me so hard that all the carefully laid Jenga pieces of my life came crumbling down.

I had read in one of those stupid self-help books that when you are doing well, you should reward yourself to reinforce the positive attitude and mindset. I was doing well in terms of "moving on", and I thought I deserved a reward. So, I went to a shopping mall to gift myself a new watch. And my fucking fate! There she was- in that watch store- right in front of my eyes. She was dressed in a leopard printed tank-top, her wet hair hanging loose, and black lipstick gaudily dancing on her lips. I had never seen her dressed like that! How much had she changed in those nine months? Hmm. Nine months is really a long time!

She wasn't alone, obviously. A guy, half bent with one elbow placed on the glass top of the counter, and looking up towards her, was encouraging her to try out the watches. And it suddenly struck me! Her birthday was around the corner. Perhaps, he was buying her a birthday gift. Last year, around the same time, I had been thinking about the gift…Our trip to Bali… 'Don't tell me what it is. I like surprises!' she had said.

Did she see me? What was her reaction? Of course, I will tell you that. Yes, she saw me. And she turned pale, as if she had seen a terribly frightening ghost. How did I feel? Well, a sharp pain gushed through my guts and my lips became parched. My heart pounded, and my knees were about to give out. I didn't want to stand for a second longer in that store. I quickly turned around and got out of the store, out of the shopping mall, and hailed the first auto I saw at the stand. When I was quite far from the mall and my heart had found its normal pace, my Nemesis No.1, my mind, said:

Did you see that guy? He seemed Okay-ish. You look better than him. Much better. God knows what she found in him.

He must be better than me in some way! I responded.

Better than you! You think so, you poor soul. No wonder she left you for him. You deserved it!

It's not a competition. I replied.

Is it not? Is he taller than you? Better built? Monied, may be? My Nemesis No1 continued.

It doesn't matter! I argued.

Shame! Shame that you ran away. You chicken! No guts, you should have confronted her. Has she even told that guy about you?

Has she even told that guy about you?

This thought refused to leave my head. Had she completely wiped away my existence? Or did I find a mention somewhere? I needed to know.

'Turn back to the mall,' I said to the Auto driver.

'What happened, sir? You forgot something.' He asked, scratching his head.

'Yes, I did,' I replied.

I entered the mall again and walked straight towards the watch store. My heart raced, and the blood jostled through my veins. I was damn excited! This time, I wanted to see if she would acknowledge my presence, and say Hi, and introduce me to her new boyfriend. I wanted to see how her new boyfriend would react. I entered the watch store with tons of anxiety and excitement. But she wasn't there! I looked around, checked each counter. They had already left the store. *They wouldn't have gone far!* My mind said. And it made me think like a stalker! Hmm. Where could she go? I knew her favorite stores. I knew the route she followed while shopping. She would start with Shoppers Stop, follow it with Westside, then visit the individual stores of her favorite brands, and finally end at Lifestyle. So, that's how I started my search.

My feet stopped as soon as I entered the Shoppers Stop. I could smell her fragrance in the air. I sensed she would be around. But that fragrance quickly morphed with other fragrances and vanished. Whatever was happening was bizarre. I realized soon, though, that the salesgirl was testing the perfumes on a piece of paper, and that was creating havoc with my senses. I passed through the perfume counter, utterly confused. I walked into the Ethnic Wear, the Western Wear, the Lingerie section, and checked everywhere. She was nowhere to be found.

I was about to leave disgruntled when I realized that she might be buying for him. This thought made me sad, but what could I do? Hesitantly, I took the escalators to Level 1, where the Men's

Department was. I walked anxiously, passing through different clothing sections, lighting up the eyes of the sales staff who looked eagerly at me. I ignored their 'Hi Sir' and 'Good evening sir' and their pleas to shop at 50% discount. I kept searching, but they weren't there. Where could they be? *Watches Section, Genius!* My Mind said, *weren't they checking out the watches?* I raced down the escalators to the ground floor where the watches section was. No, they weren't there either.

My search continued throughout the retail stores in the mall. I would get inside, take a quick look, and come out. I felt bad for all the sales staff who approached me with high expectations and went back disappointed. An hour later, when I still couldn't find her, I decided to end my mission. I was at the exit gate of the mall, about to leave when I remembered that I hadn't checked the food court. *Yes. That's where they could be!* With renewed energy, I raced towards the food court only to be disappointed again. Exhausted and hungry, I ordered from McDonald's and sat down to eat my food. As I started eating my food, I realized how stupid I had been. I was terribly embarrassed with myself for the way I had searched for her. What had taken over me? I pitied myself so much that I burst out laughing, terrifying a girl seated beside me. She watched in horror, as I laughed hysterically, and the bits of burger fell from my mouth. She finally stood up and went to the other end of the food court.

After I was done self-loathing, I decided to go back home. It was around 10 pm, and I decided to go by train. I wanted to lean out from the train, and let the cool breeze hit me. I came out of the mall and started walking towards the train station. I watched the frolicking families hurrying towards the station to get back home, and the young college crowd coming out of the station for their *night-out*. I remembered that Ada and I used to come here for such night-outs too.

Just outside the train station was our paan shop, where we used to eat her favorite Chocolate Paan. The first time there, she had raved about the Chocolate Paan she had eaten in Delhi and how much she missed it. 'Madam, you will forget Delhi's Paan when you eat this.' The affronted Paanwala had said and offered her the Paan free of charge. Ada liked the paan so much that she hugged the paanwala, leaving him embarrassed.

Our Paanwala guy waved frantically upon seeing me. I waved back at him and went to his shop. 'How are you sir?' He asked me, 'Saw you after a long time.'

'All well', I replied, 'Don't get much time nowadays, due to office.'

'That's true sir. Life changes when you start working.'

'Yes.' I nodded.

'Your regular?' He asked, preparing the Paan.

'Yes, please,' I confirmed.

'How is madam, sir?' He asked while making the Paan.

'Oh!' I was surprised by his question, 'She is fine.'

'She didn't come along.'

'No, I had some work here.'

'Madam is very nice, sir,' he said. 'She likes my Chocolate Paan.'

'Yes. Yes. She does.'

'Here,' he said, as he handed over the Paan to me.

'Thank you.' I said, reaching out for my wallet.

'Rahne dijiye sir. Aaj meri taraf se', He insisted, 'You came here after so long. I am happy to see you.'

'Thank you very much' I expressed my gratitude. 'Glad to see you too.'

As I was leaving, he handed me a packet.

'What's this?' I asked.

'Nothing much sir. Just some Chocalate Paan for Madam. Give it to her.'

'Oh! Sure, Thank you.' I said and walked away.

Poor Guy! I didn't have the heart to tell him that the packet wouldn't reach Madam.

I entered the railway station and went to my platform. A train came in, but it was very crowded. *Still!* I thought. I was too tired to jostle for space, so I decided to wait for the next train. An empty bench on the platform caught my eye. I slouched into it and watched as people fought to get out and onto the train. After a few seconds as the train moved out, to my utter surprise, on the parallel platform in front of me, there was Ada!

I was left numb for a moment. This was so unexpected! I had been searching frantically for her the entire evening, and now that I wasn't looking for her, here she was! Standing in front of me, her eyes wide open, making no effort to turn her gaze away. Wow! The same old feeling overwhelmed me- the pounding heart, the adrenaline rushing. How long had it been since our eyes locked like that! We kept looking at each other until the next train arrived.

And the reality soon crashed back in. We were not together anymore. She was standing there with her new boyfriend. I shook my body like a wet dog, got up from the bench, and raced down the platform towards the exit. Once outside the station, I got into a rickshaw and left. The packet of Chocolate Paan, I had left behind on the bench.

Chapter 29

It was a Saturday morning, and my doorbell rang incessantly. Once. Twice. Thrice… Hundred times… God knows how many times. The ringing bell pushed me out of my sleep and made me sit uptight. WHAT THE HELL! I yelled at the top of my voice. I hated being disturbed in the mornings, especially on the weekends. I checked the time on my phone; it was around 10 am. Who could be trying to wake me at such an hour on a Saturday morning?

I had specifically told my *Bai* not to come before 12:00 pm on weekends. Although she had goofed up sometimes and arrived early, I would simply put a pillow over my head and ignore the bell. Eventually, she would leave after a few attempts. However, today was different. The bell showed no signs of stopping. Filled with anger, I got up from my bed and marched towards the door. If it was my *Bai*, she had chosen a wrong day to mess with me. I was going to fire her.

As soon as I opened the door, a powerful punch struck me square in the stomach. I am sure that I was in the air for some time (like they show in the movies!) before I fell with a thud on the floor. Let me tell you, a punch on an empty stomach is the worst punch to ever have! My guts churned and I felt nauseated. I wasn't sure whether it was the pain from the punch or the morning hunger doing the *mumbo-jumbo* inside my stomach!

'What the fuck!' I shrieked in anger.

'Where the hell have you been?' Aheesh said as he entered my flat. 'I have gone crazy trying to get hold of you.'

'Ooo! It's you,' I replied, wreathing in pain.

My anger subsided on seeing him. I knew that I had brought it upon myself with the way I had treated him. I had stopped meeting him and hadn't even shared my new phone number with him. So, in all fairness, I deserved the punch. What I didn't deserve though, was getting it on a Saturday morning on an empty stomach!

'You deserve it,' he said sternly.

'I know,' I replied, still lying on the floor.

'What's wrong with you?' He asked, pulling me up from the floor.

'Nothing.' I replied.

He looked at me for a moment and then hugged me.

'Maybe you should have started with this instead of the punch,' I remarked.

'You should be thankful that you only got punched once,' he replied. 'You had breakfast?'

'It is only 10! Who has breakfast so early?' I retorted.

He opened his backpack and pulled out milk, bread, and eggs from it.

'Well, I will prepare some breakfast.' He said and went straight into the kitchen.

'Sure. Suit yourself,' I replied and headed towards the bathroom.

Fifteen minutes later when I returned, he had laid out a sumptuous breakfast on the floor, over the old newspapers. There was masala tea, bread toasts, and omelets. We sat down on the floor to enjoy the meal.

'Not bad at all.' I said, taking a bite of the omelet.

'Yeah? I make them good. If everything else fails, I am going to set up a food stall.'

'Good for you.'

'Yes. Besides that, I am also going to make new friends. The ones I have right now suck.'

'I am sorry,' I said, feeling remorseful.

'You should be. How could you just stop talking?'

'You know why,' I replied.

'No, I don't!' He stated sternly. 'Look dude, you might have your problems with Ada, and I am not getting into that. But that's got nothing to do with me!'

'I didn't know any better then, I was just stupid.' I replied solemnly.

'Do you know how many times I tried to call you? How many times I came to this wretched place? And every single time you weren't here. And I don't know why, I am a go-between. Ada keeps asking me to check upon you.'

'What?' I asked, startled. This revelation came as a bombshell! 'Why? How the hell does it concern her now?'

'I don't know what went wrong between you two. But I know one thing, she cares for you.'

'Cares for me?' I said gruffly, 'She didn't care when she ditched me. She doesn't care much when she roams around with her boyfriend.'

Aheesh fell silent for a while. Perhaps, the fact that she had ditched me was news for him. I could see the sympathy in his eyes. I didn't want him to start feeling awkward, so I tried to lighten the mood.

'You never made breakfast when we were in college. You even said you don't know anything about cooking.' I asked him.

'I lied. If I had admitted that I was a good cook, you guys would have made me your own *bawarchi*.' He retorted.

'Wow! Well done. You managed to keep it a secret. I am envious.'

'Ha! Didn't you try to keep yours?' He asked.

'Yes,' I replied, my mouth stuffed with bread, 'And I failed. But yours, my friend, is a success story.'

'She wants to meet you.' Aheesh said abruptly, catching me off guard.

All the stuffed bread came out of my mouth and fell back on my plate.

'What?' I asked, taken aback.

'She wants to meet you,' Aheesh repeated himself.

'Why?'

'I don't know,' He replied.

'You don't know?'

'No. I told you I am just a go-between,' he clarified.

'Hmm.' I said, 'You know I won't.'

'That's your call. I just wanted to give you the message.'

'Thanks. Message received.' I replied sarcastically, 'By the way, have you met her boyfriend?'

Aheesh looked at me in horror, as if I had asked him if he had ever seen a ghost! His face turned pale, and his tongue failed him. He babbled some incomprehensible words, which I'm sure even he didn't understand.

'So, you did meet him,' I said. 'That's okay with me. You don't need to die for it.'

'I bumped into them once.' He replied timidly.

'Okay.'

'I didn't mean to meet him.' He added.

'Even if you meant, I would have been fine with it,' I replied.

Aheesh stopped talking, lowered his head and quietly sipped his tea. As I watched him, so many questions arose in my mind. I wanted to ask him what he thought of them as a couple? Were they better together than Ada and I were? Was the guy better than me? Was Ada happier with him? So, so many questions! But I didn't ask. I didn't want to put Aheesh in a spot, and I was not angry at him for meeting Ada or her new boyfriend. He was as good a friend to her as he was to me.

'By the way, how is Shreya doing?' I asked him.

Shreya, do you remember? The girl Aheesh was interested in. His face lit up when I asked this.

'She is fine,' he said. 'We talk sometimes.'

'Really? She gave you her number?' I asked. I was genuinely awed with Aheesh's progress in this regard. I never expected that they would talk.

'Yes. She did.' He replied casually.

'Does her boyfriend know?' I asked.

'Yes.'

'Wow! I mean what, how…' I said, fumbling for words.

'He is a good guy. He even invited me to her birthday party recently.'

'What? And you went.'

'Yes.'

'Wow! Wasn't it awkward? I mean they are a couple, and you went alone…'

'I didn't go alone,' he said, his face blushing.

This was getting more and more intriguing now. I straightened my back and sat attentively.

'Who did you go with?' I asked, my curiosity piqued.

He hesitated for a moment before replying, 'You would have known had you not gone incommunicado!'

'Oh man! There is another girl in your life. Good. Tell. Tell. What's her name?' I prodded.

'Nyra.' He said, a smile spreading across his face.

'Nyra? Never heard the name before.' I remarked.

'She is in my office,' Aheesh continued.

'Oh! An office romance. I always thought that was fiction.'

'No, this is real. She is real.'

'So, you guys did something fun?' I asked, fist-bumping him on the arm.

He blushed and fell silent.

'Does she know about your crush on Shreya?' I asked.

'Yes.' He said, 'They have even met.'

'Wow! I underestimated you. You are a pro, bro.' I exclaimed, impressed with him.

He took my words as a compliment, and his face beamed with pride.

'Have you gone on double dates?' I inquired.

'Yes. Couple of times. Nyra likes Shreya and…' Aheesh began.

'No, I meant you guys and Ada and her BF,' I interrupted him.

He fell silent for a moment, and then muttered, 'yes.'

'Bumped into each other in a restaurant?' I teased him.

'Ada invited us…' He replied meekly.

I was amused by all the new information that Aheesh shared. The world had changed so much in such a short span of time. He spoke about our classmates. Their lives were so different now. Some had gone abroad for job or higher studies. Sushant, he told me, had taken up modelling and was about to land a major role in a movie. Ravi was running a VC funded start-up. Vani was going to Europe (I already knew that.)

When Aheesh finally left in the evening, I felt a mix of sadness and nostalgia. I was alone once again, but I was grateful that Aheesh had paid me a visit and shared with me both the memories from our past and the conversations of the present. It was a bittersweet feeling, knowing that life had changed, and we had drifted apart, but also cherishing the moments we had spent together.

Chapter 30

It was midnight, and I lay wide awake in my bed, still lost in thoughts about the conversations I had with Aheesh. The faces of all the people we spoke about flashed in front of my eyes, and I wondered if I would ever see them again and in what circumstances would we meet? Would I ever see Sushant again, now that he was going to be a movie star? Perhaps he would be too famous to even be approached by someone like me. And what about Aheesh? Wouldn't he forget me in a year or two? He had Nyra now, and a new circle of friends. And they went out on double dates, with Ada and … Hmm. Ada? She looked happy with her now boyfriend. 'One day', I mused, 'they would be married and have kids'….. Hmm. But! I wondered. Why was she concerned about me now? What had she told Aheesh about me? Did she think I wouldn't be able to cope without her and do something stupid? Was that why she was concerned about me? Huh!

And why did she look at me like that in the train station?

My phone rang. It was an odd time for a call, and I was genuinely worried. I hoped everything was fine at home. Mom had recently been diagnosed with diabetes, and despite her assurances that it was normal for her age, I couldn't help but worry. I had started calling her more often, and she teased me that she wouldn't die till she saw her grandkids getting married. I checked my phone wearily and was dazed to see the number. I jolted and sat up in my bed. This number... I hadn't forgotten it! Why was SHE calling? And who gave her my new number? Then the realization dawned on me. Aheesh, my dear friend and her messenger boy, had lost no time in giving her my new number.

Did I ever expect a call from her? No. Never. Not in this lifetime and the six others that might follow! Would I have called her again? No. Never. Not in this lifetime and the six others that might follow!

We were truly done and dusted, and I wanted no connection with her now. No amount of honey in the world could sweeten the bitterness that had crept into our relationship. But here we were! My phone blazing with her call. I let the phone ring, refusing to answer.

Why was she calling at this hour? Where was Akash? Wasn't he living with her? Was she calling in his presence? Why? What did she want from me?

The phone rang for a couple of times more. Every time I turned on the silent mode. *Thank you, Ada!* I said loudly *for ruining my night.* It was going to be a long sleepless night now. I knew, my Nemesis no.1 would not let me sleep. I had to start the preparations to keep her thoughts away. So, I got up from my bed, made myself tea and Maggi, turned on my laptop and started to watch The Exorcist! I was determined not to let her inside my head, no matter the cost.

You might think of me as a madman, sometimes even I do. After having my tea and Maggi, and while watching the movie, a part of me yearned for her call. You are right to yell at me and ask, "What's wrong with you? You resist and expect. If you were dying to talk to her, you should have picked up her damn call the first time?" I have tried to find a good reason behind this madness. And the reason you already know: that ancient disease called Love. Perhaps I still loved her, still hoped for something from her. Regardless, I didn't receive any further calls that night, leaving me angry and frustrated. You see, you don't call someone just once, twice, or thrice and then abruptly stop. That's simply not the way it's done.

A week passed by, and it was a week spent gazing at the phone millions of times during the day; a week of great self-realization about how weak, wavering and vacillating I was!

She called again on Saturday, and this time I picked up her call in the first ring, eagerly waiting for her to speak. However, there was complete radio silence at her end. I checked my phone to ensure that the call was still connected. The connection was okay, and I could hear her breathing. I waited patiently, but minutes went by without a single word exchanged. 2… 3….5 mins went by. The silence and the anxiety started to get overwhelming and after 5 minutes, without exchanging a word, I disconnected.

She called up again, immediately.

'Listen,' I said angrily, 'If you don't speak, I will end the call.'

'I…… I want to meet you.' She said hesitantly.

'What for?' I asked, shocked.

'I just want to meet you.'

'I don't.'

'Please… Just once.' She pleaded, her voice trembling.

'No,' I replied firmly and hung up the phone.

Yes, I was rude. Yes, I hung up on her. What else could I have done? Wasn't she rude the last time we spoke? Didn't she say goodbye and all. She was unbelievable! After everything that had happened, why did she still want to meet? How could she even think that she could ask and I would go and meet her?

But why did she want to meet me? And why was her voice trembling? Did she want to apologize? Or was she fearful that I might, like that phone- guy, stalk her? Did she think that the other day in the railway station, I had stalked her? Huh? Did she think of me like that? How dare she?

Or perhaps, she wanted to return the gifts. I had seen it in the movies. Maybe, those gifts reminded her of me, and she wanted to get rid of them. I began to count all the gifts I had given her. I remembered the first gift I had given her was a yellow hair band. In Goa, when she got frustrated with her hair flying all over her face while riding the scooty, I had asked her to stop near a shop and purchased the best hairband I could find. It was the only hairband she used during our time in Goa, and then I never saw it again… Until years later when she showed it to me, packed nicely in a box. "It was your first gift", she had said, "so I kept it as a souvenir".

What was I going to do with all that stuff she intended to return? As they didn't mean anything to her now, I would throw them in the first garbage bin I came across. The yellow hairband I would keep. It was my first gift to her! I was sure about one thing, though. I wasn't going to give her back the gifts I had received from her. They were mine to keep; and I was going to keep them forever. I might not want her in my life now, but I sure wanted all her memories, for good and for bad.

Next day, I woke up to the multiple messages she had sent between 2 am and 6 am, all saying the same thing: "Meet me once, please". I sat in my bed, wondering why she was doing this. A sense of fear crept over me. *Was she okay?* This wasn't the Ada I knew. She had always carried herself with pride and wouldn't behave like this. *Something must be wrong.*

'Would your boyfriend be joining us?' I messaged her back, finally.

'No' She replied. Had she said yes, it would have been goodbye from me.

'Ok. Where do you want to meet?'

'The Chinese restaurant, our place. For dinner,' she replied.

OUR PLACE? It had long ceased to be our place.

'Sorry, I already have dinner plans,' I messaged back. 'We can meet outside the Local station.'

'Okay.' She messaged, after some time.

She was already there when I came out of the station, dressed in black and beautiful as always. Her hair…… well, let's skip the description, or you might again say I am a madman. She had her earphones on and was engrossed in her phone. I paused midway and took my time to get a good look at her. It felt like ages since I had last seen her. *What had I lost?* It was almost unbearable to be near her. Part of me wanted to turn back, get on a train, and leave. But I had to chin up and go and meet her. Fifteen minutes, that's all I was going to spend with her. I was going to keep it short and transactional. I was not going to talk about her boyfriend, her relationship status or even how she was doing. Armed with these mental notes, I took a deep breath and moved forward.

'Hi.' I said, waving my hands in front of her eyes.

She looked up from her mobile, took out the earphones, and replied, 'Hi'.

'Have you been waiting for long?' I asked.

'No.' She replied softly.

She scanned me from bottom to top, and finally locked her eyes with mine. My heart began pounding, and my stomach churned. I couldn't believe that her gaze still had the power to unsettle me. *What was she searching for?*

'Why did you want to meet me?' I grumbled.

'How are you doing?' She asked meekly, her eyes fixed on me.

How was I doing? What a cruel question! How could she ask that?

'None of your concern.' I replied angrily.

She lowered her gaze and fell silent.

'I have other plans,' I said. 'So, can you please speak up?'

'Sorry,' she said, her gaze still lowered. 'I didn't mean for this to happen.'

'Somethings happen for good,' I said stoically.

I could sense that my answer upset her as the color of her face changed, and she stopped talking.

'If there is nothing else, I would like to leave.' I said after a minute.

'Can… I ask you a favour?' she asked hesitantly.

'What favour?' I asked, surprised.

'I promise you… I will never ask you anything again.'

'If it's about the photos, trust me, I have deleted them all. If it's about ever calling you, I will never do it! I swear. I had already deleted your number. I won't trouble you. Ever'

'I appreciate that.' She said meekly after a moment. 'It's something else.'

'Tell me.' I said, 'I will do that as well.'

'I… I want you to meet Akash.'

WHAT? Meet her boyfriend, Akash? What for? Was she crazy? What nonsense? This wasn't a favour, this was torture!

'I am sorry, I cannot do that.' I said, resolutely.

'Please…'

'Why in the hell would I meet your boyfriend?'

'Please. Just once.' She pleaded, tears welling up in her eyes. 'Just tell me if he is right…'

Amazing! What expectations? Why did I even agree to meet her? Stupid! Stupid! So stupid of me!

'I am not your father!' I said furiously. 'Why do you need my validation?'

Okay. Here's the thing. Some limits should never be crossed. NEVER! Whatever the situation may be, howsoever rotten the relationship might be. I shouldn't have mentioned her father. Here's the short story: She always skirted the conversation about her father whenever fathers were discussed. She was very touchy about it. Any mention would leave her sad and furious at the same time. She had spoken of him once, and that too briefly. It was for the first and the last time she had talked about him. She had lost him when she was thirteen. He had died in a car accident, along with his lover. He had cheated both - his wife by having an extramarital affair and his daughter by leaving too soon.

Today, I had let the worst of me take over and brought her dead father into the conversation. Before I realized it, she had already started moving away from me. I knew I had to run after her.

'Sorry, Ada.' I said earnestly. 'That was unbecoming of me.'

She stopped, looked at me, and said, 'I don't care about my father! But I cared for you. I care about your opinion… My mistake.'

'I am sorry,' I replied apologetically. 'When do you want me to meet Akash?'

Chapter 31

If there is one thing I never want to talk about, it's this. It must be classified as the Awkward Moment No.1 of my life. How else would you define this moment? – An Ex meeting the current boyfriend. The topping on the cake of this awkwardness was the fact that Ada had made me the arbitrator of their relationship. To me, it was unnecessary. She was going to do whatever she wanted to anyway.

So… Here I was, waiting for him at the coffee shop. I had no idea what the heck we were going to talk about or what exactly he knew about me. I wondered why he was meeting me at all. I didn't really fit anywhere in his equation. It was all so messed up that it was disconcerting. What put me at ease, though, was the fact that I had no skin in this game. As far as I was concerned, this was the last thing I was doing for Ada. And after this, it would be Sayonara, Tata, Bye Bye. From my POV, all the pressure was going to be on that poor dude. *He needed my blessings*! I sort of felt thrilled, having this villainous power over him.

I began to chart out the flow of our conversation in my head. Of course, I would wield power. I would be the Alpha male (ah yes, I had also worn my bullet pendant!), taking the lead, being vocal and going all Italian with my hands. He would have to tow my line, swim in the direction of my flow. I thumped at the table. "Yessss"! I exclaimed, shocking the quiet people around me.

After my imaginary power trip had settled, the real question arose in my head: What exactly did I have to probe in him? Ada hadn't told and I hadn't asked. *Stupid! Idiot!* I heard a familiar voice. *You are just a pet dog. She told you to do this and you wagged your tail. No self-respect. Which sane person does this?*

My table thumping had awakened my Nemesis No.1, which was now getting more vocal and Alpha Plus with me. It attacked me with such ferocity that I literally started shaking my head to get rid of it. And right at that moment, as I looked like a Bobble Head, her boyfriend stood in front me!

Ha! '*king* Alpha Male! One silly gesture and my bravado vanished without a trace. *What a fool?* My Nemesis No.1, my Mind chided me again. *You gave it to him on a platter. You weren't even deserving. He is the natural selection in this game of evolution!*

'Hi.' He said, introducing himself, 'I am Akash.'

'Vasillor.' I replied, rising from my chair to shake his hand.

Count me lucky, for he had missed my idiotic bobble-head gesture. He didn't give me a mocking look and yes, he seemed nervous. An opportunity for me to regain my composure and assert my alpha attitude once again.

'Have a seat.' I said, pointing to the chair in front of me. 'You from Mumbai?'

'Yes.' He replied curtly.

'Okay.' I responded. All the icebreakers I had prepared around the places in Mumbai were useless now.

I tried hard to think of something to talk about, but my mind blanked out. Making small talk is excruciatingly hard, particularly with someone you already don't like. Akash, too, didn't seem eager to engage in a conversation and kept looking at his flashy new watch. *Gift from Ada*, my Mind said, dampening my spirits even further.

This meeting would have been over in minutes now, had the waiter not come in. You must give it to the waiters; they always seem to know precisely when to make an appearance.

'Hi Sir,' The waiter greeted us, 'My name is Jagan, and I am here to serve you.'

'Can we have the menu cards, please?' I asked.

'Sure sir.' Jagan replied, placing the menu cards on the table.

'Give us a minute,' I said.

'Take your time, sir. I will be on standby.'

I pretended to check the entire list on the menu although I already knew what I wanted: Plain Cappuccino with no flavor. However, I took my time, reading even the ludicrously lengthy descriptions. It seemed like Akash was doing the same. We both wanted to avoid talking, maintain the awkward silence. I sneaked a glance at him, a quick X-ray glance, and I had my data points. I don't usually believe in comparisons, but if I had to, on looks, mannerisms, choice of clothes, and hairstyle, I would win hands down. Honestly, I am not bragging. But Ada had chosen him, and I was curious to know why. What was that one quality where I had been beaten down?

'I will have Cappuccino. Medium. No flavor.' I told Jagan, 'What about you, Akash?'

'Same,' he replied.

'Two cappuccinos. Anything to eat?' Jagan asked.

'I am good.' I said, looking at Akash.

'Nothing,' he replied.

'Okay. Two cappuccinos, then.' Jagan confirmed and left.

Now that the awkward silence had been broken, all thanks to Jagan, I decided to resume the conversation. 'So, how long have you known Ada now?' I asked Akash.

He took a moment to answer, as if trying to remember the exact date. 'Almost two years now,' He replied.

Two years… Two years! We were still together then…

'Where did you guys meet?' I asked, trying to sound casual.

'College.' He said, 'We did our MBA together.'

'Oh!'

'And how do you know each other?' He asked me.

'College.' I replied with a smirk, 'We did our bachelor's together.'

'You two go a long way, then.' He remarked.

'Yes. A long way.'

'I am glad to meet her old friends.'

Friends? That's what she had told him. We were friends!

'My pleasure as well.' I replied, forcing a smile 'Who else have you met?'

'Aheesh and his girlfriend. We went out together once.' He replied.

'That's nice.'

I should have kept quiet. Silence would have been better than this conversation. All this information was burning me from inside.

'Do you know how Ada and I got together?' Akash blurted out.

I wasn't interested in knowing, so I didn't respond. But that didn't stop him from continuing. He seemed too eager to share his story.

'It took me quite some time, you know. Six months to get her to look at me.' He said with enthusiasm.

I shrank in my seat, feeling uncomfortable.

'I think she was seeing someone then, but I persisted. And eventually, she came around.' He said exuberantly.

Well, the details were distressing. His words were like daggers piercing through my heart. My throat went dry, and my lips parched. Just then, Jagan came with the coffee. I took a sip from my cup and rolled my tongue over my lips. How quickly the tables had turned! How foolish of me to think that I had power over him. The truth was that all power came from Ada, and she was with him now.

'Happy for you.' I managed to say after a while, trying to hide the turmoil of emotions inside me.

'I don't know what I will do without her.' He continued, 'She is so caring and loving. And after we get married, we will get a place of our own.'

My stomach churned. Could have been coffee? Or the talk of her marriage? I couldn't tell.

'So, you guys have discussed marriage and stuff?' I asked, somberly.

'No. Not yet.' He replied, 'But I am sure she won't say no.'

'Best wishes,' I said.

'What about you? You got a girlfriend?' he asked abruptly.

'Yes,' I said. 'But my story isn't as exciting.'

You know the truth. There was no girlfriend. But he didn't need to know that.

'That's true. Mine is exciting.' He continued, taking a big gulp from his cup, 'You know they always agree. You just have to be persistent.'

'Even when they say No?' I asked, trying to hide my disappointment.

'Even when they say No.' He replied.

He wanted to talk more about Ada, but I maneuvered the conversation towards movies and cricket. There was nothing unusual or outstanding in his choice of movies or his favorite cricketing moments. He spoke highly of some Hollywood flicks, and I waited patiently for him to finish his coffee.

As soon as he was done, I called Jagan, thanked him earnestly, and paid the bill. I rose from my seat to leave. I told Akash that I had to meet my girlfriend. 'You know how it is, can't keep them waiting?' He nodded in agreement, and with that, we parted our ways.

Chapter 32

Ada called me in the evening to find out what I thought of Akash. Well, honestly, I hadn't thought much about him. After our meeting at the coffee shop, I spent some time loafing around the stores in the mall. It had been a long time since I had bought myself things. So, I got myself a sexy black shirt and a black watch, both of which I wore immediately.

After my shopping, I went to the food court and ordered a pizza for myself. It had been a while since I had one. I was about to have my first bite when my phone rang. It was Vani. She asked me to meet her for lunch. I told her, I had just ordered pizza, but she didn't listen. 'Give it away' she said, 'don't you dare eat it'.

She was already at the Gateway when I reached there. And as soon as she saw me, she ran towards me and hugged me tightly.

'Wow! Someone is looking sexy today. What's with this beard?' She commented.

'What have done with your hair? Where are your curls?' I asked her, 'I liked them.'

'Thank you for noticing.'

'Bring them back, please.'

'Soon! Finally, you are dressed properly today. You remember the last time we came out for dinner.'

'I remember telling you, I was shabbily dressed. You said I was fine.'

'You could have done better,' she said with a teasing smile. 'And look the pendant is back.'

'Felt like wearing it today. Anyway, why did you call me here? Are we having lunch at the Taj?' I asked.

'We can... some other time. Today, I want to take you to a special place.'

'So, why are we here?' I asked.

She took out her phone and clicked a selfie. 'For this,' she said, checking the picture on her phone.

She clicked our pictures at all the places from the Gateway to the Fountain, from the Art Gallery to the CST. When I asked her why she was clicking so many pictures, she said it was for a project. Finally, after we were done with the pictures, we hopped into a cab. To my surprise, she asked the driver to take us to the restaurant where we had our first dinner together!

Wow! The restaurant looked the same it was the last time we were here. Five years is a long time! And it hadn't changed a bit. The layout, the décor, the paintings on the walls- everything was the same. Even the people - the manager, the waiters- seemed familiar. It gives you a strange joy when somethings in life don't change, doesn't it? I was experiencing that surreal feeling at that moment.

We had just taken our seats (same old seats!), when the owner of the restaurant came to us. He approached Vani and told her it was a pleasure to have her in his restaurant. He spoke highly of her art. 'I am a big fan. One day, we will have your painting on one of these walls,' he said earnestly.

He requested Vani to have a picture with him. She smiled and agreed. She asked me to join her for the click, but I refused. 'The food is on us,' the owner said as he took his leave.

'So, you get free food now?' I asked puzzled.

'Yes. Sometimes.' She replied casually.

'Wow! You are living a great life.'

She smiled.

When the waiter brought in the food she had ordered, I realized they were the same items we had eaten five years back! I looked at her in wonder.

'What?' She blushed, 'I loved the food that day.

'You still remember.'

'Of course.'

She asked me about Ada, and Aheesh. I said they were fine.

'I heard.' Vani said, after a while.

I stopped eating and looked at her. 'Aheesh told you.'

'No.' she said.

'Who then?' I asked surprised.

'Ada.'

'What?'

'Yes. I spoke with her a few days ago.'

'Why?' I asked.

She did not answer.

She placed her left hand over mine, and said, 'Vasillor, I am leaving for Paris.'

'Yeah, I know that. You told me. For six months for that course….'

'I am not coming back.' She said, meekly.

'Oh!' I exclaimed, processing her words.

So, that's why she wanted to see me today. I thought.

'When?' I said, clearing my throat.

'In two days.'

'Hmm. Two days'

'Your dad would be happy and proud,' I said.

She kept quiet and pursed her lips.

'Why didn't you tell me?' she asked, after a while.

'I don't know why…'

She knew I was struggling. She patted my hand gently.

'I told her I am leaving….and…. she wants to meet me.' Vani added.

I breathed a sigh.

'Leave all that. So, you are a bigshot now. Can I at least get an autograph? You won't even recognize me after a while.' I said, changing the topic of conversation.

'You are the only person, I won't forget. Ever.' She said, with a tear in her eyes, 'My only friend.'

'You are making this too emotional, Vani! Come on! Cheer up,' I said. 'I am not letting you go like this.'

She wiped her tears and smiled. 'Will you come to Paris to meet me?'

'Why not, if you sponsor me,' I said.

'I will,' She said, 'And don't you dare not to pick up my calls.'

'When have I not picked up your calls.'

'You are a sweetheart! You always pick up my phone,' she said.

After finishing our dinner, we went for a walk on the Marine drive. This time, we walked in silence with an overwhelming feeling that this might be our last meeting.

'Is that my parting gift?' she said finally, pointing at the shopping bag I was carrying.

'No.' I said, 'I didn't know we were parting.'

'Give it me.' She snatched the bag from my hand.

'Give it back.' I said, 'It's my old T-shirt and my old watch. I will give you a nice gift.'

'No.' she protested, 'I will take this. And you had promised to give me your pendant.'

'Oh, yes, I had. What a coincidence, I wore it today,' I said as I took out my pendant and handed it over to her. 'But where is my painting that you had promised?'

'It's in the box I gave you. You can open it now,' she replied.

Well, I will be honest. I had difficulty holding back my tears once we bid goodbye, and she left in the cab.

So, when Ada asked me what I thought of Akash, I had no ready answer. I couldn't sugarcoat it and said whatever came to my mind.

'Why?' she asked.

'I don't know.' I replied, 'I won't say he isn't a good guy, but I wouldn't want to be friends with him. That's my opinion. I am sure you would be happy with him. He did seem caring.'

'Please tell me the truth,' She pleaded.

'I already told you. I am not sure what truth you want.'

'Is he better than you?'

I laughed at her question.

'You should ask this to yourself. You chose him over me, so I would assume he is better than me.' I replied.

'Why did you say you wouldn't want to be friends with him.'

'I don't want to be friends with everyone,' I replied. 'He showed me some pictures. You two make a good couple.'

'You are saying this to spite me.' She said meekly.

'Why should I? I don't care anymore.' I stated coldly.

There was no further talk, and after ten minutes of silence, she disconnected the call.

I tossed my phone aside and brought out the box Vani had given me. I was absolutely stunned to see the painting inside. It was the exact copy of the selfie she had clicked that day - Vani, me and the flamingos making a heart in the background.

Chapter 33

A week later, on a Sunday, Aheesh called me and asked me to meet him urgently. He sounded low, and I was petrified. 'What's the emergency? Are you alright?' I asked anxiously. 'Come to my place, as fast as you can,' he said.

The worst of the thoughts passed my mind on my way to his place. *Had he met with an accident? Was he in hospital, fighting for his life? Did he want to see his best friend one last time? STUPID!* My Mind said. *If he were in hospital - fighting for his life- would he be able to call? No,* I replied timidly. *What else could go wrong then? Had he picked up a fight and got beaten? Nah! He was too soft to pick up a fight, and too cute to get beaten. His puppy- face would melt even the toughest of the goons!*

I didn't even wait for the lift when I reached his building. I dashed up the stairs to his 7th floor room, and upon reaching there, frantically banged his door. I was still catching my breath when he opened it.

'What happened?' I asked.

He gave me a bottle of Thums Up that he had in his hand and said, 'come in.'

'You look fine!' I said, furiously, 'you made me run all the way here'.

'Yes. I am fine. What's gonna happen to me?' He said, calmly. 'And I didn't say come running.'

'What's the emergency, you idiot! You are making me angry now.'

'Catch your breath first! Lie down for a while.' Aheesh said, pointing to the mattress.

I gulped down the Thums Up and fanned myself with the newspaper lying on the chair. After I had cooled down, I understood that there was no emergency of any sort. Aheesh had pulled a trick on me. I stretched myself on the mattress, placed a pillow under my head and picked up an old, yellowed Archie comics book to read.

'Now that you made me come all the way here, what are we eating?' I asked Aheesh, without taking my eyes off the comics.

'Pizza.' He replied.

'Wow! What's the occasion?' I asked.

'Wait for a while,' He replied and started fiddling with his phone.

There was a knock at the door after half an hour.

'Ah! Must be the Pizza.' Aeesh remarked.

'Great! Get the door,' I replied, still engrossed in the comics. Archie was in soup. He was flirting with Veronica, and Betty had just caught him in the act. I was busy, trying to see how he would save himself now.

The 'Hi' at the door jolted me up! A sudden ache rose in my heart as I recognized the voice. I looked at the door; Ada stood there! She came in and said 'Hi' to me. I didn't reply. I was getting angry. I could understand the plot now. I looked at Aheesh and said I had to leave.

'You are not going anywhere?' Aheesh said assertively.

'Bite me!' I replied, 'You shouldn't have done this.'

'Please,' Ada said, 'If anyone has to go, it should be me.'

'No.' Aheesh said to her, 'Nobody goes anywhere.'

'I just need five minutes.' Ada pleaded.

'What are you going to talk about now? Your marriage preparations,' I said, fuming.

'No.' She said, 'I just wanted to say sorry.'

'What is this now?' I asked.

'Okay! You guys sort it out.' Aheesh interjected. 'I am going out to see where that Pizza guy has reached.'

'I am really sorry. For everything.' Ada said, after Aheesh had left.

'It doesn't matter now.' I replied, 'You made your choice.'

She fell quiet, and her eyes welled up. I went back to the comics and flipped through the pages. Well, I had lost all interest in Archie now, but I just needed an excuse to ignore her. In the silence that followed, I heard her sobbing, and I don't know why, but it began to trouble me.

'Do you have anything else to say?' I asked, putting the comics book away.

'No.' She replied, wiping away her tears, 'Nothing else... Sorry again and...'

She stopped at 'and'. Well, I shouldn't have worried about what else she had to say. I should have just let it go and get going. But, under those circumstances, in that room, that pensive 'and' forced me to ask: 'And what?'

'Nothing,' She replied. 'You can go if you want to. I have nothing else to say.'

'No, finish your sentence. And what?'

She didn't answer and looked down at the floor.

'And what Ada?' I yelled at her.

I shouldn't have yelled. The floodgates of her eyes opened, and the room was inundated with her tears.

'I love you,' she said.

I went numb. What could I say?

'No, you don't,' I replied.

'I really do.' She reiterated, 'I love you more than anything!'

'But! You are with Akash. You guys are together.' I was bedazzled with what was happening.

'We are not together.' She replied, meekly.

'You left him too!' I commented, sarcastically, 'Atleast, stick to someone'.

I can never forget the way she looked at me with her teary, red eyes.

'Don't disrespect me.' She said, sternly. 'You have no right!'

I knew I had crossed the line here. I should not have mocked her. It was her life, and I really didn't have a right to comment. But I was hurt!

'I am sorry,' I said.

'I said, what I had to from my heart. I made a mistake, and I owned it. But you don't get to insult me. I am sorry I said that I loved you. I don't want to be together with you... You are mean.' She said and broke down.

Her words struck my heart like an arrow. In her pain, I saw my own. I had dueled with that soul-tearing monster for months.

'You don't know how much pain you have caused me, Ada.' I mentioned pensively, my eyes moistening. For the first time in my life, I was having a meltdown.

As she watched the tears roll down my eyes, she came towards me and hugged me. I was surprised with myself; I didn't know I was capable of shedding tears. She wiped away my tears with her hands and said, 'Seeing you like this is my suffering for the life.'

'I still don't know why?' I asked, after regaining my composure.

She waited for a moment and then said, 'I thought you were cheating on me.'

'Cheating on you?' I asked puzzled. 'With whom.'

'Vani.' She replied.

'Why would you think that?'

'What else would I think? You were always so secretive about her. I know she called you, and you would talk to her. So many times, when we were together, you would leave me and go talk to her. I know you went out with her. You remember our Orientation? I had asked you to come. You didn't. You said you had some urgent work. And the next day, I saw your picture with Vani. You lied to me every time I asked you about her. I know you went to her college. I know…'

'You could have just asked me,' I said.

'Why? We were in a relationship; you should have understood me,' She replied.

'Hmm…And what changed now?'

'Vani told me everything.'

'Hmmm….'

'You knew how I felt about Vani. And still, you… Who wouldn't want a girl like Vani? She was everything I wasn't.'

'But I loved you,' I said, earnestly. 'I told you there was nothing between Vani and me. So many times. Why didn't you trust me?'

'How could I? When you lied and lied and kept it a secret?'

'I really wanted to tell you everything, some day. But… you left.'

'I am sorry, I left you. I didn't want to end up like my mom, in a relationship but unloved.' She said, breaking down again.

I kissed her on the forehead and said, 'No, you won't end up like your mom.'

The doorbell rang, and I got up to open the door.

'That pizza guy cancelled, so I had to get them myself.' Aheesh stated, panting. He was carrying big pizza packs.

'Don't blame the pizza guys. They never cancel.' I said, taking the packs from him.

Aheesh looked at Ada, and then at me, 'So, is this pizza going into our bellies or into the thrash-bin.'

'Bellies! Who wastes a pizza?' I said, 'What say, Ada?'

'Yes,' she said. 'I am hungry.'

'Wow! And I thought my thousand bucks were going down the drain.' Aheesh exclaimed in joy.

'We wouldn't have let that happen,' I said, smiling.

We put down the pizza boxes on the floor and sat around them. Ada opened the boxes and sprinkled the oregano and chili flakes over them.

'By the way, did you like Aheesh's girl?' I asked Ada.

'Nyra?'

'Yes.'

'Why are we talking about her?' Aheesh said, blushing.

'Because we have pizza, and we need new gossip.' I replied, unabashedly.

'And I am the easy target.' Aheesh said.

'Yes,' Ada said. 'You didn't get me hand tossed?'

'Vasillor will get it for you next week.' Aheesh commented and smiled.

'Nyra? I asked again.

Our banter continued, and we remembered the old days, laughing at the old jokes. And to you guys, I must admit, it felt nice, very nice. It had been a long time since I had laughed so much; and watched Ada laugh. That laugh... how much had I missed it. Aheesh seemed pleased. I bet in his head he was considering himself a hero. He had achieved the impossible, brought back two ex-lovers. An achievement not many people can boast of.

It was already dark when I prepared to leave. Aheesh insisted I stay for some more time, and I think Ada wished it too, but I was honest when I told them I had an early morning meeting. Natasha, the HR lady, had called me for a catch up. Ada said she would leave with me.

'Ada, let me walk you to your place.' I said, once we were out of Aheesh's building.

Ada looked at me and smiled.

This walk, our walk- it should have been familiar, right? Same two people, same old road, same brightly lit shops. There should have been the same old excitement to share the little details of the day, same old eagerness to listen to the latest gossip! But the truth is, that day, we walked in silence. Perhaps, reflecting on the events of the day and its consequences.

'Again, I am sorry, Ada.' I said as we reached her building.

She looked at me in surprise and asked, 'What for?'

'For all the mistakes I have done,' I replied, 'And for the ones I might do'.

'Let's not talk about mistakes.' She said, leaning forward and kissing my lips.

We bid each other goodbye, and as I was moving away, she shouted, 'See you next week.'

I looked back at her, smiled, and said, 'See you!'

Now, isn't this a happy ending? – An ending worthy of your 'awws' and a Bollywood movie. For you I stop here, and you can go on living happily knowing that your hero finally ended up with his heroine. Their journey of love is complete, and they will live together, happily, and forever!

Or...

Chapter 34

Or...

I can just narrate what actually happened, if you are up to it.

We met on Saturday, and on many more weekends that followed. Yes, our phone conversations resumed, and we said 'I love you' at the drop of a hat. Yes, we went on double dates with Aheesh and Nyra, and revisited the old places. Yes, we were romantic again and spoke of our future together.

But!

There was an underlying unease. Something always seemed amiss! I couldn't shake the feeling that I wasn't the only one she had confessed her love to. And I could sense that it troubled her, too, at times, knowing that I had lied to her and kept secrets.

Though we never acknowledged it openly, we were both trying to fit into each other's perspective, more cautiously than before, and it gnawed at the joy of being together in the relationship. The trust that was once solid seemed to have cracks, and we were both navigating our way through uncertainty.

One of those days after seeing off Ada, as I was waiting for the bus at the bus stop, I happened to notice an oddly familiar bus. The big purple heart stickers on the windshield, the vehicle number ending in 639, I had seen it before. The number particularly: 639. There had been a conversation about this number. Yes, I remembered! That night. That bus to Goa.

'It is a peculiar number,' she had quipped, as we got into the bus.

'What's so peculiar about it?' I had asked.

'639'

'So?'

'The angel number 639 means to let go of the past.'

'Wow! I didn't know numbers have meanings,' I had commented.

'It's a sign,' she had said. 'To move towards the new things.'

"Goa, Goa"- The bus conductor shouted. Impulsively, I rushed towards him. To my surprise, it was the same old fellow, and somehow, I was happy to see him. I smiled at him, but he kept a straight face and failed to recognize me. It didn't upset me, though. That journey was memorable for me; for him, it was just another day at work.

'Do you have tickets for seat no 23 & 24.' I asked.

'I can give you seats at the front,' He replied. 'Better seats.'

'No. I want 23 & 24.' I demanded.

'Okay. Here you go.' He said, surprised by my odd request.

'Thank you.' I said, taking the tickets from him.

I jumped into the bus and strode towards the seats. I didn't need anyone to spot them for me. I remembered exactly where they were. I slid into the seat I had taken years ago- seat no 24. The bus started moving, and I closed my eyes. I touched the empty seat – seat no. 23 that Ada had taken once- and it felt worn out and cold. How much had changed since the last time I had sat here? How much had changed in the last few weeks? How much!

I found myself in an eerily familiar place. I had a gun in my hand, and I was fighting a man. He looked familiar, but I couldn't place him. The fight, I knew, was over Ada. I pinned down the man and pointed the gun at his head. I was full of rage, but I didn't know why. I just wanted to pull the trigger.

And a trigger was pulled! But it wasn't mine. I turned around. I could see the bullet racing towards me, as clearly and as magnified as they show in the movies. It pierced my heart, and a fountain of blood sprung out. I shivered as the haze rose all around. Through that haze, with the corner of my eye, I saw Ada. She looked like an angel, with her wings spread wide. And she had a gun in her hand.

I kept looking into her chocolate brown eyes until I fell....

I was woken up by a great thud. The bus screeched to a halt as the driver applied the brakes. The conductor came rushing towards my seat with a torch in his hands. The light from the torch nearly blinded my eyes.

'What happened?' I asked, trying to shade my eyes with my arm.

'Some bastards threw the stones at the bus.' He said and moved the light towards my window.

'See!' he said, 'Bastards'.

I looked at the glass window. A small, edged stone had found its way right into the middle of the glass and got stuck there. Around the stone, the glass had broken- not in an ugly way- but in a pattern of beautiful concentric circles, much like the circles we used to draw in our geometry class.

'Rowdy bastards', the conductor cussed again, and tried to push the stone out with his torch. It didn't budge. He tried again.

'Don't push it.' I said, 'It will shatter the glass.'

He nodded and went back to his place at the front, conveyed something to the driver, and the bus moved.

I looked at the glass again. It was broken, yes. But it looked so beautiful now. I fiddled with the stone. It still didn't move. I let it be and closed my eyes again. On one of the speed-breakers, the stone fell out of the glass by itself and landed into my hands. I felt its edges- partly rough, partly smooth; partly moist, partly dry. I opened my eyes, put the stone in my jeans pocket and got up to get off the bus.

Next day in the office, I accepted Natasha's proposal – the one she had discussed with me weeks earlier- to shift to Bangalore.

*

The End